ANTIQUES BIZARRE

Also by Barbara Allan:

ANTIQUES ROADKILL

ANTIQUES MAUL

ANTIQUES FLEE MARKET

By Barbara Collins:

TOO MANY TOMCATS (short story collection)

By Barbara and Max Allan Collins:

REGENERATION

BOMBSHELL

MURDER—HIS AND HERS (short story collection)

ANTIQUES BIZARRE

A Trash 'n' Treasures Mystery

Barbara Allan

KENSINGTON BOOKS
http://www.kensingtonbooks.com

KENSINGTON BOOKS are published by

Kensington Publishing Corp.
119 West 40th St.
New York, NY 10018

Library of Congress Card Catalogue Number: 2009940495
ISBN-13: 978-0-7582-3421-6
ISBN-10: 0-7582-3421-X

First Printing: March 2010
10   9   8   7   6   5   4   3   2   1

Printed in the United States of America

For Stan and Helen Howe—treasures

Brandy's poem:

Oh, give us pleasure in the flowers to-day;
And give us not to think so far away
As the uncertain harvest; keep us here
All simply in the springing of the year

Robert Frost, 1915

Mother's poem:

Spring has sprung, the grass has ris'
I wonder where the birdie is?
There he is up in the sky
He dropped some whitewash in my eye
I'm alright, I won't cry
I'm just glad that cows can't fly

Unknown

(Mother is not taking this seriously enough.)

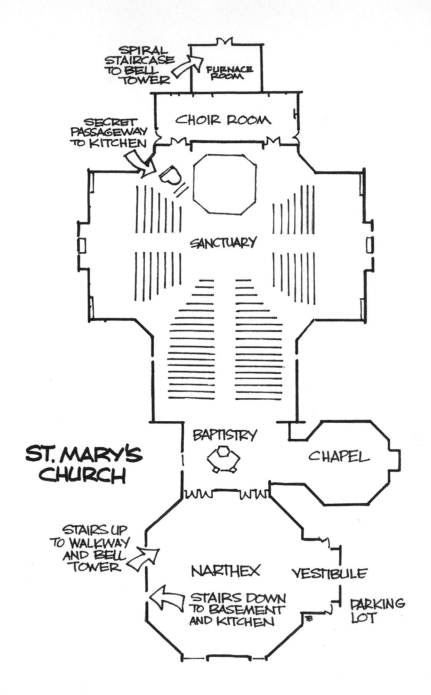

SPIRAL STAIRCASE TO BELL TOWER

FURNACE ROOM

CHOIR ROOM

SECRET PASSAGEWAY TO KITCHEN

SANCTUARY

ST. MARY'S CHURCH

BAPTISTRY

CHAPEL

STAIRS UP TO WALKWAY AND BELL TOWER

NARTHEX

VESTIBULE

PARKING LOT

STAIRS DOWN TO BASEMENT AND KITCHEN

Chapter One

Egged On by Mother

After a long and arduous winter, spring had finally deigned to show itself in Serenity, a small Midwestern town nestled on the Mississippi River like a quaint reminder of simpler times—particularly as viewed from the air. Trees were budding, tulips were blooming, and lawns were greening. People had begun to come out of their houses, squinting at the sun like moles venturing from their holes, and you could feel the collective happiness in the air.

This elation had proved even shorter-lived than the tulips. Because along with the warmer weather came the melting of ice and snow, and a particularly heavy accumulation up north came flooding down, sending the river over its banks and into our fair city, Nature taking her revenge on Serenity's idyllic pretensions—hundreds of families forced to flee their homes, dozens of downtown businesses suffering, as the muddy Mississippi sent cold, dirty water rushing into their domains.

According to Mother—who knew everything and everybody in town—this was the worst catastrophe in Serenity since the Great Flood of 1965 . . . which was before my time, I'll have you know.

I was sensitive to the travails of my fellow Serenity-ites; many were facing much worse problems than yours truly, although I did have my own concerns and the burgeoning Mississippi River had not had a drop to do with it.

At the moment, I—Brandy Borne, a thirty-one-year-old, blue-eyed bottle-blond divorcée, who had come running home last year to Mother—was looking directly into turbulent waters. Not the river, no—I had my head over the toilet bowl, paused between rounds of barfing.

Standing by, listening to my assured, if-less-than-eloquent, oratory, was Sushi, my blind, diabetic shih tzu, and Mother, a.k.a. Vivian Borne, mid-seventies, antiques lover, Red Hat Society member, director of community theater, and would-be amateur sleuth with a bipolar disorder.

And now for our first aside (and there will be others; deal with it): Mother's real age is unknown, thanks to a small fire in the 1970s that broke out in the Hall of Records, destroying all birth certificates under "J." But I'm sure Mother had nothing to do with it, even though, a) she was born Vivian Erma Jensen, b) had long since started lying about her age so she could still play younger roles, c) was the only clerk working at the time of the strangely selective fire, and d) had quit her courthouse job shortly thereafter.

When I next came up for air, Mother raised her chin to advise me, "Buck up, dear . . . it's all in your head."

And here I thought it was all in my stomach. Or used to be.

I glowered at her over my shoulder. "Do you think I *enjoy* doing this?"

Mother, wearing her favorite emerald-green pants suit, her silver hair pulled back in a bun, eyes looming large behind her oversized glasses, sniffed, "*I* never had such trouble when *I* was pregnant. And *I* was *married!*"

Now, before you start thinking that I was a wanton woman, let me explain. My best friend, Tina, and her husband, Kevin, couldn't have children because of Tina's cervical cancer, so I had offered to be a surrogate mother for them. Aren't you ashamed of yourself for thinking ill of me? (We won't go into the reasons for my divorce right now.)

I shot back, "I was *never* sick with Jake!"

Jacob was my one and only, now twelve, and living with his father in an upscale Chicago suburb.

Mother sniffed. "You most certainly *were!* Why, for two whole months, you prayed at the porcelain altar on a regular basis. You'd call me every afternoon, whining, 'Why me?' And I'd say, 'Why *not* you? What makes you so special? Join the Morning Sickness Brigade and serve proudly!' And you'd reply—"

"All right, all right," I managed, the hinges of my jaw feeling loose, "maybe I *was* sick for a few days."

She put a hand on my shoulder, and said softly, "Do not assume, my precious, that a mother upon the arrival of her little bundle of joy forgets all of the hardships that preceded the blessing event."

"Don't call me 'my precious,' " I said. "I'm not a troll."

"Of *course* you aren't, dear."

I grunted a nonresponse as I rose. Sushi, at my feet, whimpered, and I picked her up and snuggled her against my face, to let her know Mommy was okay.

Mother clapped her hands twice, then said singsongy, as if I were still her little Brandy, "Now, wash your face, and get dressed, darling—we have places to go, things to do, and people to see."

"And miles to go before we sleep," I muttered, knowing already that I was in for a trying day with Mother.

Upstairs in my bedroom I climbed unsteadily into a pair

of old jeans, which fit somehow, even though I was three months gone—I'd lost a little weight from the morning sickness. Then I slipped on a warm sweater because it was still nippy outside. What was up with God's latest little joke on me? That bringing life into the world made me feel like death warmed over?

Downstairs, Mother was waiting impatiently.

"We should take my car," she said solemnly. "It hasn't been driven for a while."

Mother had an old pea-green Audi stored in our stand-alone garage. The reason it hadn't been driven for a while was that Mother had lost her license—and I don't mean misplaced it.

"We can't," I said.

Mother frowned. "Why ever not?"

"Because I had the tires removed when you were at your Red Hat meeting the other day."

"*What!*" she shrieked. "Whatever for?"

I put both hands on my hips. "Because you keep driving it when your license has been revoked."

Mother, guilty as charged, was uncharacteristically speechless.

"And not just once . . . but *three* times!" I waggled a finger in her face. "I did it for your own good. And for the *public's* good—poor unsuspecting souls."

So far, Mother had racked up citations for cutting across a cornfield in order to make curtain time for one of her plays; causing a three-car fender-bender on the bypass after braking for a garage sale sign; and flattening a mailbox shaped in the form of a big fish because "it didn't *look* like a mailbox," which apparently she felt granted her permission to run it over.

Mother's lower lip protruded. "Now you're just being *mean.*"

"Think of it as tough love. Now can we go?"

Leaving Sushi behind with plenty of water (diabetic dogs drink a lot), Mother and I headed outside into the crisp spring air, where the sun shone brightly in a cloudless sky. You could smell lilacs in the gentle breeze, or anyway I could.

Suddenly I felt better.

My (very) used burgundy Buick was parked in the drive, and as I climbed in behind the wheel, I asked, "Where are we going, anyway?"

Mother, next to me, smiled like the cat that ate the canary. Two canaries. Three. "Never you mind, my precious . . . just go where I tell you."

"Mother—if you call me 'my precious' one more time, I will clobber you with your *Collected Tolkien.*"

"Point well taken, dear."

I sighed and fired up the engine. This was, indeed, going to be a long, trying day. . . .

We headed along Elm Street, passing homes similar to ours, mostly three-story dwellings built in the 1920s. Quite a few folks were out tending their lawns, raking dead thatch, and clearing debris bestowed by the winter. Some were even planting a few annual flowers.

At a stop sign, Mother powered down her window and addressed one such person, a man in a plaid flannel shirt, who was putting red geraniums in the ground around his front porch.

She shouted, "You're *jumping* the *gun!*"

Startled, he popped up like a jack-in-the-box and ran around the side of his house.

Mother said, "Now, wasn't that a strange reaction?"

"Really?" I smirked. "People often act like that when you yell at them."

A car behind me honked and I moved through the intersection.

"I merely meant," Mother said defensively, "that it's too early to plant geraniums. Not too late to have a frost, you know."

I said, "Well, maybe all he heard was 'you,' 'jump,' and 'gun.' "

Mother twisted in her seat to look at me. "Now why would I have a gun?"

Out of the corner of an eye, I could see Mother studying me.

"Brandy?"

"Yes?"

Her voice was arch, her words measured. "I'm not sure I *like* you off your Prozac."

I didn't figure I'd get away with my earlier, caustic remark. And I, too, had noticed that my once-censored thoughts were flying straight out of my mouth, since I'd stopped taking my daily Prozac dosage, and my what-the-heck attitude had been replaced with—dare I say it?—sensibility.

Mother went on. "I know you want to protect the baby, and that's a noble goal . . . but, honestly, dear, it's difficult living with someone who really *should* be on her medication."

This time I just thought, *Tell me about it!*

We were approaching the downtown, a small grid of four streets, containing just about every kind of business a modest community like ours might need. The main thoroughfare was (natch) Main Street, five blocks of regentrified Victorian buildings, with little bistros, specialty shops, and antiques stores.

As we drove by the courthouse—a study in Grecian architecture—Mother blurted, "Shit!"

If you are easily offended, you need to know right now that Mother rarely swears, but when she does, the "s" word is her curse of choice. Her father used it and so did her mother and her grandfather and even her grandmother, if rarely (thumb hit by hammer, for example), so this was a family tradition of sorts. I have been known to carry on the tradition myself.

Why this little scatological outburst?

Up ahead was a detour that rerouted us from the downtown.

"River must be high," I said.

Mother sat forward in her seat, instructing, "Go around the barricade, dear."

"No."

"If the river's high, I want to *see*."

"Mother, there's a reason they want us to stay away—it's not safe."

Straining her seat belt, Mother bounced in her seat like a child denied a cookie. "*That* car just went in there!"

"They probably live downtown. Local traffic is allowed."

"Well, *we're* local."

"Mother. . . ."

"Who's to say *we* don't live downtown?"

I turned right, complying with the detour. "But we don't, do we?"

Mother sighed dejectedly and sat back in her seat. "I decidedly *don't* like you off your Prozac. You used to be more . . . adventurous."

"You mean, compliant," I said. "By the way, where *are* we headed?"

"West Hill."

Leaving the downtown behind, I continued driving parallel to Main Street, then up a gradual, tree-lined incline, passing grand old homes, some large enough to be called mansions, once belonging to the early barons of Serenity—Germans and Scandinavians and Eastern European industrialists who had made their fortunes opening lumber mills and pearl button factories, and had even started their own banks.

I asked, "Where to now?"

Mother smiled deviously. "Turn left on Cherry Street, my . . . pet."

I slowed to a stop, and looked at her through hooded eyes. "Not the *Petrova* house?" It was the only mansion in all of Serenity that Mother had never dared try to wheedle her way into.

"That's right, dear."

Aghast, I asked, "We're *not* just dropping *in?*"

She pursed her lips in irritation. "Honestly, Brandy, what kind of pushy old broad do you take me for?"

"I'll plead the Fifth on that one."

She nodded crisply. "I have an appointment, dear. With Madam Petrova herself."

Nastasya Petrova was said to be nearly as old as her mansion, and the huge, dark edifice, which she rarely set foot out of, had been built in the late 1920s and perched precariously on the edge of the bluff. Any reported sightings of this Russian grandam over the years had easily been outnumbered by UFOs.

Impressed that Mother had been granted a visit, I asked, "How in heaven's name did you manage that?"

Nose high, Mother said, "You will find out when I talk to Madam Petrova. I must conserve my energy, however, for the task at hand. . . . Pull into the circular drive, dear, right up to the portico, so we can arrive in style."

In a dirty, battered old Buick, we were to arrive in style? I shrugged, and did as I was told.

When I'd turned off the car, I asked, "Should we wait for the footman?"

Mother frowned. "Don't be facetious, dear—it's unbecoming. If you're not going to behave, I'll leave you behind in the car."

"I'll behave," I promised.

I simply *had* to find out what Mother was up to. . . .

With Mother in the lead, we walked up wide steps to a massive front door bookended by large, scrolled columns.

Mother stepped forward and grasped the tarnished brass knocker on the thick, weathered wood, and gave it a few whacks.

Going on, thirty long seconds had passed before Mother reached to give the knocker another clank, only to hear a click of a lock. The door began to open slowly, creaking in protestation, haunted-house-style.

There, framed in the doorway, stood a small, frail-looking woman, coarse gray hair piled high on her head, her face as weathered as the door. Still, she was nicely attired in a navy wool dress with a sparkling brooch pinned on one shoulder, and beige pumps. In the 1940s, this outfit had been high fashion—she even wore white gloves, with diamond bracelets on the outside of each wrist. I'd seen the same from Bette Davis in old movies.

Mother drew in a quick, excited breath, then, ridiculously, curtseyed as if the woman were Russian royalty.

Maybe I did want to stay in the car, at that.

Madam Petrova smiled, bemused. "Mrs. Borne," she said, without a hint of an accent, "please do come in. And who do you have with you?"

As Mother and I passed over the threshold, I said, "I'm her daughter—Brandy."

In the large foyer of the mansion, Nastasya Petrova paused to appraise me with intense, dark, intelligent eyes. "Ah. And such a *pretty* daughter, too," she said. "Are you just visiting, or do you live here in Serenity?"

I engaged the elderly woman in polite conversation,

covering for Mother's bad manners . . . because Mother was staring openmouthed at the interior's grandeur, her bug eyes flitting up the exquisitely carved staircase to the full-length stained-glass windows on the landing, then down again and over to a huge, ornately carved grandfather clock, and up once more to an Art Nouveau chandelier.

I said, "Mother. . . ."

Mother gaped. She had the expression of a bird-watcher who'd just spotted a rare one.

"*Mother!*"

She whirled. "Yes, dear?"

"Madam Petrova would like to attend to us in her parlor."

"Yes, dear."

As I took Mother's arm, I whispered, "Don't drool," and Mother wiped her chin with the back of a hand, taking me literally.

We followed the tiny woman through the large entryway to sliding, wooden double doors, which she opened for us to step into a room whose decor hadn't changed since the 1920s.

The parlor was dark, having lost the morning sun, its furnishings somber, an eclectic combination of Victorian, Art Nouveau, and Mediterranean. But here and there were clues as to Madam Petrova's heritage: religious crosses and small statues representing the Russian Orthodox Church, as well as a framed photo on the wall of Tsar Alexander and his family, all smiling, the poor brood not having an inkling of what was to come.

In front of a fireplace (unlit) with a large mirror, gleaming mantel, and an iridescent tile hearth, Mother plopped herself down on a horsehair couch, which gave forth a *poof!* of ancient dust. I followed her example, my poof being much smaller if no more dignified.

Madam Petrova lit like a dainty firefly on the edge of an ornately carved, red velvet-cushioned chair. Then she leaned forward to reach for an exquisite silver tea set, polished to a shine, which rested on a round table. "Tea?"

I was dehydrated after my bout with morning sickness, and gladly said, "Yes, please."

Mother also responded in the affirmative, and Nastasya Petrova poured, then handed us both identical floral cups and saucers, whose colors were so rich, the blossoms looked real.

After pouring herself a cup, the woman sat back, balancing the saucer on her fragile knees.

"Now," Madam Petrova began, "what can I do for you, Vivian?"

Mother opened her mouth, but closed it again, as the woman said in an aside to me, "I don't usually entertain people anymore . . . but your mother had been so kind to me years ago, when I was in the hospital with pneumonia. I do believe she did more good than those doctors by smuggling in her wonderful casseroles and soups." The woman raised her cup of tea in a toastlike gesture. "Not to *mention* the occasional flask of vodka."

Mother beamed. "My lips are sealed."

If only.

All this must have taken place during Mother's Florence Nightingale phase, when she would haunt the hospital hallways looking for any juicy piece of gossip, until finally the hospital staff barred her from the premises.

Madam Petrova returned her attention to Mother. "So, Vivian, my darling. Do tell me what's on your mind."

Now, usually that could take some time, but Mother surprised me by being relatively concise (for Mother).

She said, "I have been busy organizing a citywide church bazaar to help those affected by this terrible flood."

I goggled at her. This was all news to me.

"So far," she continued blithely, "all of the churches I've approached have agreed to participate, and they will be asking their congregations to scour attics and basements for antiques and collectibles." Mother clapped her hands together.

I jumped a little.

Our hostess jumped a little, too.

"Now! In order to make this event competitive, and to attract good merchandise—no white elephants allowed, mind you—I suggested that we form teams, all in the name of Christian charity and good fun. The Methodists will be one team, Presbyterians another, Baptists, Catholics . . . and so on." Mother, for once, ran out of breath, and helped herself to one, a generous serving. "Some of the smaller denominations, however, must band together to form teams, and I was hoping that *you* might join with *us*. . . . 'You' being the Russian Orthodox Church, and 'us' being New Hope, of course."

When this lengthy explanation was met with silence—as can sometimes happen with Mother's community theater performances—Mother became more animated, adding, "Also, included on our team would be the Episcopalians, the Lutherans, and our Jewish friends. So we're nothing to *sneeze* at!"

I wanted to crawl under the horsehair couch, which coincidentally *was* almost making me sneeze.

"And," Mother went on, raising a finger, "here's the coup de grâce. I have attracted the interest of *American Mid-West Magazine,* whose publisher assures me that his periodical will not only *match* the winning team's proceeds, but will feature that very team in one of its issues!"

Had Mother revealed her true motivation? To be showcased in a national magazine? Or at least a regionally circulated one. (Mother had the peculiar ability to make even such a small ambition seem grandiose.)

Madam Petrova was frowning, deepening the already-well-grooved creases in her face, yet she also seemed to be nodding her approval. I just sat and waited for this mixed signal to play itself out. . . .

Finally our hostess said measuredly, "I am sure I could find several quality items that would bring in a nice sum. And I'm certainly not concerned that my nephew—my only living relative—would object to these donations. Clifford has told me quite frankly that—beyond the house itself, which will one day be his—he is not interested in my possessions, as they are not to his taste . . . nor is he a sentimental man. . . ."

Clifford Ashland, a millionaire many times over, ran his own brokerage firm in Serenity. He lived with his wife, Angelica, in Serenity's most exclusive housing development, and collected antique cars as a hobby. His aunt's treasures would be knickknacks to him.

Mother was saying, "Then I can count on you, and the other members of the Russian Orthodox Church, to participate?"

Madam Petrova responded, "Yes, of course. I believe I can speak for all of us." She laughed once. "But we are dwindling number, Vivian . . . only fifteen, now. We've never had enough members to have our own local church."

Mother cocked her head with interest. "Where do you hold services?"

The elderly woman's eyes went to the ceiling. "Up in the ballroom. A bishop comes from a Chicago diocese once a month. We attend St. Mary's on the other Sundays. I go with my nephew and his wife."

Mother most likely knew this, but—not wanting to overplay her hand—feigned interest.

Madam Petrova, finished with her tea, set her cup and saucer carefully on the table. Her intense, dark eyes went to Mother. "What kind of antiques would you want from me?" she asked. "Furniture, china, jewelry . . . ?"

Mother placed her own cup and saucer on the table,

making a clatter. "I'm thinking of just *one* item, Nastasya—if I may call you that."

Now Madam Petrova cocked her head. "Certainly, Vivian. And that item would be . . . ?"

"Your Fabergé egg."

Madam Petrova's jaw dropped almost as far as mine.

The woman gasped. "H-how do you even *know* about the egg?"

Mother's smile was triumphant. "Then it *is* true."

The little woman was shaking her head, her eyes wide and almost alarmed. "Yes . . . but . . . it's been a carefully guarded family secret. Only my *nephew* knows of the egg."

And now Mother. Tomorrow the world.

Mother smiled slyly. "Do you remember the night in the hospital when we shared that flask of vodka? Well, that's when you spilled the beans . . . or the egg, I should say. But rest assured, my dear, I haven't told a soul. Never let it be said that Vivian Borne doesn't know how to hold a secret!"

Normally, I would say Vivian Borne held a secret the way a bucket with a hole in the bottom holds water. But in all these years, I had never heard a word from Mother about the improbable notion that a Serenity resident might own a fabled Fabergé egg.

What next? "Would you fetch the Maltese Falcon for me, my precious? It's in the garage." Or maybe, "Check the fridge, would you, dear, and see if that chunk of *Titanic* iceberg hasn't suffered freezer burn?"

Nastasya Petrova stood, pulling herself up to her full five feet, and for a moment I thought she was going to ask that we leave; but instead, the woman crossed over to the photo of the Tsar and his family and removed the frame from the wall, revealing a small safe. She spun the dial a few times, opened its door, reached in, then came back with something cradled in her hands. As the woman moved to sit between Mother and me, we scooted over.

Slowly Madam Petrova unfolded the piece of green velvet, uncovering the prize inside. We leaned in, anticipating the treat our eyes were about to feast on.

Mother and I simultaneously went, "Oh!" in a good way . . . then "Oh," in not so good a way.

The egg was a disappointment. Made of light-colored wood, it was lacking the diamonds, rubies, and emeralds that were the trademark of a Fabergé egg.

Madam Petrova noted our reaction and said, "I know at first glance, the egg seems rather, well, unprepossessing. But you must remember, Russia had been at war for several long years, and—like the forty-eighth and forty-ninth egg—the Tsar felt it wasn't quite right, in such times, to have anything lavish made for him to give to his wife." She shrugged her slight shoulders. "Besides, precious stones and metals by then were harder to come by."

The woman carefully opened the egg, revealing a small crystal bird with a gold wreath in its beak.

"The dove of peace," the woman said proudly.

"Well, it's not much to look at," Mother said matter-of-factly, "but still, it *is* the fiftieth and *final* egg commissioned by the Tsar."

I asked Madam Petrova, "How can you be sure this is the genuine article?" Quickly adding, after Mother shot me a reproving look, "Not to be impertinent."

Our hostess smiled enigmatically.

Then she said, "As a very young man, my father, Peter Petrov, was an apprentice at the House of Fabergé in St. Petersburg. Then the Russian Revolution began, and one evening, when he was working late, the Bolsheviks broke down the door and ransacked the business, taking everything of value. My father had only enough time to escape out the back, but he managed to grab one item—this precious egg. Which traveled with him to Finland, then Sweden. And in Norway he caught a boat to America."

The woman's smile turned inward.

"That's where he met my mother, who was returning to Iowa after visiting relatives in Oslo. They fell in love on the crossing, and settled here, where my mother's family—who owned a lumber mill—brought my father into their business."

Again, I could tell that Mother knew all of this, and was trying hard not to show her impatience.

Mother cleared her throat. "*About* the egg . . ."

Madam Petrova took a deep breath. "I quite agree with you, Vivian."

"You do?"

She nodded. "I can't think of any better use for it. This town and its people have been good to me over these many years, and if this object can bring in a good deal of money to help those now in need . . . then, yes, certainly, of *course* I agree to donate it."

Mother smiled broadly, as if auditioning for the Joker role in the next Batman movie.

But I foresaw a possible problem.

I asked, "What about your nephew? Wouldn't he object?"

Knickknacks were one thing, but a Fabergé egg?

Mother had reached behind Madam Petrova and was in the process of pinching my side, when a deep voice asked, "Would I object to what?"

Entering the room was Clifford Ashland, the son of our hostess's deceased sister. Tall, confident, with good looks rivaling the old swashbuckling movie star Stewart Granger, he wore expensive resort clothes—navy and white seersucker jacket, butter-yellow open-collar shirt, white slacks, and white deck shoes sans socks. Seeming more Palm Beach than Serenity, the nephew bent and kissed the cheek of his aunt as she raised her smiling face to him.

Ashland's eyes went to Mother, and then me; they did not have Granger's twinkle, though in other circumstances, they might have. Were Mother and I skunks at a garden party?

Madam Petrova said with a gesture, "You know Mrs. Borne, and this is her daughter, Brandy. . . ."

"Yes, of course," he said pleasantly. "I've bought several small Art Deco items recently from your booth at the antiques mall."

Mother had been stocking our little business in Pearl City Plaza since I'd been under the weather, so this was news to me.

Mother gushed, "It's *so* nice to see you again, Mr. Ashland."

I suppressed a gag. Had Mother forgotten that before Clifford Ashland had made his millions, he'd been a used-car salesman, from whom I'd purchased my first set of wheels, which had died an unceremonious death in the middle of an intersection on our way home, after which Mother had called him a charlatan (actually a blankety-blank charlatan)? But apparently, all is forgiven if you buy from our booth.

(Look, I know I said the "s" word was pretty much the extent of Mother's swearing, and it is. What she *literally* said was, "You're a blankety-blank charlatan!")

The nephew's attention went to the Fabergé egg cradled on his aunt's lap.

"That ugly old thing," he said with a chuckle, and a kind of shudder. "Definitely *not* laid by the golden goose."

Madam Petrova gave me a knowing look. "As I said, Clifford harbors no sentimentality for this family heirloom. So I'm sure he won't mind."

"Mind what?" Ashland asked, his smile fading.

His aunt said, "I've decided to sell the Fabergé egg at a citywide church bazaar to raise money for our flood victims."

Clifford Ashland's tanned face turned ashen. He took a few steps back and eased into an awaiting armchair.

"You can't be serious, Auntie," he said in apparent horror.

"Oh, yes, I can, dear," Madam Petrova told him firmly, digging in the heels of her beige pumps. "I've made up my mind."

Ashland leaned forward in the chair, gesturing animatedly. "But you'll never get out of it what it's worth at a local bazaar! You'd be much better off selling the egg through an auction house like Christie's or Sotheby's."

Mother piped up. "And that's exactly what we're going to be doing . . . in a sense."

Ashland frowned. "What do you mean?"

"Well," Mother explained excitedly, "my plan *is* to hold an auction for that one item, and have representatives from all the large auction houses there . . . plus private buyers. Think of the publicity! And, we have matching funds promised by a magazine company."

"Then the magazine people know about the egg?"

Mother put on her vaguely insulted face. "No, of course not. Only the people in this room know of its existence. The publisher, Samuel Woods, understands that there could be some large-ticket items, yes . . . but he has no idea there might be anything of *this* magnitude. Or that the likes of Christie's and Sotheby's will be on hand. Won't *he* be surprised!"

Ashland sat back and grunted, "Yes." He raised an eyebrow. "Be sure to get the publisher's offer in writing before you announce it," Ashland the businessman said. "He won't be expecting to have to match *those* kind of funds."

Madam Petrova looked at her nephew. "Then, dear, I have your blessing to donate the egg?"

Ashland's smile couldn't have been more casual if they'd been discussing whether to lend the neighbors a cup of sugar. "Yes, of course. The cause is a good one, and Mrs. Borne has anticipated my objection—that it be given away for a song."

"You're sure you don't object, dear?"

He shrugged. "It's a charitable contribution. Should be deductible. I'll have my tax people look into it."

"Well, that's fine, dear."

"I just hope it's what you want."

"It *is*, dear."

The room fell silent. Aunt and nephew obviously needed to discuss this further, and in private. Under all those "dear's" was a certain strain.

I stood and said (much to Mother's dismay), "Well . . . I guess we should be going."

Madam Petrova placed the Fabergé egg gently on the coffee table and rose. "Yes, I am tired, now." She extended her hand to Mother. "You *will* inform me with further developments of the bazaar? I will want to attend, naturally."

Mother promised she would.

As Mother and I took our leave of Madam Petrova, Clifford Ashland announced, "I'll walk you two ladies out. . . ."

And now for our private dressing-down, I thought.

Mother, too, sensed something coming, and outside, under the portico overhang, turned to face Ashland.

He didn't mince words. "I'm not happy about this," he snapped, looking from Mother to me, then back to Mother, "but if I know my aunt, once she decides to do something, it's done." He raised a lecturing finger, which also seemed like a threat. "Understand, I don't give a damn about that egg . . . but I *do* give a damn about my aunt! And I don't want to see her hurt."

Mother looked puzzled. "What do you mean? How could she be hurt?"

"What if someone buys the egg for an exorbitant amount, then claims it's a fake?" he asked. "Next comes a lawsuit . . . and scandal. That's just the kind of thing that could *kill* my aunt."

I spoke up. "Do you have any reason to think the egg is *not* legitimate?"

Ashland shrugged. "No . . . but what proof is there that the ugly old thing is authentic, really, other than my aunt's recollections?"

Mother shrugged. "Then let the buyer beware, I say."

"That's not good enough," Ashland said flatly. "If my aunt, and her estate, can't be protected, then I'm against this."

I asked, "Is there someone with expertise who could examine the egg? Someone willing to authenticate it, and put his reputation on the line?"

Ashland stoked his chin with one hand. "There *was* a expert from Chicago, who appraised the egg some years ago—for insurance purposes. In fact, he wanted to buy it."

"Well then, there's our answer," Mother said brightly. "If he could draw up a new appraisal, I'm sure that would give your aunt the necessary legal coverage."

Ashland was nodding slowly. "Perhaps. I'll try to contact him. It was a long time ago."

With that, we left a somewhat appeased Clifford Ashland, who went back in as we walked to my car.

I had a queasy feeling in the pit of my stomach that had nothing to do with morning sickness. No one had yet mentioned other obvious pitfalls in auctioning off such a valuable and rare item—little things, like crowd control and police security. . . .

Had Mother finally bitten off more than she could chew? Was she about to meet her Waterloo? And why was I rhyming all of a sudden?

I looked at Mother, seated next to me in the car. Her face was placid.

As usual she left the worrying to me!

"Chop chop, dear!" Mother said. "So little time, and so much to do. And detour signs be darned, take us into the downtown."

If she could throw caution to the wind, why shouldn't I?

"All right," I said, starting the car, "but *you're* paying for any tickets we get."

"After this auction," Mother said, "we'll be the most popular women in town. Any minor offenses we might commit in the meantime will be forgiven. After all, we are the *Borne* girls, who brought relief to our fellow citizens, all in the form of an antique egg."

"Right," I said, and pulled out. "Just don't forget what happened to Humpty Dumpty."

A Trash 'n' Treasures Tip

At a church bazaar, the best way to get first crack at antiques and collectibles is to help unpack and set up the merchandise. When Mother does this, the other attendees are guaranteed a major discovery: there's nothing good left.

Chapter Two

Mother Lays an Egg

Suppose I awoke some night to find the Angel of Death hovering near the foot of my bed, and should he/she/it say, "Brandy Borne, you have the choice of either coming with me now, or reliving one more day . . . but it must be the day of the church bazaar!" And I would shout unequivocally, "Take me now, *please!*"

Before that excruciatingly long Saturday had ended, sickness and death would fill the air, and as for our fabled Fabergé egg . . . well, maybe I'm getting ahead of myself. . . .

The morning of the bazaar began benignly enough: the weather beautiful, breezy, and bright—a "perfect ten" on the scale of a Midwestern day.

Mother had been up since at least four A.M.; even with two pillows over my head, I'd been able to hear her downstairs, below my bedroom, clomping around like a circus fat lady in galoshes. Finally, at six, unable to fall back asleep, I surrendered to crawl out of bed and hit the shower. Sushi, who usually slept on top of the covers, gave me an "*I'm* not getting up yet" look with her spooky white orbs, and underscored her point by burrowing under the sheets.

At first, the warm water pelting my skin felt fine, like a

hundred massaging fingers . . . but then it seemed like a hundred little needles were pricking me, and I quickly got out of the shower and put on a soft white robe.

In the kitchen, Mother had thoughtfully made a cheese and broccoli quiche, but the smell of it—along with the aroma of strong coffee—sent Miss Morning Sickness of the New Millennium running once again for the down-stairs bathroom.

I didn't make it to the bowl, however, and hunkered at the sink and retched wretchedly. When my stomach finally quieted, I looked at myself in the mirror, and what I saw gave me a start.

I was thin and pale, my skin a sickly color.

Mother, in her pink robe, stood beside me. "Dear, you simply *must* eat something—it's not good for you, *or* your precious little cargo. . . ."

"I know, I know," I moaned. "But I just *can't*." I started to cry.

Mother put her arms around me, and I lay my head on her shoulder.

When my tears had subsided, she asked, "How about some cinnamon toast and chamomile tea, sweetheart?"

I snuffled.

"I'll even burn the toast just how you *like* it. . . ."

I wiped my eyes with the back of a hand. "Okay . . . I'll . . . I'll try."

Mother smiled and pinched my cheek. "That's a good girl. Now, go upstairs and get dressed. I'll have it ready in a jiffy."

From my closet I selected a girlie-pink Juicy Couture hoodie and sweatpants, and slipped on my pink short UGGS, hoping the spring color would make me look (and feel) better. But I could have easily been mistaken for a very large Easter bunny, like that poor kid in *A Christmas Story*.

When I came back down, Mother had the hot tea and burnt toast waiting for me at the small, round, table-for-two on the screened-in back porch.

Mother, now dressed in a nautical theme—navy jacket and slacks, and a white blouse with anchors (woman over-board!)—sat with me while I ate.

She said, "I don't expect you to help much today, dear, considering your condition, and how you're feeling . . . but I *might* need your assistance during the auction."

"When's that gonna be?" I asked with my mouth full.

"One o'clock—right after the luncheon."

I took a sip of tea. "What do you want me to do?" I hoped it wouldn't be too taxing, as this pregnancy made me so tired these days.

"I'd like you to help me keep track of the bids. It's going to involve large sums of money, you know."

About to take another sip, I froze, the cup at my lips. "Why are *you* worried about it? It's not like *you're* the auctioneer."

She straightened her hair.

"Mother?"

She took off her glasses and polished them with a napkin.

"Mother, you're *not* the auctioneer, are you?"

"Well, what if I am, dear?"

I groaned.

"Why look so shocked? I took that course last year. Surely you remember."

How could I forget? For days after Mother returned from a one-week course at the Worldwide College of Auctioneering in Mason City, she had talked fast in a sing-songy chant. To wit (or maybe two half-wits):

"Mother, when should we leave for the mall?"

"How about two o'clock? Two o'clock, do I hear two-fifteen? That's two-fifteen, two-fifteen, do I hear two-thirty, two-thirty? That's two-thirty . . . going once, going twice, *gone!*"

Real gone.

Mother was saying, "There's really nothing *to* being an auctioneer. My goodness, why pay good money for a professional, I say, when I can do it myself!"

"Well, that's a wonderful idea. Just because some of the most experienced bidders in the world are going to be in attendance, including representatives of Sotheby's and Christie's, plus several private collectors, among them a Russian who came halfway across the world—why on Earth would we want a professional?"

"I'm glad to see you see it the way I do."

Mother recognizes my sarcasm; she just pretends not to.

"You do realize," I said, "that everything that happens today will be recorded for posterity by local TV to be broadcast around the world, and posted on the Internet?"

"Oh, yes! Isn't that *exciting!*"

I considered telling Mother that I was too sick to go, but then somebody needed to be there to protect her from getting tarred and feathered after the botched auction. . . .

Sushi materialized at my feet, drawn from her warm bed by the smell of the toast. I broke off some crust and gave it to her.

Mother rose from the little table. "We should go soon, dear. I want to be there by eight, to get a good parking place."

I put my dishes in the sink, then fed Sushi some dog food, followed by a shot of insulin, and the usual dog biscuit treat that was her reward, or really bribe, for not running away from the needle.

With the doggie rituals completed, I put Soosh outside for a few minutes, so I wouldn't have to clean up a mess when we got back later. Then Mother and I headed out to my car, and an event I was looking forward to with the enthusiasm of one summoned to an IRS audit.

Actually, the charity church bazaar almost hadn't happened. A major stumbling block had arisen when Mother couldn't find a facility available on a Saturday that was big enough to handle the large crowd the auction would surely attract. The county fairground was under construction because the grandstand had recently burned down (thanks to Mother—see *Antiques Flee Market*); the high school gymnasium was being used for a basketball tournament; the community center, located downtown, had been half under water until recently (the aftermath *not* pretty); and all of the larger churches had weddings scheduled for every weekend.

Then, according to Mother, a miracle happened. A nuptial planned at St. Mary's Church got canceled after the bride-to-be received an anonymous phone call that her beloved intended had been seen out with another woman. (Shame on you for suspecting Mother!) (Anyway, she swore to me on the family Bible that she hadn't made the cruel call, because such shameless rumor-mongering was unforgivable, a statement followed by Mother listing five "terrible gossips" who she considered capable of the deed, including Mrs. Mulligan down the street, one of her prime sources.)

While the Catholic church was not an ideal place to hold the bazaar and auction, the main church building—with its large sanctuary, smaller chapel, choir room, meditation room, and library—could be used to hold the various church "teams." And the newly attached one-story Catholic elementary school, with its many classrooms, could also be incorporated in Mother's plan of action. Paramount, too, was St. Mary's ample parking lot, which could accommodate hundreds of cars.

At the urging of Nastasya's nephew Clifford—a respected member of St. Mary's and a major donor—Father O'Brien agreed to host the event, once Clifford pointed out that the church would gain goodwill from the community for this literal act of charity. Plus it might even attract new sheep into Father O'Brien's flock, or at least round up some old lambs who'd strayed.

When I was in grade school, Mother and I had attended St. Mary's for a while. Catholicism was just one of a long list of religions Mother "tried out" when she was searching for a perfect heavenly fit for us two earthly creatures. I enjoyed going to mass because there was always some iconic statue or deity to look at while seated in the pews, plus the ritualistic repetition of the service seemed comforting to me during times of mental turbulence with Mother.

But ultimately Mother decided St. Mary's wasn't for us, stating, "Their pomp and circumstance is *much* too theatrical," so we moved on. (Personally, I think Mother couldn't stand to be stuck out in the audience, and not performing up at the pulpit. She rarely attends plays she isn't appearing in.)

Built around the turn of the last century, St. Mary's was a gloomy, gothic limestone structure sitting high on a hill in the center of town. As a child, I'd heard members of other churches complain that St. Mary's on its perch was "lording itself over all the other lowly churches" in Serenity. Maybe so, but being on high ground during flood season made it the ideal choice for all the churches to come together for this cause.

I steered the Buick up a steep winding drive to the large cement parking lot behind the church. (About the only people who ever climbed the two-hundred-plus steps from the street level were high school jocks trying to bulk up.) Even though the bazaar wouldn't begin for another hour, dozens of cars were already there.

"Park up close to the door, dear," Mother instructed, as she opened the glove compartment to extract a handicap parking placard she'd gotten ten years ago after minor surgery on an ingrown toenail.

"Put that back!"

"But, dear, you're pregnant, and I am bipolar."

"You're also shameless. I'll drop you off at the door and park somewhere where we'd be less likely to get hit by lightning."

Mother frowned. "Dear, this high up *anyone* might get hit by lightning."

"Someday when *you* need a handicapped spot, there won't be one because you've already taken it!"

Even though that didn't make sense, Mother understood my meaning. "Don't drop me off," she said with martyred disdain. "I can manage."

I parked, not all that far away, and Mother got out of the car, and I followed obediently behind her. She was limping.

"The ingrown toenail was the *other* foot," I said.

Then, Praise the Lord, another miracle occurred, as her limp was healed.

Soon we entered a small marble vestibule. More doors led to an octagon-shaped narthex—a large lobby area—where several women were fussing over a long banquet table, preparing to take attendance money, dispense tickets, and hand out maps of team locations. A sign on the wall stated that the ten-dollar fee to get in also included a potluck lunch. Hysteria was already in the air, middle-aged and elderly ladies chattering like novelty-shop teeth.

Mother paid for us, and handed me our tickets for safekeeping; then we headed for our team's location, which was the main church sanctuary, just off the narthex.

Earlier, Mother had told the organizers that our team—dubbed by her "Team Eggs-tra Ordinaire"—would require the sanctuary because that was the best place to hold the auction; no need to bring in chairs, as the pews would serve as seating, and the pulpit had its own sound system for the auctioneer.

No one disagreed with her logic, but I wondered if this arrangement miffed some of the others, especially the home-team Catholics who were relegated to their own small adjacent chapel.

Mother and I entered the sanctuary—which was designed in the shape of a cross—and were immediately greeted by the statue of the Holy Water Angel. Skirting around the baptismal font, we passed the arched entrance to the small chapel, where a middle-aged woman in a conservative gray dress and sensible flats stood staring at us. Madeline Pierce, the church secretary, also wore a frown, showing her displeasure with her team's cramped location.

Mother nodded curtly and, smiling a little too broadly, marched triumphantly on.

I caught up with Mother in the center aisle, grabbing her arm, pulling her up short.

"Gloating is very un-Christian," I whispered.

Mother turned, asking disingenuously, "Whatever do you mean, dear?"

"Don't play innocent. Not here," I said, playing stern mother to her child. "You don't need to be rude. Teams or not, this is a community effort."

Mother's eyebrows climbed over the rim of her oversized glasses. "Who do you think *organized* this community effort? Anyway, I thought I was being friendly. I *smiled*, didn't I?"

"Like a cat with a mouse in its paws."

Mother's laugh was dismissive. "Nonsense."

I raised a finger. "*You* don't like me off my Prozac . . . and *I* don't like you up on your high horse. Let's strive to be better people, okay? Here in church, at least?"

Mother looked thoughtful for a moment, then said, "Perhaps I *was* a wee bit smug. We are, after all, guests in God's house."

I gave her an earthly smirk. "Try to keep that in mind."

While Mother hurried on, I took my time, reacquainting myself with the stations of the cross, which represented the final hours of Christ from condemnation to resurrection, and paused to gaze at the beautiful stained-glass windows, made glowingly lovely by the morning sun.

At the west transept (the left arm of the cross), I stopped to stare at the statue of St. Mary, Mother of Sorrows, which had been repainted since I'd seen it last, making the seven daggers piercing her heart more noticeable.

I moved on to the statue of St. Joseph—the Patron of Happy Death—holding the baby Jesus. It, too, had a fresh coat of paint.

I had arrived at the communion railing, where four more long banquet tables displayed a wide variety of antiques and collectibles gathered from our team's members; each item was tagged and, when appropriate, polished and carefully arranged on white linen tablecloths.

Among the donations were pottery, silver tea sets, china dishes, china figurines, lady-head vases, oil lamps, candlesticks, cookie jars, collectible toys, jewelry, and evening bags. Squatting around the periphery of the tables were a few antique furniture pieces, including a lawyer's five-shelf bookcase, a set of six caned oak chairs, a claw-footed tea table, and a waterfall Art Deco dresser.

Of the dozen or so people present, I recognized only three from our small church: Alice Hetzler, a retired teacher; Frannie Phillips, former nurse; and Harold Kerr, ex-Army captain. The two women were gal pals of Mother's, members of her Red-Hatted League mystery book club. The man also belonged to a club—the Romeos (Retired Old Men Eating Out)—and, if Mother is to be believed, the old boy had once tried to play Romeo to her Juliet (after Father passed away, of course).

The other members of our team milling around were from the Episcopalian and Lutheran churches, and the Jewish synagogue. I recognized some of them, but didn't know their names.

Nastasya Petrova was not among them. My understanding was that she was receiving the qualified bidders in her home early this morning for a private viewing of the Fabergé egg. The protocol was that each bidder would be escorted into the Petrova parlor for a private, individual examination of the artifact, for two purposes—first, to establish to each bidder's satisfaction that this was the genuine article; and second, to present a sealed bid. All of the bidders were then gathered into the parlor, the sealed bids revealed, and the highest of these would be this afternoon's opening bid—Mother had predicted three hundred thousand. We would see.

The egg itself had been locked away in Nastasya Petrova's safe deposit box since the day after Mother and I dropped by to propose the auction. And it had been delivered by local police to the Petrova mansion this morning for that series of private viewings. Those or other armed police guards, provided by Chief Cassato, would deliver the egg just in time to be the star of the big show.

Anyway, as our team was getting its act together, Harold began barking as to who should do what once the bazaar began, and I knew Mother would not put up with the ex-Army captain's orders, and had planned my retreat even before the battle had begun.

"Mother," I said, "it doesn't look like I'm needed here. Why don't I check out the other teams and see how they're doing?"

Mother always loved subterfuge. "Good idea, dear! And pick up some early bargains for our booth."

Gathering my purse and map, I decided to first check out the kitchen in the basement, to see what was being served for lunch, hoping that something might look appealing to my finicky stomach.

But instead of heading back through the sanctuary and taking the main stairs down in the narthex (hereafter referred to as lobby), I decided to use a secret passageway, which was located behind the choir benches to the left of the tabernacle, an ornately carved altar with spiral finials supported on the heads of four cherubic angels (ouch).

Years ago, when I sang in children's choir, I always sat in the back row in front of this panel, and when I got bored with mass I'd slip out and root around in the always-well-stocked kitchen, then return to my choir pew, often with food on my face, and not fooling anybody (especially Mother). I adored the secret passageway, as a child, as it was straight out of the Nancy Drew mysteries I was reading.

Even now I got a kick out of it. I slid the panel open, slipped through, and closed it again. Then, in the dark, I felt my way down the narrow stone steps, palms pressed to the cold, clammy walls.

At the base of the stairs I pushed open another panel, and reappeared in the kitchen behind a cart of pots and pans. Once a dark, claustrophobia-inducing place, the kitchen had been completely remodeled since I'd snuck my last piece of cake. Now it seemed huge—all bright white and shining chrome, with modern, restaurant-quality appliances.

I stood unnoticed as the room swirled with people in motion, coming and going as they added more and more food to the already-overflowing counters. The mixture of smells was dizzying—at once wonderful and horrible—but one really stood out: the inviting aroma of Mrs. Mulligan's stew.

She stood a short distance away, at the oversized stove,

stirring her famous concoction in a large vat with a long wooden spoon. (She wasn't in the vat—the spoon was.)

As I approached, she glanced up from her task, and said, "Well, well . . . I'll be a monkey's auntie. . . . If it isn't Brandy Borne."

And she did look like a monkey's aunt—a orangutan to be exact, with her short Lucille Ball–red wig (a little off-kilter), facial hair, and close-set beady eyes. She had the kind of unpleasant appearance that made it difficult to think kind thoughts even in church.

Mrs. Mulligan was well-known in Serenity as *the* town gossip, running rings around Mother. Unlike Mother, this woman was indiscriminate in her scandalmongering; she didn't care if the gossip was true or not, or who it hurt. Still, that hadn't stopped Mother from going over to Mrs. Mulligan's, once or twice a week, and not for stew.

With a nod, I said, "Mrs. Mulligan."

An eyebrow arched, she replied, "I can't say I *approve* of any woman renting out her womb. . . ."

At first I thought she had said "room," Elmer Fudd-style, but then her ball-bearing eyes drifted to my stomach.

I said, "It's rent-free. My best friend couldn't have a child and I'm helping her out."

But then, the town gossip knew all this.

Mrs. Mulligan raised another eyebrow, a lecturing one. "Our bodies are God's *temple* and should not be used other than for his purpose."

"Funny. I thought helping out a friend was a Christian thing to do."

She sniffed and shrugged. "Still, what's done is done. . . ." She frowned. "You look *terrible*, dear."

"Thank you for your concern."

"How about some of my famous stew?" she asked, returning her attention to the cauldron.

It did smell good. She might have been a horrible woman, but her stew was legendarily wonderful; sometimes I suspected she was the *original* Mulligan. My mind said "Yes," and I waited for my stomach to concur.

To my surprise it growled a long, loud affirmative.

"I'd love some," I said. "Is it done?"

Mrs. Mulligan smiled proudly. "Oh, yes—I made it yesterday and it's just reheating."

I retrieved a bowl from a cupboard, and a bent soup spoon from the silverware drawer, and Mrs. Mulligan used a ladle to fill my dish.

I ate two bowls—it was that delicious.

MRS. MULLIGAN'S SPICY BEEF STEW

Ingredients:

2 Tbl. olive oil
1 ½ lbs. lean chuck roast, cubed
¼ cup flour
1 can (14 oz.) beef broth
1 cup beer or dry red wine
1 onion, chopped
1 clove garlic, minced
1 Tbl. brown sugar
1 tsp. dried thyme
1 tsp. sage
½ tsp. cumin
½ salt
1 Tbl. mild chili powder
6 medium potatoes
4 large carrots
4 stalks celery

Preheat oven to 350 degrees. In Dutch oven, brown beef cubes over medium-high heat. Remove beef and stir in flour. Add all other ingredients, including beef, and bring to a boil. Cover and transfer to oven. Cook for 2 hours.

After eating the stew, I thanked Mrs. Mulligan, who responded warmly (suddenly she didn't seem so bad), then left the kitchen for the dining hall area where I sat in a folding chair next to a bathroom. After fifteen minutes or so, satisfied that my stomach wouldn't change its mind about the spicy meal, I headed upstairs to the lobby to begin trolling for bargains . . .

. . . and what I found was that there were none to be had!

Every team, in every location, had priced their antiques and collectibles way too high. Understandably, many of the items were family heirlooms going on the block for a worthy cause; but unless dealers—a significant part of the crowd—could make a profit in resale . . . well, basically, the only sales the teams had made so far were to each other.

I reported back to Mother.

"This is *not* good," she responded, dismayed. "Everything will hinge on the auction, and we have our proverbial eggs in one basket."

"Egg. Just *one* egg, Mother."

I will now fast-forward through the luncheon (which I didn't attend, having already eaten), and get to the auction itself.

To say that the sanctuary was filled to capacity is an understatement—people were packed into the pews like the Pope was speaking, and there wasn't even standing room left. There were many familiar faces, including such cronies of Mother's as various members of her Red Hat social club, lovely African-American Shawntea, who drove the local gas-powered trolley, and local barfly Henry Something-or-other, looking surprisingly sober. The church was definitely in violation of the fire code, but no one seemed to care, since Our Heavenly Father apparently didn't.

At the back of the sanctuary, the media had set up camp, which included several TV camera crews—local affiliates that would no doubt be sending their feed to national channels. But a few renegade reporters had sneaked up to the front where the bidders were sequestered in the first pew, the press squatting in the aisles, their camcorders at the ready.

Mother and I sat in the two celebrant's chairs next to the lectern (stage left), while Father O'Brien stood stiffly at the pulpit (stage right).

He cleared his throat and a pin-drop hush fell over the crowd. The white-robed priest—a slender, middle-aged man with receding hairline and ruddy complexion, his shoulders hunched, perhaps by the weight of the world—raised a benevolent hand and gave a benediction.

Was a blessing really necessary today? I think the priest probably provided one in response to criticism from certain of his parishioners who reportedly felt the sanctuary should not be used for raising money, even if for a worthy cause. Christ throwing out the money-lenders had been cited. But what did these Christians think collection plates were all about?

After the benediction, a stirring at the back turned heads, and the standing crowd parted for Nastasya Petrova—looking elegantly regal in a long-sleeved, high-necked royal-blue evening dress—carrying the surprisingly unprepossessing Fabergé egg on a small red-velvet pillow.

Two policemen followed close behind her: tall and gangly Officer Munson, and sandy-haired, brown-eyed handsome Brian Lawson, my once and maybe future boyfriend. Our relationship was on hiatus while Brian tended to a personal matter with his ex-wife (their daughter was battling an eating disorder), and while I had Tina and Kevin's baby.

The presence of police security, by the way, was a Mother touch, to heighten the suspense of the auction; but considering the value of the egg, their presence wasn't just stagecraft.

All eyes followed Madam Petrova as she made her slow, royal walk down the center aisle, trailed by the two officers, whose expressions suggested they were none too happy to be a part of Mother's theatrics.

Brian spotted me in the celebrant's chair, and we exchanged looks—his, exasperated; mine, chagrined.

At the communion railing, the little procession parted ways—Officer Munson taking a spot to the right of the pulpit, and Brian to the left of the lectern—while Madam Petrova ascended the two steps of the inner sanctuary and placed the pillow on the altar table. She then crossed over to the lectern and stood behind it, her head barely visible to the audience.

Mother jack-in-the-boxed up, rushed over, and bent the microphone neck to accommodate the tiny woman, in the process making a loud, amplified *THUNK!*

After mother returned to her chair, and I did my best to crawl inside my skin, Madam Petrova—looking even more frail than she had during our visit—began to speak, sharing with the attendees the history of the Fabergé egg and how it came to be in her possession, much as she'd related to us at her home.

Honestly, I didn't hear much of what she said, caught up in anticipation about the potential disaster that would soon follow in the form of auctioneer Mother. Would her performance find its way onto YouTube, I wondered, and/or Keith Olbermann's "Oddball" segment on MSNBC's *Countdown*?

I looked slowly down the row of bidders, seated near

me in front of the lectern. Resting on my lap was a legal pad with their names written down, along with a column for their bids, so that I could prompt Mother if (make that *when*) she got lost in the process.

The well-attired players were: handsome, businesslike Don Kaufman, representing the Forbes family, owner of eleven of the Imperial eggs; attractive gray-business-suited brunette Katherine Estherhaus, New York, representing Christie's Auction House; slender, dark-haired, bespectacled John Richards, here for Sotheby's of London; stocky, solemn Sergei Ivanov, wealthy Moscow industrialist; and white-maned, distinguished-looking Louis Martinette, the private dealer (and collector of other Fabergé works), who had originally appraised the egg. The dark-eyed Martinette had an oval face with half-lidded eyes and deep grooves of character or anyway experience.

Also seated among the players was the publisher of *American Mid-West Magazine*, Samuel Woods, a relatively young man in a dark pinstriped suit; he seemed a bundle of nervous tics, sweating profusely, most likely contemplating the next stockholders' meeting where he would have to explain a drop in profits due to having to match today's winning bid.

Madam Petrova ended her ancestral story to thunderous applause (I noticed, however, that the Russian attendee wasn't clapping) and then she traded seats with Mother, who approached the lectern to start the auction.

I, too, had broken out in a cold sweat, knowing what disaster likely awaited, wishing I could be anywhere else— Mars or Kentucky or maybe that island on *Lost*. And yet—like a bystander at a bad accident—I couldn't take my eyes off Mother. . . .

She began by leaning toward the microphone and blurting ridiculously, "Is this *on*?" So loud that everyone jumped a little.

The reps of Christie's and Sotheby's, seated next to each other, exchanged wide-eyed looks. They had come to Podunk in the middle of Flyover Country expecting just about anything—anything but *Mother*, that is. . . .

I grinned to myself. *You ain't seen nothin' yet.*

Mother straightened her shoulders, produced a gavel from beneath the lectern, and banged it.

"The bidding for the Fabergé egg will begin!" Mother announced.

A cheer went up from the audience, echoing in the sanctuary.

Mother said crisply, "Bidding starts at three. Do I have three?"

Earlier, at our kitchen table, Mother had created some homemade bidding placards, using recycled cardboard and old Popsicle sticks; but I'd convinced her it would be more dignified if the bidders simply used their heads or hands.

And the first bidder—a chubby, local thrill-seeker—now did so, waving his hand wildly like a kid in class who had to use the bathroom.

Mother, flushed with excitement, said, "I have three hundred thousand dollars—do I have three-fifty?"

The Russian nodded his bucket head, and the thrill-seeker appeared relieved to be off the hook for three hundred grand when he may have thought she meant three thousand or even three hundred.

"Three-fifty—do I have four?"

The Forbes rep, Don Kaufman, nodded.

"That's four . . . four. . . . Do I have four-fifty?"

Christie's Katherine Estherhaus raised a red-nailed finger.

"Four-fifty—do I have five?"

John Richards from Sotheby's nodded.

Mother picked up the pace; the crowd stayed with her, their excitement mounting.

"Five hundred thousand dollars! Do I have five-fifty?"

Sergei Ivanov swiped the air with a bear paw.

"Five-fifty! Six? Do I have six?"

Don Kaufman nodded.

"Six hundred thousand! I have six hundred thousand. Is there six-fifty?"

The audience began egging the bidders on with chants of "More! *More!*"

John Richards aimed a forefinger at Mother.

Mother, red-faced, shouted, "Do I have seven?"

When none of the bidders twitched, Mother looked pointedly at Katherine Estherhaus, and asked incredulously, "Are *you* going to let your cousin across the pond win the bid? Have you so soon forgotten the Boston Tea Party?"

I was squirming in embarrassment, but darned if Estherhaus's red-nailed hand didn't fly up, and the audience cheered.

"I have seven hundred thousand! Do I have seven-*fifty?*"

Louis Martinette, until now silent, seemingly bored with the proceedings, intoned, "One million," drawing gasps and shouts of exultation from the crowd. The white-haired gent appeared as casual as somebody ordering a cheeseburger. Or in his case, maybe, a filet mignon.

But suddenly, strangely, there were other sounds emanating from the crowd: cries of alarm, and fear.

Mother, oblivious to anything but her own performance, shouted in her best Dr. Evil style, "One *million* dollars! Going once . . . going twice . . . *sold!*"

And she banged the gavel.

My eyes were on Brian, who—along with Officer Munson—had been standing at parade rest during the auction.

Brian's body tensed as he, too, became aware of a disturbance in the crowd, beginning with those standing in
back.

Here and there, people were moaning, some keeling
over, while others cried out for help. The audience was
falling ill, a response apparently not inspired by Mother's
performance, which by her standards had been remarkably tame.

Brian moved quickly up the center aisle to aid those
who were sick, but his effort was impeded when a gentleman toppled from a pew into his path, and lay curled and
convulsing.

Mother, frozen at the lectern, added to the unfolding
drama, when the microphone picked up her astonished
words, "Dear Lord, what *is* this? *Anthrax?*"

Well, maybe *not* remarkably tame. . . .

Panic ensued as the crowd tried to flee, moving en masse
toward the back of the sanctuary, pushing and shoving,
and jumping over those who had fallen. Did *everybody*
have morning sickness?

My plan of escape was via the rear of the room, which
is to say the *front* of the sanctuary, through the chambers
located behind the tabernacle. I turned to gather Madam
Petrova, still seated in the other celebrant's chair.

She was leaning back, staring straight ahead, though
she seemed not to be looking at anything.

"Mother!" I called out, alarmed.

Mother rushed over, then knelt, her knees making a
popping sound. She peered into Nastasya's face, and felt
for a pulse in the woman's neck.

She shook her head somberly. "She's gone, dear."

"Are you *sure?*"

Behind the big lenses, her eyes were wild. "Don't you
think I know a *corpse* when I see one?"

The question was both blunt and rhetorical: Mother indeed had firsthand experience with dead bodies since I'd returned home and gotten unwillingly caught up in her amateur sleuthing.

I asked pitifully, "Isn't there anything we can do?"

I was specifically thinking about finding Nastasya's nephew, Clifford Ashland, but the last I'd seen him, he was standing at the back of the sanctuary, and would likely have been swept out into the lobby by the current of the panicking crowd.

Mother stood, supported by the arm of the celebrant's chair, her knees now making a grinding noise.

"The best thing we can do, my dear, is to get out of here . . . out into the fresh air . . . until we know what is happening."

The stench of sickness was in both our nostrils. Could Mother have been right—could it be Anthrax? Or Legionnaire's Disease?

I said, "There's an exit door in the furnace room."

Mother shook her head. "You know it's locked, dear. . . . Security." She raised a finger. "But the spiral staircase can take us up to the bell tower, where we can go across the walkway to the front of the church, and down the stairs into the vestibule."

It sounded like a plan. But when I hesitated, looking at Madam Petrova, Mother said softly, "Come, dear, she's in God's hands now. We must think of ourselves—and your little forthcoming bundle from above."

With Mother in the lead, we fled to the arched wooden door behind the tabernacle, then on through to the choir room, where white robes, hanging like limp ghosts on a clothes rack, flapped their arms as we hurried past.

Through another door we entered the dim, dreary maintenance room, greeted by a water pipe dripping somewhere. We skirted around the ancient metal furnace, shut down for the season, and Mother suddenly stopped short; I stumbled into her, nearly losing my balance.

Father O'Brien was on his knees near the spiral staircase, bent over as if praying, and perhaps he was; if so, it was inspired by the sprawled body of Louis Martinette, who lay on his back, eyes staring upward, head cracked open like an egg, spilling not yellow, but a bright terrible red.

A Trash 'n' Treasures Tip

When attending a church bazaar—where money is being raised to help the disadvantaged—leave your price haggling at the door. Don't be greedy about the needy.

Chapter Three

A Curate's Egg

We didn't arrive home until late evening, because Mother felt a responsibility to linger at St. Mary's Church until the last of the sick had been transported to area hospitals.

Before you attribute caring compassion to Mother's various traits, keep in mind that the diva also wanted to find out as much as she could from the authorities about what had caused the sudden illness of over one-hundred-plus people, with the only fatality an ironic, especially tragic one—Madam Petrova herself, whose Christian spirit of generosity had been rewarded most bitterly.

Then there was also the matter of the unfortunate Louis Martinette, the winning bidder of the Fabergé egg. . . .

According to what Mother had overhead at the scene from the coroner, Martinette's body was (she vividly put it) "a sack of broken bones," indicating the man had fallen down the high spiral staircase—which he had apparently, trying to exit the scene of mass sickness, climbed after finding the back door locked.

So the question seemed obvious: was the fall an accident, or had he been pushed?

At various times I have referred to Mother's tendency to

view herself as a great detective. She and I had, bizarrely enough, been involved in several murder cases over a year or so that seemed no longer than the War of the Roses. From Mother's point of view, we have solved three cases for the local police; from the local police's point of view, they solved these cases despite our interference.

By the way, I once asked who she (Mother) thought she was—Miss Marple? Jessica Fletcher, maybe?

"I'm more the Angie Dickinson type, dear—remember *Police Woman?*"

Consequently, extracting Mother from the church premises was as tricky as removing a burrowed-in tick from a child's scalp. Finally, an exasperated Chief Tony Cassato—Serenity's top cop—put a figurative hot match head to Mother's swollen back, forcing her to leave (or anyway me to take her away), since Vivian Borne has sucked all the blood out of that crime scene that there was to suck . . . *ugh!* That analogy made me more nauseous than another bout of morning sickness. Apologies.

By the way, I was exhausted, having actually helped out at the church, corralling the sick in various areas as those in the most trouble got the first rides to the hospital; I helped distribute water and aspirin and encouraging words, and emptied the pots and pans that had been provided for the upchuckers. Aren't you glad I'm sparing you the details?

Meanwhile, Mother was flying high, and don't think my hackles weren't tingling, seeing her manic self kicking in.

"The cause of the sickness has been tentatively linked to the lunch served," Mother said as we rode home on the lovely moonlit spring evening. "Now, that was *withheld* from the media, dear . . . so do keep that to yourself."

And here I'd been planning to hit the bars tonight and troll for media types to peddle scoops to.

"Most likely salmonella poisoning," she was saying. "But tests will have to be conducted to pinpoint the offending food, which will take time, because so many different dishes had been eaten. That's potluck for you!"

"Food poisoning, then," I said. "That egg winner—Louis Martinette? *He* didn't die of something he ate. But I suppose you could write it off to collateral damage from the panic the food poisoning set in motion."

"You could, dear—but the police aren't."

"No?"

"No. Mr. Martinette's death is being treated as suspicious."

"I think I know why."

Mother's eyes were gleaming like the jewels on one of the better Fabergé eggs. "Do you, dear? I would love to hear your theory! We are a *team*, you know."

"Well," I said, ignoring the latter, "I don't think you can fall all the way down a spiral staircase. You'd get caught up in the works, maybe a quarter of the way down—and the way that staircase is constructed? You couldn't fall through the side rungs to the floor. There's a railing up there on the wooden landing, but not much of one. Pushing someone over wouldn't be *that* much of a challenge. . . ."

"Brandy! This is wonderful! You're thinking like a detective."

I sent my eyes from the road to her disturbing face. "We're just *talking*. We're not getting involved in another of these things. This isn't *Murder, She Wrote*, Mother, or *Nancy Drew*, either. You can't—*we* can't—go snooping around without getting ourselves into real trouble this time."

She touched her cheek with a forefinger. "I'm afraid I *am* in real trouble, dear."

"Why is that?"

"The auction . . . I'm afraid it was a fiasco."

"You think?"

"Oh, I don't mean the hundred people throwing up, or

even our Russian benefactor being the only food-poisoning fatality. It was Mr. Martinette's death that has put my mammaries in an old-fashioned washing machine."

"Huh?"

She whispered, looking around to make sure no one else was in the car, eavesdropping. "Titties in a wringer, dear. Titties in a wringer."

She really hadn't needed to repeat that.

"You see," she said, "each of the credible bidders had arranged a line of credit up to at least a million dollars with First National. The paperwork, and the actual transfer of funds, were to take place *after* the auction, off the church premises, at Father O'Brien's request."

"Why?"

"He apparently found it undignified. Too much like money lenders in the temple."

As if allowing Vivian Borne to run an auction in your church was the *dignified* way to go. . . .

"Anywhoo," she went on, "Mr. Martinette obviously did not have time to make payment, nor had he taken care of any of the paperwork. With his death, and Madam Petrova's, the egg goes back into her estate and the auction is null and void."

"How do you *know* this?"

"The bank president was there—Mr. Ingstad? He answered all of my questions, which was very kind of him, considering he was intermittently—how shall I put it delicately?—sitting there filling a pan at his feet."

I closed my eyes. This nasty image reminded me of the smell in that church, which I hoped one day to banish from my sensory memory.

"So then the guy who really benefits," I said, "is Clifford Ashland."

"One would think, but then he's already wealthy in his own right. So I hardly see why he'd kill Martinette, much less his beloved aunt! I mean, can you imagine anyone wanting to kill a beloved elderly relation?"

I looked at her. "Am I under oath?"

"No, dear." Her smile was wicked. "But I can tell you that the death of Mr. Martinette has been deemed suspicious *not* because of the nature of his injuries, rather due to . . . now, you simply *must* promise to keep this from press!"

"*Mother!*"

"Sorry, dear. But imagine how excited the media will become when they learn that the Fabergé egg . . . is . . . wait for it, darling . . . *missing.*"

"*What?*"

"Several people gave statements confirming that Martinette moved from his seat and claimed the egg on the altar table, just as panic broke out." She raised a finger skyward and waggled it. "And yet the valuable item was not found with his body!"

"Father O'Brien was right there. . . ."

"Yes, dear . . . and Father O'Brien says he did not notice the egg. Of course, he didn't search the poor man—he was more concerned with checking for signs of life, and of course giving the last rites."

"Wow. Gotta hand it to you, Mother—you sure can soak up a lot of information when people all around you are getting sick."

"Thank you, dear. But all is not bleak."

"Really?"

Her smile was wide, making her face nothing but teeth and magnified eyes, like a cartoon animal. "Yes, our team brought in more money than any other . . . even *without* the million-dollar egg! So, technically, we were the winners, and will be featured in *American Mid-West Magazine!*"

"Well, I'm glad to see the tragedy hasn't blurred your sense of priorities."

"Thank you, dear."

We pulled up in front of our house. "Mother, you have to promise me something."

"Yes, my darling girl?"

That was bad—"my darling girl" meant that any promise I extracted from her was worth the air it was written on.

But I tried anyway. "I have that 'bundle from above' coming, remember? Can we please let the police do their job, and stay on the sidelines of this?"

"We don't even know if there's a *murder* yet!"

I was pretty sure there had been, but I said, "That's right, Mother. That's very sensible. Shall we go in and not talk about this?"

Sushi didn't greet us at the door, which meant she was hiding somewhere because she'd been bad. At her age, this meant either number one or number two, because she wasn't chewing furniture, anymore. In a house full of antiques, dogs who chew on furniture don't last long.

Soosh did, however, on occasion, when she was feeling particularly put upon, sink her tiny teeth into an available shoe. . . .

I called out that it was okay for her to show herself (sort of an olly-olly-oxen-free for dogs), but when she still didn't appear, I surmised that the little doggie must have been *really* bad. Maybe the dreaded *three* (number one and two). . . .

I left my shoes on. Not a good time to go barefoot.

You see, Sushi can be quite vindictive if I miss her dinnertime, and we'd been gone much longer than that. I just hoped she hadn't chewed up my new, black-leather Donald Pliner sandals that I'd left on my bedroom floor; I'd bought the expensive shoes end-of-season last year at seventy-five percent off, then stored them away. (Don't you just *love* discovering a sale item you'd forgotten you had? If that isn't guilt-free shopping, I don't know what is!)

Whatever Sushi's dastardly deed had been, and there surely had been one, I decided I'd rather deal with it in the morning; so I said a quick good-night to Mother and went upstairs. Despite my orders to Mother about not talking about the church fiasco, my brain hadn't got the message.

Why, it asked me, *didn't you get sick? You don't even need the excuse of food that's gone off to throw up, do you? And yet you were one of the few who kept it down!*

Of course, so had Mother, which only meant she hadn't partaken of whatever the particular dish was that carried the nasty bug. And Martinette had felt good enough to snatch his egg and run . . . and die.

A cursory scan of my bedroom indicated nothing had been disturbed—the Donald Pliner shoes still in their box on the floor. (*Phewww!*) I shut off my brain, clicked off the light, stumbled over to the bed, and fell in, not bothering to take off my clothes.

My head hit the pillow in delicious anticipation of deep slumber, but an instant later I bolted upright.

Sushi had peed on my pillow!

"*Sushi!*" I said, not calling the dog, rather invoking her as a nemesis, the way Seinfeld used to with Newman.

It was the little pooch's ultimate "gotcha," which she employed only to show her most extreme displeasure—as when, a while back, we had taken in an orphaned dog named Brad Pitt-bull until a new owner could be found. She had marked her territory, all right—with my pillow as her territory.

I ran into the bathroom and scrubbed my face—which, by the way, was a rarity for me, since I often opt for leaving my makeup on at night. (Not a suggestion—an admission.)

Then, muttering, "I'll get you later, you *dog* you," I made for the guest room and crawled under the covers . . .

. . . where I found Sushi hiding.

She sheepishly inched her way to my face, then licked it. All over. And I forgave her, of course, kissing her furry little forehead, tucking her close to me. People were sick and dying, and I had a warm doggie who loved me.

Anyway, I'll take a piddled-on pillow over gnawed-up Pliners any day.

The next morning, Sunday, I awoke with a start, remembering that I had a lunch date at noon with my BFF, Tina. And as she would no doubt be concerned over my wan appearance, I would need several hours to get ready to look healthy and happy.   `

The first clue that something wasn't right in the Borne household came when I walked by Mother's bedroom and saw that her bed was made.

Why suspicious? Well, *she* never made the bed, leaving that task to me—so that meant it hadn't been slept in.

Then downstairs, in the living room, I found that my childhood board games had been dragged out of the front closet and scattered around the floor, as if Christmas had come way early, the presents all been opened, but the tree had been stolen.

I wondered if Mother had been so keyed-up that she couldn't sleep. Had she stayed up all night, playing games? Wasn't hard to envision her rolling the dice, making a move, then running around the game board to play against herself.

I found Mother in the dining room, wearing the same clothes as yesterday, her eyes wild behind her large glasses, hair disheveled—as if maybe she'd inserted a wet finger into a light socket. She loomed like God Almighty over the Duncan Phyfe table, where, taking up most of the surface, was a large cardboard replica of the inside of St. Mary's Church!

Vivian Borne had been a busy girl.

The model was quite detailed: Popsicle stick pews; cereal box pulpit (single-serving-size—Cocoa Puffs); ditto for the lectern (Froot Loops); empty tuna can celebrant's chairs (lids opened for back rests); and taped-together toilet tissue tubes to represent the tall spiral staircase.

Into this miniature playhouse, Mother had placed an assortment of board-game pieces, which I quickly ascertained represented the key players in last night's melodrama. For example, the chess queen behind the Froot Loops lectern was Mother, while the white pawn from the Clue game, resting on a tuna can, signified Madam Petrova.

I frowned at the other tuna can. "You're a chess queen, and I'm a *Tiddly Wink?*"

Mother's eyebrows scaled her forehead, seeking escape. "Why not, dear? Didn't you love to play Tiddly Winks as a young sprout?"

"I also loved Old Maid but I don't want to be one! Anyway, *you're* the Borne who liked *that* game. I thought it was stupid. Peggy Sue hated it." My older sister. "Why can't *you* be the Tiddly Wink?"

Mother put hands on hips. "Because then *I* couldn't be seen behind the Froot Loops!"

She had a point.

"Then make me Michelangelo," I suggested, referring to the Teenage Mutant Ninja Turtle among the other game pieces in the front Popsicle stick row.

"Sorry, dear. *That's* the man from Sotheby's."

I stuck out my lower lip. "Well, I could be one of the other turtles you didn't use . . . there *are* four in the TMNT game, you know."

Mother shook her head vigorously, and amazingly nothing rattled. "Absolutely *not*. They all look alike. I might become confused."

"First of all, you are often confused anyway. And second of all, the turtles do *not* look alike. Leonardo has a blue mask and carries a sword, while Donatello has a purple mask and uses a *stick*—"

Mother stomped her foot, in the manner she'd employed when little "sprout" Brandy used to get under her skin. Which had been frequently.

"*Dear!*" Mother said, exasperated. "If you didn't want to be the Tiddly Wink, you should have gotten up earlier."

"What? I'm psychic now? And when would that have been—like . . . three in the *morning?*"

Mother ignored that, saying testily, "I have already written down who is what and have committed it to memory. To do otherwise would make it difficult for me. I'm an older woman and you must make allowances."

As astonishing as her admission to being an "older woman" might have been, it paled next to her disingenuousness. I happened to know that Mother learned her entire part of "Everybody Loves Opal" in one night, when she stepped in to replace the lead actress after a stage light dropped on her (the actress, not Mother) (no, Mother didn't drop the light) (at least, she had an alibi).

Mother reached behind the dining room table and, with a dramatic flourish, produced another piece of cardboard that she placed on a chair, making an easel out of it.

Printed with a black marker in large capital letters was:

MADAM PETROVA = CLUE®—MRS. WHITE
DON KAUFMAN = OPERATION®—LEG BONE
KATHERINE ESTHERHAUS = CLUE®—
    CANDLESTICK
SERGEI IVANOV = COOTIE®—HEAD
JOHN RICHARDS = TEENAGE MUTANT NINJA
    TURTLE®

LOUIS MARTINETTE = PARCHEESI®—
   ELEPHANT
SAMUEL WOODS = MONOPOLY®—TOP HAT
MOTHER = CHESS®—QUEEN
BRANDY = TIDDLY WINKS®—TIDDLY WINK

I ignored the redundancy of the last entry, even though it described my own role, and said, "I don't think chess needs a registered trademark."

Mother had become a stickler about crediting trademarks after she'd gotten into trouble producing a play she wrote that had used the Coca-Cola logo in the title. She might have got away with it had she not sent the script to Coke's Atlanta HQ, asking if they'd like to back her in a nationwide tour of said play. (Her next original work was entitled: "Cease and Desist.")

Anyway, Mother looked at me for a long moment before asking tersely, "Don't you have somewhere to *be*?"

I checked my Chico's watch, which I hadn't removed from my wrist last night.

"Oh, yeah . . . I'm supposed to pick up Tina in an hour."

Mother's eyebrows climbed again. "*Well?* You wouldn't want to be late for your BFFF."

"You put in an extra 'F,' Mother."

"Did I? Well, I'm *sure* it doesn't stand for anything *nasty*. . . ."

That's the closest I'd ever heard her come to dropping the "F" bomb, and it showed just how long she'd been up, and how manic she was getting. Houston, we could have a problem—Vivian Borne might be about to launch into orbit . . . .

"Never let it be said," I said, "that Brandy Borne can't take a gentle hint."

And I turned on my heel and left her to her cardboard theater of the absurd.

As long as I was a Tiddly Wink, I had no intention of taking Mother's new "murder case" seriously.

A Trash 'n' Treasures Tip

Sometimes an auctioneer may change the description of an item, at the start of bidding. Make sure you base your bid on that description and not a prior catalog listing. You don't want to wind up buying a pig in a poke. And what is a pig in a poke, anyway?

Mother explains:

Back in the Middle Ages, a "pig in a poke" was a rat or cat in a bag that got passed off as a suckling pig to hungry suckers. It's a perfectly good expression, and if my daughter encourages you not to use it any longer, please feel free to ignore her.

Chapter Four

Egg Poachers

In the kitchen, an unusually subdued Sushi sat by her bone-shaped dog dish (one side, food; the other, water), apparently still feeling guilty for moistening my pillow.

I opened a small can of Mighty Dog®, which was the only dog food she would tolerate, and dumped the contents into the dish. (Free crates of the aforementioned pet food will be forwarded to the author by the publisher.)

After wolfing down her breakfast, Sushi waited patiently while I prepared a syringe of insulin, then, pinching a fold of fat at her neck, I gave her a quick poke.

And she put up with this, why? As I indicated briefly in passing, *after* the shot, Soosh always got a special treat: today, a homemade cookie from Serenity's own Doggie-Woggie Bakery Shop. (It's just possible, by the way, that a bakery shop for dogs may be one of the Seven Signs of the Coming Apocalypse.)

Bribery transaction complete, I put Soosh out the back door on a long leash, left her to do her business, then hurried upstairs to get ready.

After a quick shower, I dashed to my bedroom and rummaged through my messy closet for something to wear that would disguise my skin and bones. I put on a bulky blue Free People sweater over a Three Dot tee, and retro flare-legged Joe's jeans. (Effective now, unlike Mother, I'm dropping *all* trademark indicators.)

To detract from my sallow pallor, around my neck I wrapped a ghastly Technicolor designer silk scarf that my older sister, Peggy Sue, had given me, and which I'd never worn.

Then, seated at my Art Deco dressing table with its big round mirror, I piled on twice as much makeup as usual—going especially heavy on the blush—and moussed my hair to double its size until I looked like Chewbacca in drag. Makeup hadn't gone on this trowel-heavy since the eighties.

Back in the kitchen, I retrieved the yapping-to-come-in Sushi, then bid Mother—who was still fussing over her cardboard church replica and her various pawns—a warm good riddance, I mean, good-bye. After grabbing my Betseyville purse, I headed out to the Buick.

Tina and her husband, Kevin, lived in a white ranch-style house on a bluff overlooking the Mississippi River. The view from their home was year-round spectacular, but never so much as in the spring, when the trees lining the riverbank were beginning to bud and flower, nature working with a soft-color palate of pink, lavender, yellow and green.

In the driveway, in white T-shirt and cut-off jeans, was Kevin—hunky, sandy-haired, early thirties—washing both of their cars (Tina, black Lexus; Kev, silver Mazda) and getting himself a good deal wetter than the vehicles. As I pulled in, I wolf-whistled out my powered-down window. If we're ever going to even out this battle of the sexes thing, turnabout *has* to be fair play.

He grinned, shut off the hose, then jogged over, leaning in.

"Fries and a cheeseburger with everything," I said. "Diet Coke with extra ice."

"Sounds like you're eating for two," he said, his eyes drifting downward for any sign of a baby bump.

"Yeah, but I don't look it, I know," I admitted. "Won't see anything for a while—too early."

"But everything's fine?"

"Everything's fine."

I hoped.

Kev glanced back at the house, where a beaming Tina was coming out the front door, no faster than somebody fleeing a burning building.

"Just a heads up," he whispered. "She's been looking at baby catalogs all morning—don't let her spend *too* much."

I nodded solemnly. "I'll keep her in check." As in, I would make sure she didn't write any more checks than were left in her checkbook.

Tina and I, fast friends since high school, were a gleefully terrible influence on each other, where shopping for clothes was concerned. We had honed our fashion skills while at community college, often buying identical items independently, because we were so much alike in our tastes. We each considered the other a sort of fashion genius, the way a conceited fool stands admiringly before a mirror.

Tina, wearing an olive-green DKNY shrunken jacket and dark skinny jeans, skipped around the front of my car, then jumped in on the passenger side. She had a radiant glow—*hey, who was the expectant mother around here, anyway?*—with her prettiness framed by natural blond hair falling like liquid gold to her shoulders, her light blue eyes and fair skin reflecting her Norwegian ancestry.

I gave Teen the cheeriest smile I could muster.

"And how are we doing?" she asked, twisting in her

seat to face me, her eyes flicking down and back from my still-flat belly.

I wasn't sure if she meant me and her, or me and the baby, or me, her, *and* the baby. (I had ruled out Kevin, who was back to his husbandly hose duties.)

But I replied, "Just great! Couldn't be better."

Her eyes widened at the sight of my scarf. Her expression said she might indulge in some sympathetic morning sickness.

I shrugged. "Yeah, I know. Hideous doesn't cover it. Peggy Sue. Last Christmas. Where Sis is concerned, there will always be a *test* later, and I have to be able to say truthfully that I wore it."

"*And* be seen in public?"

"Witnesses may be called."

She pursed her pretty pink lips. "Didn't come with a gift receipt, huh?"

"Nope. Anyway, what would I say? The scarf didn't fit?"

She made a clicking in her cheek. "A real pity. . . ."

"Just be glad I didn't regift it to you."

I backed the car out of the drive; Kevin paused in his work to wave. We didn't deserve him. (For the record, I didn't get preggers for Tina by shacking up weekends with Kevin—I had gone the much more socially acceptable, if less entertaining, test-tube route.)

As we headed in the direction of the mall, I employed a trick I often use when I'm with someone and don't feel so good: I get them talking about themselves.

"So," I said, "Kevin says you've been poring over baby catalogs. See anything you like?"

This kept the ball in Tina's court for a good five minutes (with me interjecting the occasional "uh-huh") and long enough for us to arrive at our destination, which was the elaborate mall that conspired with its competition—the quaint shops of downtown Serenity—to make our little town a shopping destination for the greater area and weary travelers.

Indian Mounds—so named because of an adjacent Indian burial ground—was located on gently rolling hills, with pathways winding through an asymmetrical layout. That the Mounds was outdoors—unusual for our versatile climate—didn't seem to deter shoppers in the least, even in the coldest of winters. Many people—myself included—preferred it to stuffy enclosed malls, where you can get all hot and crabby going around in your coat.

In recent months, a tasty tableau of new restaurants had sprung up around the mall, ranging from formal to family-friendly, and hitting just about every ethnicity.

Tina said, "Your turn to pick."

My joke to Kevin about cheeseburgers and fries had stuck in my brain, and suddenly I had a craving for drive-in food. This was no doubt one of those pregnancy urges, and I saw no reason not to give in to it. Anyway, a fattening malt might do me good.

"How about the Corvette Diner?"

We had not yet eaten there, opting for healthier fare, and also waiting for the fuss to die down—when a new restaurant opens in Serenity, you need to wait a good two months before the crowds subside.

Tina smiled sideways. "Happy days! I was *hoping* you'd say that. . . ."

Maybe Teen, who rarely veered from her salad sans dressing, really was experiencing a sympathetic pregnancy.

I wheeled into the parking lot, lucking into a nice close space, and we got out and headed toward the restaurant. If the outside decor—which featured a vintage Corvette embedded in the wall, its stylish tail toward us, as if the car had come crashing into the diner—was any reflection of the inside, we were in for a treat, or anyway a good time.

We opted for one of the red, plastic-padded booths instead of a round chrome table, our eyes taking in the assault of fifties memorabilia plastered on the walls and ceiling, while a jukebox blasted away, Elvis singing "Blue Suede Shoes."

A waitress plopped down next to Tina, saying, "Shove over, honey—my feet are *killin'* me!"

The woman, like the Corvette, had a lot of miles on the odometer, and was tricked-out to accentuate it: over-bleached hair (a wig), heavily-penciled eyebrows, false eyelashes, and goopy lipstick. Her white uniform dress was too tight, bursting at the bosom, and a button pinned on one shoulder announced TAKE ME FOR A RIDE."

"What'll ya have?" the waitress asked, chewing gum, to boot.

I recognized her—Selma Lewis, one of mother's chief competitors for eccentric gal parts in local theater. The waitresses and waiters here were not just hired but cast, and were either local theater types or area college kids from drama programs.

Playing along, I asked, "Anything good in this dive?"

She partially covered her mouth with a chipped, red-nailed hand, and said sotto voce, "*Not* the meat loaf . . . and *I'm* fresher than the cherry pie."

Tina asked, "How's the coffee?"

"What's available right now, you could break a spoon on. Some fresh is brewin', though, sweet cheeks."

I asked, "And the burgers?"

"That's what we're famous for, honey! The cows come around and line up to participate. Ask for grilled onions, and you may experience true love."

Tina and I ordered the same thing: cheeseburger with grilled onions, fries, and a vanilla malt.

Before the waitress left, she dropped character briefly to whisper, "How's Viv doing?"

"Okay."

"With the theater closed 'cause of the flood, she must be climbing the walls."

"No, that would be me, living with her."

Then back in character, she said, "I *hear* you, honey! I *hear* you!"

With that settled, Tina and I got down to the business of catching up—only amateurs do their visiting while they shop.

But before I had a chance to steer our conversation into placid waters—for certainly Tina had heard all about the fiasco at the church bazaar—my friend leaned forward and said, pleadingly, "Brandy . . . *please* tell me you're *not* getting caught up in your mother's latest shenanigans."

"Shenanigans" was possibly the nicest way Teen could have put Mother's penchant for involving herself in local crimes.

Teen rushed on. "When I heard that you could have had food poisoning like the rest of those people—well, I cried for hours. Honestly, Brandy, *you* might have died. *And* the baby!"

I reached for her hand, squeezed it, and said reassuringly, "Nothing is going to happen to me. I'm not going to do anything foolish. I know how much the baby means to you and Kevin."

She was nodding, but her blue eyes asked, "*Do* you?"

The tenseness of the moment broke as a college-girl waitress flashed by on roller skates, throwing a handful of bubble gum on our table.

I let go of Teen's hand, sat back in the booth. "Sweetie,

you have nothing to worry about—the church thing was just a freak accident. Anyway, the chief has told Mother in no uncertain terms that she's to stay out of the police investigation."

Tina gave me a rumpled smile. "And since when has that stopped her?"

I leaned forward. "I admit I can't always control Mother, but I most certainly can control myself. And I'm not going to get involved in anything that will jeopardize either me or the baby. I promise."

She frowned at me. "You're not . . . parsing words, are you?"

"Of course not!" I frowned at her. "What do you mean?"

"You stopped short of saying that you wouldn't get yourself involved, or allow your mother to, either. And if the TV is to be at all believed, this was no 'freak accident.' That Chicago art dealer may have been murdered. And who's to say the food poisoning was accidental?"

"You sound like *you're* the one who's involved."

Her eyes flashed. She wasn't cross with me, but she wasn't fooling around, either. "I am involved, if you're involved. You're carrying our child!"

Again, whether "our child" referred to me and her, or her and Kevin, or me and her and . . . forget it.

"I'm sorry, Teen, but I'm already involved. I'll try not to get any *more* involved, but you have to understand—these deaths, not to mention serious sickness among over one hundred people, all grew out of something Mother put in motion."

"That stupid auction."

"That stupid auction is going to raise a lot of money for flood relief in this town, so while Mother always has ulterior motives, her heart was in the right place. Teen, she was up all night, worrying about this."

I didn't go into detail—Tina hearing about Mother making a cardboard replica of the church and peopling it with game tokens would have hardly been reassuring.

"Well," she said almost timidly, "just let the police handle it. Just you girls stay out of it."

"That's just it—we'll *be* involved somewhat, because we were at the scene, and this was Mother's idea in the first place, the auction. She ran it. I helped. We'll be questioned and all that kind of stuff. Can't be avoided."

"I . . . I understand. I do understand."

"And the way Mother is reacting . . . I'll admit she's talking this amateur-sleuth silliness again, but the real reason is not that she's delighted to have another crime to 'solve.' She blames herself. Holds herself responsible for the two deaths. And the churchful of sick people."

"And you're saying she'll try to do something about it?"

"Teen, I'll do my best to prevent that. But she's going to make noise. That much we know about Vivian Borne—she *is* going to make noise."

How could Tina argue with that?

And when Tina smiled in defeat, I segued into, "Have you thought about baby names?"

She nodded. "Both boy and girl."

When she didn't provide the prospective monikers, I raised my eyebrows in question. Anything went these days, as names for offspring; I just hoped it wasn't anything *too* weird. . . .

Tina smiled again, warmly now. "Kevin and I have agreed that . . . if it's a girl . . . we'll name her Brandy."

"And . . . if it's a boy?"

"*Brandon*, for a boy."

Tears sprang to my eyes—heartfelt, not hormonal. "Oh, Teen," I said softly, "that is so sweet. I'd be honored, of course. You are the best."

She shook her head, a little embarrassed. "We always planned on doing that . . . even before the surrogate thing."

Our food arrived, and I immediately took a big bite of the cheeseburger and swallowed before my stomach had a chance to know what hit it. Then I followed with a large dose of vanilla malt to show my tummy who was boss.

That tactic worked for a while, but then I had to quit eating, when my stomach warned of impending disaster, should I continue.

"Anything wrong?" Tina asked.

"Just had a big breakfast," I lied. "This on top of that. . . ."

While my gal pal worked on her fries, I excused myself to use the ladies' room, because . . . Why do you think? I was pregnant! I had to pee a lot. . . .

I used the bathroom, then took a different route back, passing a private dining room, where a small group of people were in the midst of a party, being serenaded by some of the female waitstaff. (Imagine alley cats meowing "Happy Birthday," with somebody tugging on tails to help them hit the high notes.)

I stopped to watch the guest of honor, stocky Sergei Ivanov, blow out the candles on a huge, quadruple banana split sundae with all the trimmings, sending some of the whipped cream across the table. As solemn as a priest preparing to give communion, he grabbed up a spoon and dug in, not sharing with the other guests, although utensils and plates had been brought for them.

The other guests included his fellow Fabergé bidders, as well as *American Mid-West Magazine* publisher Samuel Woods. If I wasn't going to be involved in this mystery, the suspects simply couldn't go around having group meetings like this.

While I stood there gaping with the manners of a goldfish, they morphed into Mother's game pieces: bald Sergei

"Cootie Head" Ivanov; blond, slender, handsome Don "Leg Bone" Kaufman; curvaceous, sophisticated brunette Katherine "Candlestick" Estherhaus; boyish, bespectacled, British John "Ninja Turtle" Richards; and of course nattily-attired Samuel "Top Hat" Woods.

As the waitstaff filed out, I stepped in and said, "Well, I see *someone* has something to celebrate."

And was greeted with a horde of hostile eyes.

"Brandy Borne?" I prompted. "I assisted my mother, Vivian, who brought all of you together?"

Cootie-Head Ivanov slammed down his spoon and flecks of whipped cream flew. *"You!"* His Russian accent couldn't have been thicker if he'd been a local actor Mother was directing. "You have *nerve* to crash party!"

"Actually, no. I was just using the rest room. I wasn't expecting to come upon the cast party for *Murder on the Orient Express.*"

This crack earned alarmed expressions from one and all, which they traded amongst themselves like kids swapping baseball cards.

Only birthday boy Ivanov wasn't speechless: "You, Miss Borne, are *reason* we cannot return home! You and that *stupid* woman."

I went on the defensive—nobody calls *my* mother stupid! Besides me.

"My mother and I aren't the reason you're still in Serenity, having birthdays and ice cream. . . . You know, you *could* share a little with the other children, Sergei. Has the Communist spirit totally died in you? Anyway, it's the police who are keeping you here, because of at least one suspicious death. And it could be that someone in this room is the *real* person keeping you here—if one of you nice people shoved Louis Martinette over the staircase railing."

Have I mentioned I was off the Prozac?

Leg Bone Kaufman was patting the air. His expression was conciliatory as he said, "I'm afraid—*what's* your name again?"

"Brandy Borne. You can call me Brandy. We're all friends here, right?"

Kaufman's smile was as crinkly as wadded-up paper. "I'm afraid, Brandy, meaning nothing personal, that we *all* feel that way about your mother, and the incompetent way she conducted this event. There *should* have been more security."

"As is all too obvious after the fact," Ninja Turtle Richards said, his British accent as crisp as Sergei's Russian one was thick. "You and your mother knew that you had a precious object that would go for hundreds of thousands of dollars. You should have known what kind of people that would attract—and you should have known what kind of sideshow the auction would create."

It seemed to have attracted a roomful of self-righteous snobs, who were having ice cream at the carnival.

Candlestick Katherine snorted in a most unfeminine manner for such a beauty. "Come *on*, guys—we all craved the publicity. Even for the losers, it created attention for our clients."

"Clients?" I asked. I was still just standing there. For some reason, no one had invited me to sit down at the table with them.

"Yes," the sophisticated yet down-to-earth brunette said. "We aren't employees of Christie's or Sotheby's or Forbes. We're independent agents, who took on these roles as freelancers. Any publicity brought to our clients would be viewed as positive, whoever won the bid."

"Not just *any* bloody publicity," Richards said snappishly. "This kind of publicity—people retching, people dying, the precious art piece poached. . . . This is *hardly* the kind of event that will lead to further assignments."

"It's not the kind of event," I said, "that Mother and I planned or intended. When *can* you go home?"

"When the police give us the go-ahead," Kaufman said with a pitiful shrug. "Whenever *that* is." The good-looking blond seemed the least combative of the lot.

"Then—you've not given your formal statements?"

Katherine shook her head. "Just preliminary ones, at the church. We've been dealing with small-town police and they are horribly understaffed and in over their heads. They were hardly expecting anything like this."

"Somebody was," I said.

This sank the little group into gloomy silence. The Russian Cootie Head returned his attention to his melting dessert, regarding it like a sculptor who didn't know what to do next.

Their silence said I'd been dismissed, but I had more to say.

"I guess most of you are out a hefty commission," I said.

The agents for Christie's and Sotheby's exchanged glances.

Katherine said, "In an auction situation, my dear, there is always that strong possibility. We receive a flat fee and expenses for our trouble, and a potentially high commission is the brass ring we all reach for . . . knowing only one of us can snag it."

"I see."

"But we're *all* suffering, because this job, this auction, is over . . . and we're captives here in Podunk-land. Prisoners. It's hard to imagine a more bitter fate."

"Not *that* hard," I said with a shrug. "There's dying of food poisoning, or falling from a high place. Were any of you poison victims at the church, by the way?"

No one said anything.

"Well?"

Head shakes all around.

"*None* of you?"

Kaufman said, "We ate together at our hotel, before going to the auction. None of us wanted to take, uh . . ."

"Potluck?"

"Yes."

Richard pitched in. "One never knows what is in the food at such functions."

"I guess not," I admitted. "But it's interesting to note that this group, one and all, did not partake of food that no one knew would be off. Maybe you were psychic."

Or maybe this really *was* the cast party of *Murder on the Orient Express*. This little knowledgeable group would have known full well the extreme value of that egg to a private collector—a million or more dollars would divide up handsomely among a handful like this.

One of them might have poisoned a certain dish at the potluck dinner, or even provided a doctored dish . . . and another could have been assigned the task of snatching the egg from the winning bidder. Perhaps the group had inside knowledge that Martinette intended to outbid them. . . .

But these thoughts I did not share with them. At the same time, I knew I had best not do so with Mother, either, or she would really be off and running. Make that flying. Maybe I'd have the chance to share my notions with Chief Cassato, somewhere along the line.

"*You* should be happy," I said, looking at Top Hat Woods, the Yuppie-ish magazine publisher, "because now your publication won't have to cough up any matching funds."

"Your mother must not share all her responsibilities with you," Woods said patronizingly. "If she did, you'd know our commitment to match auction funds was capped at $100,000. That was in *writing*, Ms. Borne. But you're correct that we are now no longer obligated, since the artifact will surely be returned to the estate, and the auction, if there is another, will start from scratch at some other time and date."

"And what about you?" I asked the Russian Cootie Head. "How disappointed are *you* not to return to Mother Russia with the Tsar's grade A egg?"

He pushed his banana split aside, the dessert having gotten the better of him, the contents of the dish looking like Vincent Price at the conclusion of a sixties horror film.

"I am disappointed," Sergei said with strained dignity. "But if this foul egg is mine? I *not* return it to Russia." He made a fist with one bearish paw. "I *crush* the shell in my hand . . . like *this!*"

That revelation left me slack-jawed. But the collective eye-rolling from the others around the table told me the Russian's plan was anything but news to them.

Kaufman explained, "Sergei's great-grandfather died in prison, thanks to the Tsar."

"Brother," I said, "do you Rooskies hold a grudge!"

The Russian's chin rose and he oozed pride, much as his dish oozed melted ice cream.

"Let me get this straight," I said. "If you had won the egg, Sergei—you'd have destroyed it?"

"*Da.*"

The Brit with the dark-framed glasses sniffed at that. "That's an easy claim to make, when the egg is not in one's grasp. I have enough faith in what remains of the Capitalist system to think anyone at this table would do the right thing . . . and sell the damned bauble to the highest bidder!"

"But that," I reminded them all, "was Louis Martinette. And where did it get *him?*"

I was my Mother's daughter—I knew a curtain line when I heard it, and got off stage.

Back at the booth, Tina was miffed by my long absence, which I deflected by telling her I'd run into some friends, and then giving her the news about an online-only sale on Kate Moss Topshop.

Soon, we split the check and left.

The next hour was spent in the baby department of Ingram's department store, and I have to admit, I was miserable, although I tried hard not to show it. You may have already discerned that I am not the most noble human on the planet, and I admit that the person I really love to shop for most is . . . you guessed it . . . *moi*.

What was wrong with me? Why couldn't I share in my best friend's joy? Was I putting up an emotional wall of protection, since the baby wasn't mine? Or wouldn't be, after I delivered? Or was I just being my usual selfish self?

No answers are required—these are what we call rhetorical questions. You don't need to post at Amazon about what a bad person I am.

Thankfully, our baby shopping excursion came to an end, and we hauled our purchases—mostly little unisex outfits the size of doll clothes—out to my car.

After dropping Tina off, I drove home in a funk. I felt I'd made a fool of myself in front of that room of suspects, right down to thinking of them that way. I was no more Nancy Drew than Mother was Jessica Fletcher. Couldn't I get real?

But my thoughts screeched to a stop when I spotted Chief Cassato's unmarked car parked in our drive. *Why was* he *here?* To get our official statements maybe? Or had Mother gotten into (more) trouble. . .?

As I wheeled into the drive, Mother rushed out the front door and down the porch steps.

I got out, and met her halfway on the sidewalk.

"What is it?" I asked, alarmed.

Mother was breathing hard, her face flushed. "Dear, he *insists* on seeing you. I've *told* him you shouldn't be interrogated in your tender condition. . . . She's *expecting*, you brute!"

I looked behind her to where the roughly handsome fortyish, barrel-chested chief now stood on the porch, having followed Mother out. His arms were folded, his expression probably the same as Sitting Bull surveying the aftermath of Custer's Last Stand.

"Interrogated about what?" I frowned. "I gave a statement at the church. What more can *I* tell?"

Tony Casatto, stony-faced, moved to take my arm. "It's not called interrogation anymore, Vivian—it's a simple interview. But you do need to come with me, Brandy."

I gaped at him. What had *I* done? Or what did he *think* I had done? Good Lord, had the birthday party called and complained about me harassing them? Can you call the cops and complain about *civilian* harassment?

We were moving toward the unmarked car, his hand on my elbow, Mother on our heels. This was what walking the Last Mile must have felt like for Death Row inmates. (Well, okay, that may be a bit of an exaggeration. . . .)

"Is she being charged?" Mother demanded indignantly. "Is she a material witness?" To me she said, "Dear, don't answer any questions without talking to our lawyer."

Our attorney happened to be around ninety, and most likely was in bed asleep right now. If he wasn't in bed, he was still likely to be asleep.

Chief Cassato opened the back door of the vehicle, saying over his shoulder to Mother, "She'll be back in a few hours."

Then he deposited me inside.

Just another confused perp.

A Trash 'n' Treasures Tip

Charity bazaars can turn up unexpected treasures, like the time Mother bought a coat, and found a hundred-dollar bill in one pocket. The Christian thing would have been to return the money to its rightful owner, but in Mother's mind "Do unto others as you would have them do unto you" is trumped by "Finders keepers, losers weepers."

Chapter Five

Good Egg or Bad Egg?

Chief Cassato's unmarked car lacked the mesh screen separating front and back that squad cars have, so it wasn't like I was a prisoner, right? I mean, on TV and in movies, you see bad guys in back with no door handles and no way to roll windows down or anything, making escape impossible (or anyway hard, because—on TV and in movies—they often do find a way to escape).

Not that I was thinking of escaping. But if this wasn't official, if I wasn't some kind of witness if not suspect, why had he deposited me in back? We were friends, weren't we? Why wasn't I sitting up front with Daddy?

I was just telling myself there was nothing sinister about my backseat banishment when we drove past the police station, and before long were heading out the river road.

I leaned forward. "Ah . . . Chief? Tony? Where exactly are we going?"

He eyed me in the rearview mirror. "You just sit tight, young lady."

Young lady! Normally, a thirty-one-year-old woman being called "young lady" might be viewed as a compliment of sorts, left-handed maybe but reassuring on some level. But there was nothing reassuring going on in my Prozac-free mind. The chief might not have been speeding, but my brain was shifting into overdrive, concocting all sorts of scenarios—none of them good.

Good Lord, what if Serenity's top cop was actually involved in either the murder of Louis Martinette or the theft of the Fabergé egg? Did he think that I had seen, or heard, something that could implicate him in one or both of those crimes?

All of this was ludicrous, of course, and such thoughts would never have gone running wild in the canyon between my ears if I hadn't shared DNA with Vivian Borne. And the silly paranoia was not aided by the chief turning off the scenic blacktop highway onto a secondary country road, the tires kicking up gravel and dust.

I leaned up. "*Where* are you taking me?"

But this time he didn't even reply. Not even a glance from his steel-gray eyes!

"Look, you can't just throw somebody in the back of your car and go riding off without explanation. This is America! This is Iowa! Just because you're the chief of police—"

"Relax," he cut in gruffly. "I'm not going to bury you in the woods or anything."

Good to know!

And over the next fifteen minutes or so, the car twisted and turned along remote backroads, making my fantasies of jumping out a door and rolling to freedom seem as silly as they sounded, and then suddenly the vehicle veered into the mouth of a private lane, nearly obscured by a row of thick bushes.

We bumped down a long narrow strip of gravel before coming to an abrupt stop in front of a rustic structure, a slightly oversized log cabin, as dust settled around us like smog.

What *was* this place, and why were we here? Was this the backwoods equivalent of a dank secret cell in the basement of the Serenity police station, where suspects and uncooperative witnesses were given the Third Degree? And what were the First and Second Degrees, anyway?

Maybe Mother was right—maybe I did need to get back on the Prozac. . . .

Chief Cassato got out of the car, then came around and opened my door in a gentlemanly fashion.

When I didn't budge, he leaned in. "What's the problem?"

"What's the idea of throwing me in the backseat and doing whatever you want with me?"

That came out a little wrong. . . .

"If I'd put you in front," he said, his tone bland, "your mother would have thought this was a date. Needed to make it look official, Brandy."

"Is *that* what this is? Your idea of a date? Drive me in the country and scare the daylights out of me?"

"If I'd told you what I had in mind," he said, "you might have said no." Then he frowned, as *that* had also come out a little wrong. . . .

Finally I got out of the car, then stood with hands on hips and worked up a little indignation. "Do you *mind* telling me why I'm here?"

He gestured to the cabin. "This is where I live. I don't bring just anybody out here."

My eyes swept over the rustic home, finding nothing at all sinister about it. "You don't?"

"No. I keep kind of a low profile."

I knew that already—Cassato was Serenity's resident Man of Mystery, which is partly why my paranoia got out of hand on the drive out here.

"Then you *weren't* trying to throw a scare into me. . . ."

His smile was small but wicked. "Maybe a little."

I pounded on his chest, once, with a fist. Not hard. "What did I do to deserve that?"

"How about, help your annoying mother interfere in countless police matters over the past year? How about, put your own welfare and life itself stupidly at risk, any number of times?"

"Well . . . besides that."

He chuckled, gave up half a grin. "You seem a little surprised by the Cassato homestead. What did you expect?"

"I guess a condo, maybe—in a gated community, so you'd have a little privacy. And to keep Mother out."

He waved a hand at his place. "This is just as safe—unless you tell her where it is. I'm trusting you, Brandy."

"Yeah, I guess Batman doesn't just show every chick the Bat Cave."

Everyone in Serenity knew Tony Cassato protected his private life—both past and present—like a bulldog does a ham bone.

And speaking of dogs, a snarling canine with teeth bared was rounding the side of the cabin and making straight for yours truly. I grabbed on to the chief's nearest arm as if I'd fallen from a cliff and needed a branch to cling to.

The chief moved me behind him, stepping protectively in the path of the barking hound, then barked his own warning, stopping the animal in its oversized tracks.

"*Sit!*" the chief said.

"You talking to me or the mutt?"

But the mutt—and it was a mixed breed critter, white and black and coming up to about his master's knee—was sitting there dutifully, slobbering and wagging his tail (the dog, not the master).

"I guess even a watchdog needs a watchdog," I said.

"He's a good boy. Stays in his doghouse and gives trespassers hell. But he's all bark and no bite."

Like his master, I wondered?

"So what's his name?"

"Rocky."

"After the flying squirrel or Italian stallion?"

"Stallone. I love the first of those movies."

"Me, too." I pointed, gingerly, at the dog, not moving too quickly. "It does look like he got K.O.'d."

Rocky had a black circle around one eye.

"You ever see *The Little Rascals* on TV?" he asked. "Or are you too young?"

Loving the sound of seeming "too young," I said, "Mother used to show us tapes of them—Spanky and Alfalfa and a dog who looked like Rocky, but smaller."

"Right. Go ahead and call to him. He's friendly."

I'd had a taste of his friendliness already, but I called to the dog, and he trotted over for a sniff, his stump of a tail starting to wag once he'd gotten a whiff of Sushi on my clothes.

Soon I was following the chief up a few wooden steps, and across a small porch where a log-wood rocker with a green cushion kept company with a few potted plants. He unlocked the front door, then stepped aside for me to enter, which I did, an impatient Rocky pushing past me (and letting me know who rated first around here), nails clicking on the floorboards.

Inside, the cabin had a predictably pleasant, woodsy aroma—like pinecone-scented freshener, only the real deal—and was roomier than it had appeared from the outside. To my left was a cozy area with fireplace and overstuffed brown couch, along with a matching recliner; to the right, a four-chair round oak table shared space with a small china hutch. A hallway led to a few other rooms—

bed, bath, and beyond. The place had a nicely masculine feel.

Tony hung his sport coat on one of several wooden pegs in the entryway, exposing a shoulder holster on his white short-sleeve shirt with blue tie. He undid the apparatus and slung it over another of the pegs. When he turned and realized I'd been watching the procedure, somewhat awed frankly by the whole shoulder-holster gun rigamarole, he twitched a smile, loosened his tie, and motioned me over to the sofa.

I sat and watched silently as he bent before the fireplace, putting a match to crumpled papers beneath the logs and flames danced upward, bringing a soft yellow glow to the room, and chasing the chill away. This homey side of city-boy Tony was brand-new to me.

He straightened and pointed. "Stay put."

Again, I wasn't sure if the command was for me, or Rocky, who had plopped down with a world-weary sigh near my feet. Maybe he meant both of us.

Then the chief disappeared into a side room, where soon came sounds of pans banging, and utensils clanking, as if he were ransacking his own kitchen.

Now what?

Oh, well, like Rocky, I'd had my orders—mine was not to reason why, mine was but to . . . stay put.

I began to make mental notes about my surroundings, knowing that Mother would grill me over every single detail of my visit to the chief's secret hideaway. Tony might want me to protect his privacy, and the whereabouts of the cabin were safe with me, but Mother's questions would no doubt wear me down. She'd seen me ride off with the chief, and I didn't have the imagination to create a fake scene for her about being grilled at the station, or believably come up with a story about the chief taking me out dancing or dining or whatever.

And, I have to admit, part of my curiosity was personal. I longed to learn more about the mysterious chief of police, who had come from the East three years ago to take over the top cop job.

Since then, a myriad of stories had circulated around town about his untold history, ranging from the scurrilous (he had been a bent cop in New York and got relegated to the boonies) to the ridiculous (he was in the witness protection plan after ratting on the mob, and used to look like a young Cary Grant before surgery). I was pretty sure Mother spread most of the stories, attempting (without success) to flush out the truth.

My eyes traveled to a pair of antique rifles hanging above the fireplace, then to an assortment of fishing gear piled in one corner (creels, poles, hip boots, nets), to a collection of snowshoes (arranged haphazardly on one wall), and to framed photos displayed here and there, of fishermen and hunters, sepia shots of days long gone by.

My shrewd Nancy Drew–like detective's mind quickly deduced that a) the chief was a man's man, b) he used to live somewhere where the snow got even deeper than around here, and c) he preferred fake, sepia memories to real ones.

A crash came from the kitchen—a plate dropping, possibly shattering—followed by cursing.

"Everything okay?" I called.

"I'm on it!" Tony called back, gruffly.

Rocky's shrewd Rin Tin Tin–like detective's mind quickly deduced an opportunity for fallen food, and he abandoned his warm place by the fire to investigate.

Yummy smells were emanating from the kitchen—freshly baked bread, and apple pie. . . .

Now *I* went to investigate.

"Okay, what is this?" I asked from the kitchen doorway.

The chief, looking no more frazzled than he might have after running down a bank robber (on foot), stood at the stove, swathed in steam, stirring the contents of a saucepan. The only thing that would have made him look more comic was a zany backyard chef's apron.

"Out," he said, gesturing with the ladle, sending an arc of orange across the floor.

Rocky, finished with whatever had been on the broken plate, pounced on the new spill.

I grinned at my host. "Are you *sure* you don't need help? I'm pretty good at accident scenes. Or is this a crime scene?"

"Go!"

"Anywhere special?"

"Sit at the table."

"Yes, sir."

And I gave him a crisp salute.

Retreating to the outer room, I pulled out a chair at the table, only now noticing (some detective!) the two place settings.

Maybe he *had* taken me out dining. . . .

A few minutes later the chief—or was that *chef?*—emerged from the kitchen like a harried waiter, carrying two steaming bowls of soup, then hurried back, returning with freshly baked bread on a wooden platter, which he placed in the center of the table.

He pulled out the chair across from me, making a fingernails-on-blackboard screech, sat, picked up a spoon, and dipped it into his soup.

When I didn't move, he looked up.

"It is a little hot. You may want to blow on it."

I just stared at him.

"Oh . . . sorry—did you, uh, want to say grace or something?"

I laughed.

"What's funny?"

He'd reminded me of when I was a little tyke, when Mother would help me put my hands together, and do her best to teach me the Danish table prayer she'd said as a child.

Vlesign vort maltid, Herre kaer
Velsign os alle haver isaer
Og lad din ve og vel os finde
At du har lyst din fred herinde.

But I'd mangled the words so badly, Mother had in desperation taught me the simplest of prayers.

Lord, bless this food
Which now we take
And make us thine
For Jesus' sake.

Around age ten, I finally realized that it wasn't "food-wich" (apparently a kind of sandwich), and that I need not fear a food-stealing creature called "Snoughy" (*now we take*), or that we weren't meant to "make a sign" (*make us thine*) . . . for Jesus' sake!

I said to Tony, "You brought me out here to . . . feed me?"

"Well, it's not a kidnapping."

"Now he tells me."

He shrugged a shoulder. "Your mother said that if you didn't start gaining weight, you were going to the hospital."

Mother's meddling knew no bounds.

"You have been talking to my mother?"

"Not because I want to," he assured me. The chief's steely eyes softened with concern. "Well? *Do* you have a weight problem?"

The kind of weight problem every girl dreams of—not weighing enough. . . .

Now I shrugged. "Hey, it's not *that* serious."

Yet.

He frowned just a little; he seemed to be searching for words. "Carrot soup helped my wife when she was pregnant with our daughter."

This was the first I'd heard about a wife.

Or child.

"You're married?" The question carried certain unspoken baggage—the cabin seemed clearly his alone, with no sign of either a female or an offspring.

"I was."

"Divorced then?"

He shook his head.

"Your wife. . . ?"

It was a moment before he answered. "Gone."

I wanted to ask if he meant she had died, or maybe were they just separated, and what about that child he'd mentioned? But I was afraid to push it.

So I did my best to match my host's graciousness (weird graciousness maybe, but graciousness) and tried the carrot soup. It was delicious—rich and creamy with just a hint of spice.

"This is wonderful," I said.

"It's a nice recipe, isn't it?"

One of his wife's? I wondered.

Despite the unspoken and unanswered questions hanging in the pinecone-scented air, we ate in comfortable silence. Which was strange for me, because I'd been around talkers all of my life—first Mother, then my ex, Roger. The table was a raucous place in my life; but not here. Not that I minded.

After the soup and bread and some cold cuts for sandwich-making (keeping a sharp eye out for the evil Snoughy), we had warm apple pie à la mode. I had two pieces. How wonderful to be asked to pack on the pounds! And my stomach, perhaps as happy as I was to be out on a sort of date, cooperated just fine.

After dinner, Tony refused my offer to help with the dishes (I did clear the table), so I returned to the fireplace, threw another log on, and plopped down on the couch.

Eventually Tony joined me, drawing up a small ottoman, which he positioned under my feet. I kicked off my shoes and, sans socks, wiggled my Technicolor toes.

He smirked. "What's the deal, Brandy? Couldn't decide on a nail polish?"

"Nope. Tried them all—mostly to see if they were usable. Didn't realize I might be showing them off to a man tonight."

"You shouldn't take anything for granted."

"I think I like the neon green. What's your favorite?"

But Tony was studying me quizzically.

"What?"

He shook his head. "You're so different from when I first knew you."

That had been three years ago, back when I was married, living in an upscale suburb of Chicago, wearing tailored clothing, and acting mature and responsible. . . .

I had returned to Serenity to attend to Mother after she went off her medication and landed in the county jail. After the crisis, with Mother once again stabilized, I had a meeting with Serenity's new chief of police, one Tony Cassato, whom you've met.

I argued that mentally ill prisoners should not be incarcerated with the rest of the inmates, but should have their own segregated section—pods—to keep them away from the hardened criminals (and vice versa). I'd been pushing hard, reading the chief's silence and apparently glowering expression as an unspoken counterargument. But Tony had surprised me, and agreed wholeheartedly, and over the next six months, we worked together to accomplish what became a mutual goal.

I said, "Hate to disappoint you, but that wasn't the real me. That time in my life? I was trying to please my husband, who was much older than I, a successful businessman. . . ." I stretched my toes toward the warmth of the fire. "It just didn't work."

"What didn't work?"

"Me pretending to be that together. Also, my marriage. My fault."

He didn't pry further.

Anyone else would have asked how it was my fault, but he gave me space.

Still, it *had* been my fault. At my ten-year high school reunion, I'd done something really stupid involving too much wine, an old boyfriend, and a condom. The perfect storm to break up a marriage.

"So what's the real you?" Tony asked.

I watched the fire dance, graceful but mocking. "Still trying to figure that out, I'm afraid. Unfortunately, the *real* me would seem to be an irresponsible, self-absorbed dope, who can't learn a lesson, and is easily influenced by her cuckoo mother."

Tony smiled one-sidedly. "Aren't you being a little hard on yourself?" His eyes drifted to my stomach. "I can think of one selfless thing you've done, at least."

"Maybe I don't completely suck. Not sure."

"I'm sure."

"I notice you didn't say I was being too hard on my mother."

"No, she's cuckoo, all right."

We both laughed a little.

The log snapped and cracked, and we fell silent, watching red-hot embers drift upward.

After a while I ventured, "You're gonna have to give me something."

"Something more than soup and sandwiches and pie?"

"Something that will appease Mother."

He frowned. "Can't we leave your mother out of this?"

"She saw me go off with you. She'll want to know what I pried out of you."

"Tell her you didn't pry anything out of me."

"No. That's not how you keep Mother at bay."

"How about, give her an inch and she'll take a mile?"

"Not Mother—it's more like, deny her an inch and she'll take the highway."

He said nothing.

"Hey, we're involved, Mother and me. She feels responsible for all of this."

"How?"

"She put the auction in motion. It led to all those people getting sick, and poor Madam Petrova dying of food poisoning, and that Martinette character maybe getting murdered."

He was staring at the fire. "No maybe about it."

"It *was* murder?"

"Just about had to be. Coroner says the nature of the injuries is consistent with a fall from the platform above. With that railing, you would have to be shoved to go over."

"He couldn't have slipped?"

"Possibly. I suppose a stray banana peel might have

found its way up there. Or he could have had a sudden urge to kill himself."

"Neither likely."

"Neither likely. And there was bruising on the arms, indicating the man had been grabbed, hard, before he'd been sent on his way."

"So it's a murder." I felt a chill despite the fire. "With all that media there, you have video to look at, don't you? That can show you who followed Martinette, after he grabbed the egg?"

He shrugged. "We've been going over the tapes, but so far they're not proving useful. When the crowd fled, the cameras on tripods in the back got knocked over."

"And the ones up front—the hand-helds?"

He shrugged. "Focused on the stampede."

"Kind of a coincidence, isn't it? Everybody getting sick right on cue? Covering up a murder?"

Another shrug. "Killing Martinette could have been spur of the moment. The food poisoning might just have given somebody an opportunity to get that egg."

"And somebody followed Martinette up those stairs to that platform, and took the egg away from him. And shoved him over to cover it up."

"Could be."

He was going taciturn on me. The chief didn't like being interrogated, particularly when the "transcript" might be shared with Vivian Borne.

"You don't really think everyone getting sick was a co-incidence, do you?"

Tony shook his head. "More like a diversion."

"Really," I said flatly. "Then someone *deliberately* poisoned the food."

He nodded.

"What with?"

"Rat poison."

"Good Lord."

"Arsenic-based."

I shuddered. "That's evil. Which dish did they put it in?"

"The coroner tested the remains of every dish served—it was the stew."

"Mrs. Mulligan's stew?" I gaped at him. "But it *can't* be!"

He gave me a quizzical look.

"Tony, that's what *I* ate!"

He frowned, cocked his head like his mutt might have. "What, just a smidge of it?"

"No! *Lots* of it!"

"You ate with the others at the church?"

"Why . . . no. Pregnant women eat when they feel like it. I had my servings of stew about, oh, an hour and a half before lunch was served."

I told him about sneaking into the kitchen through the secret passageway, and getting a preluncheon sample of Mrs. Mulligan's stew. I'd of course heard the rumors that the stew had been the source of everyone's sickness, but hadn't thought much about the fact that I hadn't gotten sick—not till I heard rat poison had been an added ingredient, anyway.

Tony's brow furrowed. "Then the poison must have been added between ten-thirty and noon. That's helpful to know. Thank you."

I almost said, "The Borne Girls Detective Agency aims to please." But instead I had the sense to just nod.

"My Lord," he said. His steely eyes had softened. "That might have been a close call for you. And your baby."

"Yes, but there was only one fatality. Madam Petrova. Because she was elderly, I guess, and her system just couldn't take it."

"She *was* the oldest person there," Tony said with a nod.

"Does Mrs. Mulligan know that someone doctored her stew? That she isn't responsible for this tragedy?"

"Not yet. None of this is for public consumption."

Sort of like stew with rat poison in it. "Look, you need to tell her. She probably feels terrible about it. The word is all around town that it was her stew that was tainted, you know."

"Well, we haven't released that info yet."

"No, but Mother overheard the coroner speculating about the stew as the source at the scene. And if Mother knows, Serenity knows."

Tony closed his eyes. "How can you stand it?"

"I love her. You don't have to, but I do. Listen, something else about that stew—I don't know if you're aware, but none of those five out-of-town bidders ate at the church."

"I do know—we interviewed them today. They ate at their hotel. How do you know? If this is more amateur detective nonsense—"

"Not guilty! I just ran into them at a restaurant—they were eating together again. Do you think one of them is your murderer?"

His eyes widened, then narrowed. "Possibly. We searched their hotel rooms and rental vehicles—they cooperated fully, no search warrants required—but an artifact as small as that egg could be easily hidden. Could even have been discreetly shipped somewhere by now."

"And you've searched the church?"

"Top to bottom. Father O'Brien has been very helpful. We still have police stationed there. Considered a crime scene." He sighed. "That's how I got the media out of there so quickly, and we've been very lucky on that front, actually."

"Yeah, we had all the Quad Cities stations represented.

Which are all the networks, including Fox. I expected to see them hanging around."

He waved as if batting an invisible fly. "They took off shortly after the auction went to hell. They'd come expecting a fun story about a Fabergé egg helping bail out a flood-wracked town, and instead got a church filled with people puking. But when this murder stuff hits the local papers, that might attract national attention."

We just sat there a while and he even slipped an arm around my shoulder. No more talk of murder or anything else. We just enjoyed the fire and each other's company. I fell asleep briefly, nestled against his shoulder.

Then I woke up, feeling a little embarrassed, yawned and stretched, and said, "It was a lovely supper, Tony. A lovely evening. But Mother will be worried—you better run me home."

He did.

But I sat in the front seat this time.

A Trash 'n' Treasures Tip

Bidding at auction is not for the shy. Hold your card up high, or speak loudly when you bid. Mother can go too far in this regard, however, jumping up and blocking other bidders. It's just remotely possible that she does this on purpose.

Chapter Six

Walking on Eggshells

At around nine o'clock that evening, Tony dropped me off at my house. He pulled up at the curb, turned, and asked me if I had my cell phone with me.

"Sure," I said. "Why?"

"I want to give you my unlisted number. You have any problems, of any kind, day or night—just call."

I didn't quite know what to say, but finally mumbled, "Thanks," and he gave me the number and I entered it on my contacts list.

He gave me a crisp nod, and a nice sort of asexual Lone Ranger smile, hands on the wheel, as I said good night and got out. Then he was gone and I was heading for the front steps, wondering why the front light wasn't on for me, when I noticed the familiar shape seated on the top step that led to the enclosed porch.

Mother.

Okay, so she was sitting in the dark, her pink fuzzy robe over her pajamas, shod in matching pink slippers. Why was that a biggie? Vaguely nutty behavior on Mother's part was par for the course, and the night was pleasant enough to be sitting out in it. Still, an ominous vibe shimmered my way. . . .

"Is he gone?" she asked in a hoarse whisper.

I was at the bottom of the several steps looking at where her eyes were, able only to make out the big glasses in the dark. "Of course he's gone. You saw him go. Mother, is something wrong?"

She sprang to her feet, looming over me like a gargoyle. A gargoyle in a pink bathrobe and slippers, that is.

"There's something you must see," she said portentously.

And she floated down the steps and moved past me down the walk toward the street.

"Mother!"

"Come along, dear!" She gestured back with a crooking finger.

Suddenly I felt like Scrooge following the Ghost of Christmas Future into the graveyard for some bad news.

There were halfhearted streetlights along Elm and part of a moon, too, which conspired to make Mother look even more ghostly as she took a right and headed down the sidewalk.

I fell in along beside her and asked, "Mother! Where are we going?"

"To see Mrs. Mulligan, dear."

"Is that wise?"

"There's something you must see."

Mrs. Mulligan lived just two and a half blocks down from us. Mother was a fairly frequent visitor, though she professed not to care for the woman, condemning her as the worst gossip in town. She denied that she dropped by Mrs. Mulligan's once or twice a week to catch up on the juiciest tidbits.

"What's going on, Mother?"

"This is my second visit tonight."

"What? What are you talking about?"

We were at the shared driveway that separated Mrs. Mulligan's yard from her next-door neighbor's. Her well-maintained two-story clapboard house was yellow with blue trim, though the moon washed both colors out. Lots of shrubbery hugged the front of the house, and four front steps went up to a cement stoop. No light shone above the stoop, but lights were on behind drapes in the living room, and another light was on upstairs.

Mother was trotting down the driveway, where the lawn sloped, and seemed clearly headed for the side stairway up to the kitchen entrance. We were ignoring the front door, and I wasn't surprised—Mother and Mrs. Mulligan would sit in the kitchen together and share secrets (not their own—everybody else's).

No light was over this side door, either, but one was on in the kitchen. I followed Mother as she padded up the flight of wooden steps and bent to pluck a hidden key in a potted plant on the landing. The screen door onto a small back porch was open, and I trailed after Mother as she unlocked the door onto the kitchen.

She went in, and so did I. A light over the sink on the driveway side was burning, but the overhead one wasn't. The kitchen was neither spacious nor small, but did have room enough for a round maple table with four chairs. A counter with cupboards was next to us where we'd entered, and the refrigerator was opposite. At right was a stove and oven, a small pan on a burner, switched off.

Mrs. Mulligan, in a plaid flannel robe but with her red fright wig on, was slumped at the table, her head on her folded arms like a grade-school student taking a nap at her desk. On the table nearby was a large ceramic cup that said IOWA STATE FAIR '66 on it. Also her glasses.

"Is she . . . asleep?" I asked.

"No, dear. She's dead." She turned to me and the eyes behind the big lenses would have been huge even without the magnification. "This is what I wanted you to see."

I went over and checked—the shrunken old lady looked strangely peaceful, if pale as, well, death. I felt guilty for once thinking she resembled an orangutan, though truth be told she still did. I couldn't find a pulse in either her wrist or throat.

Mother came close and said, "I did what Archie Goodwin always does, dear! In the Nero Wolfe books? I got some fabric threads from my bathrobe, and held them under her nose, and they didn't flutter. Then I got a makeup mirror from the bathroom and held it under her nose and it didn't fog up at all."

Wincing in rage, doubting that Archie Goodwin had ever plucked fibers from his pink bathrobe, I walked her by the arm into the nearby dining room, where a table was stacked with mail and obviously hadn't been used for company for some time. Mrs. Mulligan had no living children and her best friend had been the telephone, where she gathered and passed along gossip. For a woman who had thrived on the misfortunes of others, her house had (to me anyway) a creepy cuteness—lots of worthless knicknacks and curios, frog and kitty and puppy collections on display.

"Talk," I said, holding on to her arms.

"I came over to see how Mildred was doing."

Mildred Mulligan.

"Keep talking," I said. "Make it fast."

"Some girls I spoke to on the phone today said Mildred was down in the dumps because everybody was blaming her . . . well, her *stew* . . . for the outbreak at the church! A woman died, after all."

Now another one had.

"And you haven't called the police?"

"No, dear."

"Or 911?"

"Obviously not, dear."

"Instead you just sat on the porch and waited for me?"

"That's right, dear."

"Because no doctor was needed, since you'd determined by means learned from old mystery novels that she was likely dead."

"She *is* dead, dear."

"Well, she is now! Maybe if you'd . . ."

That was when Mother started to cry. There was nothing theatrical about it, nothing fake at all. I helped her to a chair and went to the bathroom off the kitchen and brought her some Kleenex.

Snuffling, she managed, "You're saying I . . . I killed her?"

"No, Mother."

"She was gone. She was already *gone*. There was nothing that could be done!"

"I'm sure you're right, Mother."

"I'm such a stupid, stupid, *stupid* woman. . . ."

I said nothing. Just patted her back gently.

"Three people are dead, Brandy! Three people! All because I tried to do a good deed."

All because you wanted to star in a big-time auction and appear in a regional magazine, I thought, but was not cruel enough to say.

"It wasn't your fault," I said, pretty much meaning it. "But we have to call the police. Right now."

Her tears stopped, though their trails glistened on her cheeks. "We could just go home. What good will it do if we're here and just make your friend the chief mad at us? We can go home and make an anonymous phone call!"

The only light in the dining room spilled in from the kitchen and the shadows on her face made her crazy. More crazy.

"Mother, I'm pretty sure the police have caller I.D. This isn't a *Boston Blackie* movie from 1945. Anyway, your fingerprints are all over the place! And as we *know*, the Serenity P.D. has your prints on file."

"Oh, please, can't we just go home and call from there, and not wait here?"

This from the woman who was making her second trip to the crime scene.

"No," I said, and I got my cell phone out of my purse. I dialed the number and got Tony.

I said, "I'm afraid you're not going to be very happy with me. . . ."

We didn't wait inside the house, but I have to admit we lingered in the kitchen for a while. I was curious about a couple of things.

Mother stood behind me as I positioned myself between the late Mrs. Mulligan and her stove. I pointed to the little pan on the burner. "That looks like broth. Chicken broth?"

Nodding, Mother said, "Mildred had trouble sleeping. It was her habit to have a cup of broth before bedtime."

"You knew this how?"

She shrugged. "Everyone who knows Mildred knows her routine. Never went out much—people came around to talk to her, share the latest, uh, news."

"What did she do before she had her cup of broth?"

"She showered at bedtime." Mother gestured to the bathroom off the kitchen. "She was always in bed by ten o'clock. Like clockwork."

"So if someone who knew Mrs. Mulligan's habits wanted to sneak in here, and doctor her broth," I said, remembering the key in the potted plant, "that would be child's play."

"Oh yes, dear. Is that what you think happened?"

"I don't know what happened. Just trying to think it through." I went to the cupboard. Touching the lower handle carefully, I opened the door and saw two well-stocked shelves, with the two higher shelves empty. The lower shelf had household cleaning products and their ilk; the upper shelf held food items.

"How was Mrs. Mulligan's eyesight?" I asked.

"Why, not good. She has cataracts."

"I notice she's consolidated her items onto two shelves, so she didn't have to get up on a stool or ladder to reach the higher ones."

Mother's head bobbed. "Yes, and of course her flour and sugar and other canisters are out on the counter."

Not wanting to get Mother going, I did not point out that among the items on the lower shelf was a box of rat poison.

We exited the kitchen and went around to the front and sat on the steps, much as Mother had back home when she'd been waiting for me. A squad car with two young officers I didn't recognize arrived first, and I gave them a brief rundown of the events, and they told to us to wait while they entered the crime scene.

Five minutes or so later Tony arrived. He was in the sport coat again and the tie was snugged—which meant he'd gotten all the way home before I'd called him. He looked pale and I don't think it was the moonlight.

I got to my feet and allowed Mother to remain seated and met him halfway up the walk.

"It's not what it looks like," I said.

His eyes were unblinking and cool. Make that cold. "What does it look like?"

"We live just down the block, you know . . ."

"Yes, I remember."

"And Mother was a friend of Mrs. Mulligan's. She regularly dropped over, and just stopped by to check up on her. There's been some nasty talk around town, because of the stew and all, and Mother was just being a good friend."

Briefly I explained that Mother had come home and taken me to Mrs. Mulligan's, but did not mention that she'd been waiting for me in the dark when he dropped me off. I thought we might get away with being a trifle loose about the timing of events. . . .

"Did you touch anything?" he asked.

"Mother did. She found a makeup mirror to try to check for breathing. She may have absentmindedly touched other things in the house. I don't think I touched anything."

I told him what Mother had said about Mrs. Mulligan's habit of having broth just before bed, to make her sleep. And that she showered before bedtime, and that a key to the house was in a potted plant by the side door.

His sigh started at his toes. "Go home."

"You don't need us anymore tonight?"

"You'll hear from me if we do."

"Okay."

"Go. Home."

We went.

Home.

The next morning, Mother was suspiciously chipper. She was in a pale blue velour pants suit (cousin to her green one) and we had English muffins and jelly and hot tea on the porch. Neither of us was very hungry.

"In all the excitement last night," she said, "I failed to get a report."

"Report?"

"Were your rights abused by that brute?"

After a good night's sleep, or anyway *a* night's sleep, she was ready to get the skinny on my evening with the chief.

"He spared me the rubber hose and fingernail pulling," I said, nibbling at a toasty edge. "As a matter of fact, we didn't even go to the police station."

"If you weren't at the station, where *were* you?"

She used to ask something similar when I was eighteen: "If you weren't at Tina's, where were you?" (Probably in the park drinking champagne.)

"The chief was very sweet, really. He drove me to his house and made me dinner."

For a while Mother just goggled at me, then eventually regained her powers of speech. "I simply must hear *all* about it!"

No surprise there.

"After breakfast," I said.

Back in the house, I let Sushi in—I'd put her out in part so that I could enjoy my muffins without her begging—but she smelled the food in the air and started dancing and pawing at me, as best she could, as chubby as she's gotten.

I filled her bowl, dry and wet, and refreshed her water dish, and was further going about my business when Mother materialized like a movie monster and grabbed my arm.

She steered me into the living room and over to the high-back Queen Anne armchair with the needlepoint flowers in rich colors of brown, burgundy, and gold. It was *her* throne, and neither I nor Sushi could sit there without getting a disapproving look from the Queen.

She pushed me down. "Comfortable?"

Now, I have yet in my time on Planet Earth found a comfortable "Queen Anne" *anything*. That style of formal furniture was designed to discourage Victorian Age visitors and suitors from overstaying their welcome.

"My back hurts," I complained. "I'm expecting, remember?"

Mother rushed off, then returned with a small velvet pillow, which she stuffed behind me.

"How's that? Comfy now?"

I crinkled my nose. "I'm a little dry. A little thirsty. . . ."

"You just had *tea*, dear."

"But hot chocolate would be so very nice."

"Hot chocolate, of course." Her smile seemed no more forced than Dick Cheney's at the Obama inauguration.

"With marshmallows."

She hurried off again. Soon the microwave dinged, and Mother returned, handing me a warm mug.

I slurped, then frowned. "Thanks. But these marshmallows are kind of on the *stale* side. . . ."

Mother stomped one foot. "*Brandy Ingrid Borne!* Stop toying with me and tell me what happened last night at the chief's!"

I smiled smugly; for once *I* was in the cat-bird seat!

By the way, what the heck is a cat-bird, anyway? And what seat is the cat-bird sitting in? (Certainly not a Queen Anne.) Honestly, if an old saying doesn't make sense anymore, it should be lost to the ages. Now that barbershops are all but extinct, isn't it time we stopped hippity-hopping down to them?

Anyway, with new intel on the chief, let's just say I had Mother over a barrel. *Wait a minute* . . . what does *that* mean? Did I have the old girl bent over a barrel? Was she going over Niagara Falls in a barrel, maybe? Or was that just wishful thinking. . . ?

Finally I set my mug on an end table. I folded my arms. "No info until we have a few changes around here."

Her eyes were narrow, wide slits behind the big lenses. "What *kind* of changes?"

"For one thing, no more bursting into my room in the morning, singing, 'Uppy-uppy-uppy,' like I was still three years old."

Mother guffawed. "Oh, I don't do that. I didn't *ever* do that."

"Yes. You did. You do."

She frowned in thoughtful consideration. "What if instead I sing, 'Oh, What a Beautiful Morning'?"

"No. No singing whatsoever."

"*Fine*," Mother said. "Anything else, my pet?"

"No more 'borrowing' my car in the middle of the night to run and buy chocolate-mint ice cream at Wal-Mart."

Mother gasped. "However did you *know*?"

"Are you *kidding*? I can hear that old muffler a mile away." I waggled a finger at her, relishing this reversal of roles. "You'll go to jail next time they catch you driving without a license, you know."

"You win," Mother said dramatically. Arms high. "I surrender, dear!"

"I said no singing. . . ."

"All right. Is there . . . anything else?"

And here's the heartbreaking part, folks—I couldn't think of one other thing.

So I let Mother off the hook. (Once again—was she a fish? Or a slab of beef in a meat locker maybe?)

"No," I said magnanimously. "That's all I ask . . . with perhaps one small exception."

"Yes, dear?"

"No amateur sleuthing . . ."

Her face fell.

". . . without telling me what you're up to, first."

She beamed. "You do agree, then, dear, that we have a responsibility in this situation?"

Surprised to hear myself say it, I said, "I do. We'll not interfere with the police, but we might . . . *might* . . . ask a question or two around town. And now, if you'll take a seat. . . ?"

Mother settled at my feet like a child eager to hear a bedtime story, and I proceeded to recap the events of last evening, leaving out the conversation the chief and I had about the murder of Martinette and the poisoning of the stew.

Also, I admit that I downplayed anything that might seem romantic, although I further admit that I wasn't sure anything really romantic had occurred. Tony Cassato wasn't the easiest guy to read.

And after the nasty coda to our evening, that is, having to call him about Mother finding Mrs. Mulligan's body, any romantic inclinations he might have had for me might now just be more smoke up his fireplace.

When I had finished my monologue, Mother began to clap like a trained seal. "Well *done*, dear!"

I smiled, basking in such rare praise from Mother on my theatrical abilities.

But then—like a critic whose review begins well but ends with a wicked barb—she raised a finger. "There are just a *few* questions I must ask. . . ."

Uh-oh.

Here came the Spanish Inquisition: Why hadn't I inquired further about his wife and child? What was the recipe for the carrot soup? And hadn't I gotten *anything* out of him about Martinette's murder?

"No," I said, holding up my hands, palms out. "That's all you get."

Mother pulled herself up off the floor; it was like watching a building reassemble itself, a demolition video run backward. "Get out of my *chair,* dear."

And I was forthwith dethroned, relegated to the hard floor, while Mother sat regally, gazing down at her court jester.

"We are in a pickle, dear," Mother said. "We set in motion events that have taken three lives. So there must be no secrets between us."

"*You* were the one who—"

"Shush! You will share with me now, and in complete detail, every new piece of information Chief Cassato revealed."

"You can't make me do that. I'm of voting age and drinking age, too. It's my judgment that it would bad for your mental health for me to—"

A finger settled against her cheek and she gazed ceiling-ward in contemplation. "Of course I could go down to the police station, demand to see Chief Cassato, and tell him how outraged I am that he threw my daughter into the back of his car and drove off with her into the forest . . ."

"The *forest?*"

". . . and apparently had his way with her . . ."

"Did not!"

". . . and perhaps the mayor and my friends on the city council would like to hear from me on the subject at the 'Citizens Speak' segment of their next meeting, which is televised on public access, as you know, and—"

And I spilled. All of it, from Martinette's death being ruled a homicide to the media folks being banished from the crime scene, from the rat poison in Mrs. Mulligan's stew to the four out-of-town bidders having their hotel rooms (unsuccessfully) searched for the missing egg. Even the obvious deduction that the rat poison had to have been added after I ate my early portion(s).

Satisfied with both my humiliation and declamation, Mother stood, then strode off to the dining room, not even bothering to grant me a dismissal. I followed, finding m'lady studying her cardboard church and list of suspects, one hand stroking her chin, like a silent movie villain.

Finally, Mother sighed irritably. "This case is *too* complicated! There are too many suspects with both motive *and* opportunity."

She sat down dejectedly at the table.

Mother was displaying uncharacteristic defeat, yet I had a sudden suspicion that she might at any moment regroup and start terrorizing the suspects willy-nilly, thwarting the police investigation, not to mention my own efforts.

I joined her at the table. "Maybe you're not looking at this the right way, Mother. Maybe you should go in a *different* direction. . . ."

Like *away* from the investigation. . . .

Her eyes met mine. "What do you mean, dear?"

Settling more comfortably in the chair, I asked, "Who are our two favorite mystery writers?"

Mother raised her eyebrows, but played along. "Well, I would have to say Agatha Christie and Rex Stout."

Ol' Rex "Fibers Under the Nostrils of a Corpse" Stout.

"Our two very favorites," I confirmed. "And they *both* have a lot of suspects in their mysteries. Right?"

"I'm listening."

"But each author goes about constructing his or her brand of mystery quite differently."

Mother nodded, and her eyes flared. Nostrils, too. "How true! In Sexy Rexy's novels, any *one* of the suspects could be the murderer, right up until the very end, when Nero Wolfe sits his considerable bulk down in his over-sized chair and closes his eyes and begins to purse his lips in and out. That's why I can read those books over and over again! Because I can never remember who did it."

"Could be anybody," I said with a nod. "Agatha Christie, however, designs her stories so that really only *one* of the seemingly interchangeable suspects has the right motive and psychology to be a killer."

"Oh, yes. She's wonderful."

"Dame Agatha loves to put the murderer right under your nose, at the very start—then give him or her a cast-iron alibi, moving that suspect off-stage until the very end, when she reveals that the cast-iron alibi, or lack of motive, is made of Silly Putty."

Mother beamed, liking that image; but then she frowned and cocked her head. "What exactly are you *saying*, dear?"

"I think we need to concentrate on suspects with no motive and great alibis."

This nonsense made Mother's eyes dance with excitement. "Such as who, dear?"

I stood, then approached the board and, using the black marker, added two names to the suspect list.

Mother gasped. "You can't be serious—*Father O'Brien?* Why, he was busy tending to the sick!"

I raised an eyebrow. "The sick, such as the murder victim's corpse we both saw him bending over?"

"But Brandy!" She paused, then said emphatically, "He's a priest! How can a *priest* be evil?"

"You want me to refer to some former altar boys?"

Mother frowned in displeasure. "What a terrible thing to say!" Then she pursed her lips and nodded, adding, "Good point, dear. But your *other* new suspect . . ."

"Yes?"

"Clifford *Ashland?* You're way off base there, darling—he was stuck in the back of the sanctuary." She pointed to the cardboard church, paused, and then added, "Besides, he has no motive. He is wealthy as sin, and anyway, rumor has it that his aunt was leaving everything to two churches—the Russian Orthodox 'sister' church in Chicago, and St. Mary's here in Serenity!"

"Which brings us to Father O'Brien again! And as for Ashland, it's true, he really doesn't to seem to have a motive"—I cocked my head Sushi–like—"but then, Vivian Borne hasn't gone *looking* for one yet, has she?"

Mother was regarding me with new appreciation.

"Dear," she said finally, "I like the way you're thinking. Don't *ever* go back on Prozac. You're much more use to me *not* mellowed out."

Funny thing: I liked the new me too.

I especially relished the devious way I was about to send Mother down the proverbial garden path.

"How should we proceed?" Mother asked. "Rex Stout style, or à la Dame Agatha?"

"This feels more like an Agatha than Rex, to me."

She slapped her knees with her hands. "I wholeheartedly concur! I'll start investigating Father O'Brien and Clifford Ashland *right* away."

Moving in the opposite direction of the police investigation of the bidders.

But my smugness caught in my throat when she added, "Besides, with Mrs. Mulligan as our third murder victim, it's very unlikely one of the out-of-towners is responsible. How could they know her habits, or where the house key was hidden?"

I was shaking my head. "Maybe it *was* suicide, Mother. Maybe Mrs. Mulligan felt terrible about what her stew did to all those people, and what was worse for an old busybody like her, uh, rest her soul, suddenly she herself was the object of gossip!"

"Please, Brandy—listen to yourself. We have a death by poisoning, and another murder that was made possible because, as your chiefie put it, that widespread poisoning created a diversion. And now a third victim, the second in the case to die by poison, is a convenient suicide? Would Stout or Christie ever do such a thing?"

"Sure! All the time!"

But Mother was ignoring me. "Of course, with the good father in the game, and the loyal nephew, we'll need two more game pieces." Mother gestured to the replica church. "What do you suggest?"

"You decide." I checked my wristwatch. "I'm due over at Peggy Sue's in half an hour."

And I left Mother rummaging around in the assorted boxes of board games.

There are mysteries and then there are mysteries, and in my life—despite the bizarre circumstances of the past year that included several murder inquiries—the biggest mystery for Brandy Borne had been that of her own parentage.

Before the Fabergé auction had gone Humpty-Dumpty, I'd set up a visit with Sis at her home for this morning, so we could finally clear the air on the subject. As readers of my previous books already know, Peggy Sue is my biological mother, a secret which had been kept from me until a few months before, when I received an anonymous letter in the mail.

A while back I had confronted Peggy Sue, and she'd admitted that she'd become pregnant the summer after high school, just as she was preparing to leave and study abroad. She'd gone off to Paris anyway, returning just before I was due, with a detour to Maine where she stayed with discreet relatives.

Meanwhile, my recently widowed Mother had been back in Serenity pretending to be pregnant, and what a performance *that* must have been—never had a "pregnancy pillow" been given a greater workout.

After I was born, Mother joined Sis in Maine, and they returned together with a bundle that was Brandy, passing me off as Peggy Sue's new baby sister.

So we'd resolved that issue—with one major exception being that Mother did not know that *I* knew she was really my grandmother. For various reasons, Peggy Sue and I had decided that it was for the best that Mother remain Mother and Peggy Sue remain Sis. Never provide Vivian Borne with melodrama if you can help it.

But recently I'd received another anonymous letter, claiming that Peggy Sue hadn't told me the truth, at least not the whole truth, and nothing but the truth. So help her God.

Before leaving the house, I noticed that Mother had made fitting choices of board game pieces for the two new suspects—Father O'Brien, a white rook; and Clifford Ashland, the wealthy Mr. Green from Clue—placing them in position in the cardboard replica.

I bid Mother good-bye—she barely noticed—and went out to my car.

Sis, along with her accountant husband, Bob, and college-student daughter, Ashley, lived in an exclusive subdivision on the outskirts of Serenity, meaning I had to cross the treacherous bypass. But at least there was a light at the intersection now, thanks to a ten-car pileup a while back, and soon I was entering the upper-class housing addition, where the homes ran half-a-mil and up, even with housing prices down.

At Sis's mansion (to me it was), I turned up a wide cement drive to a three-car garage, which stood open, revealing Peggy Sue's white, gas-guzzling Caddie Escalade. Bob's hybrid was gone—indicating he was working today at his office instead of at home—as was Ashley's sporty red Mustang, which my lucky niece had taken with her to college.

Just to be obnoxious, for a few moments I let my battered Buick rumble and belch—recalling the old VHS tapes of Jack Benny shows Mother used to play, where his famed Maxwell would come to a long-shuddering stop.

Then I Dorothy-ed up the yellow brick road to the Emerald City, where I rang the bell, which was no louder nor any more pretentious than Big Ben.

Peggy Sue answered right away, her chin-length dark brown hair perfectly coifed, her attractive face fully painted; she was dressed head-to-toe in Burberry plaid, an outfit that could pay a month's rent for a family of four, and give me eyestrain for a week.

She greeted me somewhat sheepishly as I trooped by, heading down the gleaming floor hallway, passing a living room on the right and formal dining room on the left that were worthy of an *Architectural Digest* spread, and on into a state-of-the art kitchen Rachael Ray would kill for.

There, I settled into a modern, black-lacquered chair at a square glass-topped table with real flowers in the center.

Sis, her back to me, busied herself at one of the endless marble counters, filling two china cups from a combo espresso-latte machine, then delivered them on matching plates, along with almond biscotti.

She took the chair next to me, asking, "How are you, Brandy?"

I answered by opening my small L.A.M.B. purse (couldn't afford the bigger one) to produce a folded white piece of paper. This I placed in front of her, clearly in a mode of accusation.

Peggy Sue picked up the note, read it, then slowly put it down again.

"Well?" I asked. "Is it true? Is my real father a senator?"

Her troubled eyes met mine. "It's true."

"But you told me my father was a *grease monkey* you had a one-night stand with, who died in Vietnam in a helicopter crash!"

"I know what I said."

"*Well?*"

"Well . . . I'm sorry. I did it to—"

"To what? Deceive me?"

"No. Protect *him*."

"What's his name?"

Peggy Sue looked pained. She sighed. She looked everywhere but at me.

I gave her the evil eye. "If you don't tell me, I'll start

contacting every senator in the state, and every man who has been a senator in this state since—"

"*Not* state senator, Brandy. United *States* senator—Senator Clark? Edward Clark?"

My jaw fell as if the hinges had come loose. The media was buzzing about the veteran senator from our state making a gubernatorial run, as a prelude to an eventual presidential try. Suddenly, I was a mutt with a pedigree!

"Does he . . . *know* about me?"

Peggy Sue shook her head. "I never told him I was pregnant." She looked down. "He . . . he was married at the time. I'm sure he would have done the right thing, but I didn't want him in my life. I didn't want an abortion. I wanted *you.*"

Wasn't that flattering?

"Did he take advantage of you?" Dirty old man—or dirty *young* man, back then.

"No! The attraction was mutual." She paused, then went on. "The summer after high school, I worked for his campaign—it was his first election, and we grew . . . close."

"I'll say."

Sis took deep breath, let it out slowly. "I guess I was lonely and starry-eyed, being around such a handsome, powerful man. I'd just broken up with . . . anyway . . . and of course Mother was . . . difficult. I had dreams of marriage, even though he was already . . . ."

The sentences just wouldn't come together for her.

Finally she said, "Brandy, I was just a stupid kid." But there were tears in her eyes when she added, "I really *did* love him. . . ."

I was seeing Peggy Sue in a new light—vulnerable and sad, compassionate and caring. She had made mistakes—like me.

"I'm sorry, Brandy, that I made up that other story—

please don't hate me for it. I didn't want Edward's career to be ruined. I *still* don't."

"I understand," I said. "But that *did* happen a long time ago."

"It could still hurt him. I was only seventeen, although I became of-age a month later."

Oops—even a long-ago whiff of statutory rape could feed the twenty-four-hour news cycles for a good long time. . . .

Peggy Sue snatched up the note. "Who's been sending these awful things?" I wasn't used to seeing that much anger on her face. "First, telling you that I'm your mother, and now *this!*"

I smirked. "Who do you think? Connie Grimes."

Connie Grimes—nastiest of Peggy Sue's snotty gal pals, with whom I'd had several run-ins lately. It made sense that that mad cow would go after her revenge.

Peggy Sue was shaking her head, the perfect hair swinging. "But how would *Connie* know?"

I shrugged. "Where was *she* thirty years ago? She didn't work on the campaign with you, did she?"

She frowned. "Yes, she did. But—"

Something was forming in Sis's mind, but then she shook her head. "I don't know. If it *is* her, I could *strangle* that witch!"

I tried to get the conversation back on track.

"About Mother," I said. "We agreed before that I didn't want her to know that *I* knew about you. . . ."

"And now you don't want her to know that *you* know about *him*." Peggy Sue nodded. "I agree it's for the best."

"Let's maintain the status quo."

"Let's."

She warmed up our cold coffee, which we sipped as our conversation turned to more pleasant subjects, like how my pregnancy was going, and what courses Ashley was taking at college, avoiding any discussion of the botched bazaar.

When we'd run out of things to say, Peggy Sue gathered up the cups and leftover biscotti, then walked me to the front door.

We stood out on her expensive inlaid stone stoop, in the cool, spring air, and Sis said, "I don't suppose there's any way you can keep Mother from attending Nastasya Petrova's funeral. . . ."

"Not a chance."

Sis pursed her pretty lips. "I can't believe she's in the middle of a murder again. How can that keep *happening?*"

"Just lucky I guess."

"You *have* to rein her in. You have to promise me that. Is she taking her medication?"

"Yes, but she's pretty keyed-up over all this. Don't worry, Sis—I'll do what I can to keep her under control."

She sighed. "It's really been embarrassing for me, living so close to the Ashlands." Her eyes traveled to another half-mil-plus monstrosity down the street.

I followed her gaze. "Is that where they live?"

She nodded, "Clifford and Angelica. Lovely, isn't it?"

So now the real Peggy Sue was back, worried about what the neighbors might think, concerned about her own community standing. Old habits die hard. Actually, they don't die at all.

"You know," I said, "I hear Ashland's aunt left all her money to St. Mary's and her Russian church in Chicago."

"I've heard the same. Wonderful people, the Ashlands. So many brokers are doing poorly in this economy, but Clifford is thriving. Smart, conservative investments. Bob and I have done very well with him."

"So it's not likely he'd kill his aunt for her money."

Her eyes widened in horror. "Brandy! He's a millionaire

many times over, and his aunt's wealth doesn't go to him in any case. Don't *say* such terrible things. Not *all* rich people are evil, you know! He'd be the *least* likely suspect. . . ."

That gave me a sick feeling as I walked to my battered Buick. I'd read enough Christie and Stout to know all about least likely suspects, and was suddenly hoping the garden path I'd sent Mother down wasn't a thorny one.

A Trash 'n' Treasures Tip

Examine auction items before bidding, using the same scrutiny you would for any purchase that can't be returned for a defect. (If I forget to bring along a magnifying glass, I just use Mother's glasses.)

Chapter Seven

Cracked Egg

In my previous accounts, I have always allowed Mother her own chapter, which seemed only fair—after all, she is privy to certain information that I am not. Besides which, I make certain comments and even accusations about her along the way that might seem to warrant an opportunity for her to respond.

But on our previous outing, *Antiques Flee Market*, she wheedled me into giving her two chapters. And in an effort to make sure she does not view that practice as a precedent, I am limiting her once again to a single chapter. As usual, The management is not responsible for, nor necessarily in agreement with, the following content, and therefore will not be held accountable.

Ah, my dear ones!

How wonderful it is to have your collective ear once more. My darling daughter is precocious and well-meaning, but she does occasionally reveal an unflattering point of view where her mother is concerned, and I am grateful for the chance to straighten all of you out.

We'll begin just after Brandy left the house to visit Peggy Sue. That was when I flew into action, with not a moment to lose, because due momentarily to pass by the house was Serenity's gas-powered trolley—my only form of transportation other than Brandy and her car (or my own car in an *absolute* emergency. And assuming I could get the tires back on).

It is basically true that I have lost my driver's license due to some silly infraction involving a tractor and a cow, which I won't go into right now, not because I couldn't defend myself, but due to Brandy limiting my word count.

And my sincere thanks to all you who wrote to sympathize with me after the ungrateful child cut me off in midsentence last time around. I had just been about to share with you an account of the time Billy Buckly (the town's little person, grand-nephew of one of the original MGM *Wizard of Oz* munchkins—talk about a local celebrity!) had been sitting on my lap, not out of affection but due to a shortage of seats, when the trolley inexplicably braked. Unfortunately I must reserve the exciting conclusion of that tale for a later time, when I'm not so carefully watching my word count and staying on point.

Super-heroine quick, I changed into navy slacks and sweater, and put on my most comfortable walking shoes, then grabbed a tan trench coat, as the spring weather was still a little nippy, and of course that's what *all* true detectives wear, particularly this time of year.

I knew I needn't worry about putting Sushi outside one last time, because Brandy had installed a small doggy-portal in the back door—I tell you, that animal has to relieve itself more than *I* do! I could ascertain, however, that Sushi was miffed at being left alone again, by the way she stuck out her lower teeth, much as Marlon Brando did in *The Dogfather* (typo: *Godfather*).

On one occasion, after we'd had the little door put in, Brandy and I happened to be away for a very long afternoon of yard-sale snooping in the neighborhood. When we depart on foot, Sushi expects to be part of the group, but our expedition that day would have been too much for her (she is *blind*, if she doesn't know it). On our return we discovered that the little demon had gotten hold of Brandy's car keys and buried them in the backyard. This had taken detective work on our part because the animal might have hidden them *anywhere*, but her paws were filthy and signs of fresh digging out back led us to the treasure (although I was *still* late for rehearsal at the Playhouse). Sometimes that dog can be very vindictive. Wherever does she get that?

But I digress.

I caught the trolley just in time, hopping aboard an already-full car. You see, the ride is free, *if* you're going downtown, presumably to spend your hard-earned money, a service underwritten by the merchants who compete with the mall. These days, though, with high-flying gas prices and low-riding economy, many folks who work downtown join shoppers in taking advantage of the free ride.

"Hello, Shawntea," I bid the young, attractive African-American woman at the wheel.

I had met her in Chicago last summer when four of us Red-Hatted League gals drove into the Windy City for a Cubs game and lost our bearings, ending up with a flat tire somewhere called Cabrini-Green.

Shawntea, who had just disembarked a bus, enlisted help from her brother Trayvon, who belonged to a young men's club called Gangsta Disciples (apparently something on the order of the fine boy's clubs we set up during the Depression to keep the young 'uns out of trouble). Trayvon changed our tire and I, in exchange, offered to change Shawntea's life with a new start in Serenity, where, a few months later—to my complete surprise—she arrived on my doorstep with two little boys in tow. But Vivian Borne never makes a promise lightly, and I managed to find her this job.

" 'lo Viv." The young woman smiled, flashing perfect white teeth. "Been a while."

"Nice to have the trolley running again, my dear."

The service had been shut down for several weeks because of the flooding, but the downtown was open for business again, with the exception of River Drive, which was still waterlogged.

A young man seated just behind Shawntea stood to give me his seat.

I bowed to him. "Thank you, young man! It does a mature person's heart good to see that, in these trying times, chivalry among the younger generation is *not* dead!"

He gave me a odd look—probably embarrassed by the praise—and the trolley stopped and he got off. Perhaps I'd jumped the gun a trifle on the kudos.

Seated now, I returned my attention to the driver. "And how are Kwamie and Zeffross?"

"Oh, fine, Viv, fine. They *love* school! Isn't that something?" Her eyes were on the road.

"And how are *your* educational efforts proceeding, my dear?"

"Gee, Viv, I feel terrible I didn't call you! I finished school, completed my GED! You are bein' chauffeured this morning by a *high-school* grad."

"Why, that's wonderful, dear! I *knew* you were up to the challenge."

"That's just the start, Viv—why, I'll be attendin' community college in the fall." She paused, adding, "Thanks to you, sweet thing."

I lifted my chin in all modesty. "I'm sure I had nothing to do with it."

She risked a glance back. "Come on, now—I know you musta had *something* to do with the full scholarship I landed!"

"I'm sure you accomplished that all by yourself, young lady."

On the other hand, my recommendation to the foundation board might well have been taken to heart. Several of the members have minor indiscretions in their past that could prove embarrassing should they come to light. Brandy calls this approach blackmail, but I insist it's just good citizenship.

We had arrived downtown at the trolley's first stop, where I always get off, and I gathered myself.

Shawntea said, "Viv . . . Miz *Borne*. . . ?"

That struck an ominous note. "Yes, dear?"

"I'm afraid . . . afraid I won't be driving the trolley anymore, not after next week."

"Oh, no! Give me your boss's name and I'll have a word with him! There is no room in this modern world for that kind of—"

"No, no, Viv, ain't nothin' like that! I have a *new* job, at the Children's Care Center." She beamed proudly at me. "That's what I want to do, you know—run a preschool someday."

I summoned my sweetest smile. "How nice, dear. How wonderful for you. And you will be *splendid* at it, I'm sure."

"Thanks, Viv. Couldn't have done it without ya."

I disembarked, then stood on the sidewalk in front of the courthouse, somewhat miffed, watching the trolley depart.

Honestly! You do something nice for someone, and this was how they repaid you!

Oh, well, as Scarlett O'Hara put it, tomorrow was another day. After all, it wasn't like I couldn't train the next driver to break the rules and take me off the beaten trolley path where and whenever I wanted.

I turned and gazed at the magnificent courthouse, a white sandstone study in Grecian architecture with a wonderful clock in its tower. The apple and cherry blossom trees, dotting the lush, manicured lawn, were in full bloom, their sweet scent lifting my mood. Just because Shawntea had been selfish didn't mean *I* had to be. . . .

The courthouse was the heart of our small downtown, with City Hall (down a block) acting as the lungs, the police station (kitty-corner) as the kidneys, and the new county jail (across the street) as the liver. The heart pumps life's blood, the lungs take in air, the kidneys purify, and the liver deals with unwanted bile. It's so simple, isn't it?

Every once in a while, however, a few nincompoops over at the lungs want to cut out the heart and replace it with a new one. I'm all for adding a stint or a pacemaker, for efficiency sake, but I will *not* tolerate tearing down a beautiful courthouse just to make way for some nondescript soulless pancreas of an edifice. *That's* when I march on the lungs, and sometimes end up in the liver. . . .

(I hope you appreciate the lengths I'm going to to add some literary value to these presentations, i.e., the previous lovely extended metaphor. Brandy has a certain bounce to her prose, but she lacks a classical sense.)

I power-walked over to the police station, a modern though inoffensive red brick building that also housed the fire department. Upon entering the small lobby, I strode up to an unfamiliar female dispatcher (short red hair, severe features) who was sequestered behind glass, working at a bank of computers and monitors. I wondered where the regular dispatcher was—Mona the Mole, I called her. (But not to her face.) Every great detective needs his or her system of informants and snitches, you know.

While it is common to have a high turnover in dispatch-ers—due to the stress of the job—I was dismayed that once again I would have to spend precious time cultivating the friendship of yet another one, to gain access to inside information.

However, I buoyed myself in the knowledge that I had a certain amount of influence now, due to the chief's budding romance with Brandy. (My daughter may not have realized it was a romance yet, but after she'd recounted their evening in starry-eyed detail, I knew things were about to change in the way our local chief viewed the Borne girls and their amateur sleuthing ways.)

I spoke through the microphone embedded in the glass. "I need to see Chief Cassato, please. Tony."

The dispatcher looked up. "And you are. . . ?"

"Why, Vivian Borne." I smiled. I thought everyone employed by the department knew me! Sotto voce I added, "But you'll learn that soon enough, dear."

"Excuse me?"

"I said, I hope you're earning enough for such an important job. Now, will you *please* inform Chief Cassato that *Vivian Borne* is here to see him."

She arched a skeptical eyebrow. "Is it important?"

I laughed once. "Would I take time out of my day for something trivial?"

She didn't respond, but then it had been a rhetorical question, so she wasn't necessarily being rude, even if her expression did seem to further sour as she turned to use an interoffice phone.

After a moment, she looked at me, somewhat taken aback. "Well—I guess he'll see you now. He said to go right on in."

Well, dear reader, in all candor, I admit to being mildly surprised myself. Even in the best of circumstances, before seeing me, Serenity's chief usually sentenced me to half an hour of cooling my heels in the dreary waiting area, where I would pass the time removing dead leaves from the corner rubber tree plant.

This was proof positive of my new, improved status with the chief—my stock had indeed risen! (Unlike everyone else who had invested in the market.)

The dispatcher was saying, "You can go on through," nodding her red head toward the heavy steel door at the end of the short hall.

"Thank you, dear," I said sweetly. "And I feel quite certain this is the beginning of a beautiful friendship."

She did not respond, just gave me a wide-eyed, frozen stare, before shaking her head, as if to clear the cobwebs, and turning her attention back to the monitors.

I made a mental note to speak to the chief about her attitude. If she treated Vivian Borne in this unacceptable fashion, how did she behave for your average routine taxpayer?

I entered the inner police station sanctum, and strode confidently down a long beige hallway, where photos of policemen of bygone days broke the boredom of the tan walls.

The chief's office was at the end of the hallway, and as I neared, he stepped out to greet me.

Anthony Cassato was not a tall man, but I wouldn't call him short—blessed with a barrel chest, bucket-shaped head, full head of dark hair, and the kind of rugged face some woman find attractive. Not me—I'm more drawn to the Errol Flynn type (before he got pickled, at least).

The chief wore his usual attire of starched white short-sleeve shirt, blue tie, dark gray slacks, and black Florsheim shoes. But there *was* something different about him—today he wore a smile.

"Vivian," he said, "I'm glad you're here. I was just about to call you."

So!

Tony Cassato had *finally* decided to take me seriously, to view me as a resource, a valuable asset, belatedly coming to the realization that my sleuthing was not trifling, but real, honest-to-goodness, effective detective work. Hadn't I handed him three killers on a platter (well, respective platters) (three platters) over this past year or so?

I was certainly in the cat-bird seat now!

(For you younger folks—are you listening, dear?—this refers to an Australian bowerbird, a.k.a cat bird, known for the extraordinary lengths that the male will go to in order to. . . . Perhaps you should look it up yourself. I have my chapter length to consider, and can't just go off yammering about anything.)

The chief escorted me into his annoyingly uncluttered office—annoying, because it revealed nothing about the man, no personal papers lying around for me to eyeball, or to surreptitiously slip into my handbag.

He offered me the padded chair in front of his desk, but instead of going around and taking a seat himself, he perched on the desk's edge, looking down at me over his somewhat crooked nose.

And suddenly his smile didn't seem so friendly.

I cleared my throat. "You said you were about to call me—which is good because I have a few theories about the death of Mr. Martinette—"

He cut me off with "Not interested," his smile disappearing altogether. "I wanted to see you to give you a piece of good news."

"Really?"

"Yes. I've decided not to press charges against you."

I was speechless. (Really.) (I tell you, I was!)

"Mrs. Borne, you left the scene of a crime last night. A woman at the scene was dead, and we have no way of knowing whether she was still alive when—don't interrupt! When you first found her. Instead of calling 911 or the police, you went home and gathered your daughter. Now, the coroner feels Mrs. Mulligan was probably deceased when you arrived. But nonetheless this is unacceptable, possibly criminally negligent behavior. Because of your age—do not interrupt! Because of your age, and because your daughter did in fact promptly contact the authorities, that is, me, we are willing to overlook this lapse in good judgment and display of bad citizenship. There is one condition—you must henceforth stay out of this police matter. Otherwise, I will cite you for obstructing our investigation."

"I want to see my lawyer."

"Do it on your own time." The chief pointed a finger at me as if aiming a gun at my poor head. "And *stop* involving Brandy in your nonsense. You're putting her *and* the baby at risk." He withdrew the finger. "That's all."

"That's all?"

"Just one other thing."

"What?"

"Get out."

What a *terrible* way to speak to his future mother-in-law!

Shocked, unable to find the words to properly express my outraged indignation (or perhaps my indignant outrage—hard call), I rose, summoning every ounce of dignity within me, then headed slowly to the door, stumbling only once.

"Oh!" he said to my back. "There *is* one more thing."

I rotated my head to look at him, my chin up, nose high, my displeasure on display. "What is it, Chief Cassato?"

"The next dispatcher who gives you sensitive police information will find herself out of a job. Understood?"

I nodded numbly, and made my way into the corridor, numb as a dead gerbil. (There is a gerbil story that you must simply remind me to tell, but not at this time. Not when I'm watching every word.) (Richard Gere not involved.)

My visit with the chief could have gone better.

But Vivian Borne is not one to buckle under even the greatest pressure, and the unfairest persecution . . . and the day was still young. . . .

I hoofed it over to Main Street, five blocks of regentrified Victorian buildings housing quaint little bistros and shops, accentuated by old-fashioned lampposts and wrought-iron benches.

Hunter's Hardware was my next destination, a uniquely Midwestern aberration: the front of the elongated store—which hadn't changed an iota since I was in bloomers (figuratively speaking—I'm not old enough to have actually worn bloomers). The place retained the original wood floor and tin ceiling yet sold everything one might expect from a modern hardware outlet.

The rear, however, contained a small bar area that offered hard liquor to its customers, a practice called into question after one man got too loosey-goosey imbibing, then went home with his new nail gun and affixed his foot to the floor. (The most disturbing thing, reported by the man's wife, was that the nailer alternately screamed and laughed about his mishap. Men can be strange.)

I breezed into the store/bar, weaving in and around various displays, successfully managing to avoid Mary, coowner of the store, who could talk your ear off about the most unimportant things, wasting precious time.

Mary was a squat lady, who wore a prosthesis ever since losing a leg some years back in a freak accident while visiting the *Jaws* attraction at the Universal theme park in Florida. Soon after, she and her husband, Junior, bought the hardware store with the money she got from the settlement. Always a silver lining!

I found Junior in the back, where he was polishing glass tumblers behind the scarred mahogany bar. Sixty years ago, his nickname had accurately described him, but now he was paunchy and balding, with a puffy face and dark circles under his eyes.

The bar was deserted at this morning hour, the only other customer being Henry, a barfly who was as much a fixture in Hunter's as the old ceiling fans.

(Just so you know, the following sentence originally began, "As a matter of fact," but I deleted it to save precious word space.) Henry was the reason I was here, as Junior was a terrible gossip—and by "terrible" I mean the old fool couldn't retain and retell a good story if his life depended upon it.

Henry, however, sitting quietly in his cups all these years, absorbed town gossip like a bar-sponge does a spilled Blatz. He was my number one informant, and not one the chief could take away from me.

Junior spotted me first, serving up his usual buck-toothed grin. "Vivian! Nice to see you!"

"Must be nice to be open again." I slid up on a well-worn leather stool next to Henry. "Any water damage?"

"We got some in the basement. Just a block closer to the river, it's *still* a foot deep, first floors."

"Terrible tragedy. We all do what we can."

"Well, *you* sure do!" Junior snorted. "I heard that was one wild party you threw over at the Catholic church." He chuckled. "I always say, wherever there's a catastrophe, Vivian Borne's gonna be right there on the front line."

"Why, thank you. Very sweet of you, Junior."

Henry swiveled toward me. "Hello, Vivian."

I did a double take (double and triple takes are part of my comic bag of tricks for stage performance, and I must admit a touch of theatricality has tended to creep into my off-stage persona—just a tad).

My surprise was due to this not being Henry's usual slurred, " 'lo 'ivian," ending with a hiccough.

The one-time surgeon had famously (or infamously) taken to drink after losing his license many years ago, upon removing a patient's gall bladder instead of the intended appendix. Now he was sitting in a bar—stone-cold sober!

No longer was Henry the rheumy-eyed, mottled-nosed, and sickly-complected barfly we all knew and loved. Instead of his regular tumbler of whiskey, he was having the only thing *I* ever ordered—a Shirley Temple!

"Huh . . . Huh . . . *Henry!*" I sputtered. "You've finally done it! You've finally kicked the monkey off your back!"

For *years* I had tried, in my simple Christian way, to get Henry off the sauce, always to disastrous results. The latest in a long line of failed attempts to dry Henry out had been to take him to a hypnotist. But susceptible Henry had been sitting in the hypnotist's reception area and overheard instructions intended for a heavy smoker. Apparently, the hypnotist had been at an early stage of therapy when telling the subject that cigarettes would begin to taste terrible to him, because Henry arrived at Hunter's the next day and, between drinks, smoked cigarette after cigarette, snuffing them out, and making terrible faces and loud comments about the horrible taste. You see, Henry hadn't smoked before.

(Editorial comment from Brandy Borne: Please understand that you are not expected to believe everything Mother says. I'm told she is what's known in literature as an "unreliable narrator," and if you feel this particular tall tale is just too much, you are not alone. Now we return you to Mother's chapter, already—unfortunately—in progress.)

Henry's smile was unfamiliar—his mouth no longer lopsided! "Been dry a whole month, Vivian."

"Well, I'll drink to that!" I replied.

Junior, who had begun making my nonalcoholic concoction (with extra cherries) the moment he saw me,
placed the drink on the counter. I picked it up and clanked
glasses with Henry, and then we both took sips.

"How did you do it?" I asked.

"I went back to that hypnotist—wasn't really her fault a
few signals got crossed—and anyway, this time she got it
right."

"Tilda Tompkins, you mean."

"Yes. Have another session with her this afternoon, at
three. Once a week and works like a charm."

"Well, congratulations," I beamed, glad that I had
played at least a small role in his transformation.

Henry frowned. "But Tilda says I can't have even a single drop of liquor. Otherwise, I'll fall of the wagon and hit
real hard."

By this time I'd heard quite enough of Henry and his
success story, itching to get to my reason for dropping by.

"Henry," I began, "what can you tell me about Clifford
Ashland?"

The ex-surgeon took a moment before answering. "He's
wealthy and runs an investment firm."

"Well, *I* know that! What else?"

Henry shrugged. "I don't know anything else."

I found that hard to believe. But I moved on. "What
about Father O'Brien? Tell me all about him—surely he
must have some deep, dark secrets. . . ?"

Henry's eyeballs rolled back in his head, as if searching
for information in his brain, or maybe reliving an exor-
cism his hypnotist had stirred up. When his eyes reappeared, they were somewhat crossed. "Well, all I know is,
Father O'Brien is the priest at St. Mary's."

I was beginning to get peeved.

"Henry," I snapped, "you know *everything* there is
about *everybody* in this town—past and present!"

He shook his head, then slowly, soberly said, "Not any-more, Vivian."

"What do you *mean*, 'not anymore'?"

His shrug was elaborate. "I don't remember much of anything since before I got cleaned up."

Well, dear reader, I nearly toppled from my stool! This bit of news meant utter disaster. Henry was my go-to-snitch, my snitch of snitches, the Snitch-a-tola of Serenity. He was where I went when I wanted, when I *needed*, sensitive information.

"Henry, I'm working on a case, and I really need your help. Would you consider falling off the wagon just for this afternoon, and I'll pick up the tab on all your future hypnotherapy?"

Henry's eyes popped. "Vivian—how you can suggest such a thing?"

Junior seemed to be thinking my idea hadn't been bad at all.

"I'd love to help, if I could," Henry said, and shrugged again, less elaborately. "What are you working on? The theft of that egg? The murder of that fellow Martinette?"

Now *my* eyes popped. "You may have forgotten your yesterdays, but you're certainly up on current events, Henry."

"I read the paper. Watch the TV. Anyway, I was there. I was at the church—I got pretty sick. I had some of that bad stew. Really something about Mrs. Mulligan dying, too. Is that another murder?"

This was way off base—Henry asking *me* questions. The world had really gone topsy-turvy today.

"Funny thing," he was saying, studying his nonalcoholic beverage somewhat wistfully, "that fellow Martinette? I'm sure I've seen him before."

"I don't think so. He came in from Chicago as a bidder."

"No," Henry said forcefully. "I know I've seen him before. Maybe more than once."

"Where? When?"

Henry turned his palms up. "I'm sorry, Vivian. I just don't remember."

Beyond frustration, I addressed Junior, "Where are the Romeos having their lunch today?"

The Romeos—Retired Old Men Eating Out—were friends of long standing who had sometimes been helpful with information for me, when I was cracking a mystery. But they were a dwindling group, Father Time catching up with them.

Junior frowned. "Haven't you heard?"

I hated it when a) this simple soul knew something I didn't, and 2) when he made me ask him, "What?"

I asked, "What?"

"They're on hiatus," Junior said. "Not enough of 'em around to get together anymore, between death and Florida." He paused, adding, "And they kinda lost heart after what happened to—"

"Yes, I *know*," I cut him off, holding up a "stop" palm, not wanting him to spoil *Antiques Flee Market,* for those of you who haven't read it (yet).

Pushing my Shirley Temple aside, I demanded, "Give me a whiskey, Junior. Neat!"

Junior's eyes widened. "Are you sure? What about your medication? And do you even know what 'neat' means?"

"You're not my doctor, or my conscience. Just serve it up! Uh . . . what *does* 'neat' mean, in this regard?"

"Straight, Viv. No mixer."

"Fine!"

Junior hesitated, then poured amber liquid into a tumbler.

I downed it. "Another one," I demanded.

Henry reached a hand out. "Don't *do* it, Vivian."

"*Another* one."

Junior sighed. "Okay, Viv. But no more."

I sat glumly with the second drink untouched, wondering what my next move might be, when Mary appeared and asked her husband to move a large box.

When Junior left, I turned to Henry.

"Maybe you should lend a hand, too," I suggested. "We don't want Junior having a heart attack, now do we?"

Henry nodded, climbed off his stool, and sauntered off to help.

After Henry had gone, I studied his glass. Who would ever know if I poured my whiskey into his tumbler? He'd kicked it once. Surely he could kick it again, and I would gladly guide him back to sobriety.

But it must have been the whiskey talking, or anyway thinking. I couldn't do that to my old friend, my loyal one-time snitch. Yes, my better nature and my conscience got the better of me, and I refrained from such sabotage.

Please don't judge me too harshly—remember, I had a killer to catch.

When Junior and Henry returned, I paid my tab, then slid unsteadily off my stool—that whiskey packed a wallop!—but I soon found my land legs.

Outside the establishment, I stood for a few minutes, breathing in the fresh air, though nasty river smell still touched it; finally the world stopped spinning, and I headed to my next destination.

At the end of the business section of Main Street was a unique Victorian four-story building with an ornate facade and corner-set front door. The old structure—yet to be refurbished—had a checkered past, several former owners having died under unusual circumstances. But the current owner, Raymond Spillman, had the building blessed by Father O'Brien and, ever since, the Grim Reaper had kept its distance.

An antiques mall occupied the entire first floor (the others currently not in use) and Brandy and I rented a booth there—number thirteen—which was situated to the right, just inside the door.

A quick word about the number thirteen (I think I deserve *one* small digression). I've always considered thirteen to be lucky—it's only unlucky if you *think* it is. Our booth—the best location in the shop because most people turn right when they enter a store—had been available thanks to silly superstitious renters. Doesn't that *prove* thirteen's a lucky number? So don't shy away from the number thirteen—that's all feeble-minded nonsense . . .

. . . unless it falls on a Friday, and then *look out*!

I hurried over to our booth, my eagle eyes searching out any missing objects—occasionally something might have been shoplifted, but mostly empty spaces meant our pockets would be filled with some extra cash.

S word!

Everything was still there—including that smiley-face clock that I had cautioned Brandy not to buy. She claimed it was the perfect retro piece for a certain age group. Apparently that age group didn't have a measly three dollars to spend, because that's how far we'd marked it down.

My dears, forgive me, but I absolutely *despise* tax time, when people act responsibly, and hold on to their money to pay Uncle Sam, instead of blowing it at our booth.

I marched over to the center circular counter, where Ray—as everyone called him—was working on an old sewing machine, parts laid out like instruments for a surgery.

Ray was a small, spry man in his late seventies, with a slender build, thinning gray hair, bright shining eyes, bulbous nose, and a slash of a mouth. Out of the corner of an eye he caught me coming, but before he could utter a greeting, I said, "*Please* don't tell me you're going out of business!"

Because that's how bad my day was going. I hadn't had

a day this bad since they canceled *Magnum P.I.* (don't you just *love* that Tom Selleck?).

Ray looked stunned. "What are you, Vivian? A witch? How did you know *that*? I only came to that decision last night!"

My piercing scream was worthy of my performance with the Midwest Shakespeare Company's 1982 production of *Hamlet*, as Queen Gertrude in Act V, Scene II. (All right, you smarty-pants out there who know your Shakespeare—she wasn't *really* supposed to scream, just moan loudly, but I had spotted a few snoozing patrons in the audience, and needed to provide a wake-up call.)

A few shoppers poked their heads above booth walls to see what had happened, while Ray tried to calm me down.

"Vivian," he said, patting the air with his palms, "I'm *sure* I'll have no trouble finding a buyer."

"In this depressed market? I highly doubt it!"

But I knew that once Ray made a decision, he stuck to it, like chewing gum to a shoe. Stubborn! Some of these older people are like that.

So I turned on my heel and left.

Outside, I decided that bold action was needed to salvage my day (and this chapter). At the curb, a young man with tattooed arms, wearing a worn T-shirt and torn jeans, had just dismounted his motorcycle.

"Young man," I hailed, "would you be so kind as to help a lady in distress?"

"Huh?"

"I need a ride to St. Mary's Church—mustn't be late for confession—and I'm recovering from a sprained ankle, so walking is out of the question." Anyway, I *was* still wobbly from the booze.

"Lady, this is a *motorcycle*."

"I can see that—I'm not blind, I just have a sprained ankle."

He shrugged. "Well, okay—why not? It's a nice day. Hell—hop on."

He straddled the bike, jumped up and down, and the motor came to life. Gingerly, I climbed on behind, thankful I was wearing slacks, and hooked my arms around his slender waist.

And we roared off.

"*Wheeeeee!*" I said. Actually I said it several times.

This was the most fun I'd had in a very long time, flying along with the wind in my hair, feeling like a teenager again. This must have been how Isadora Duncan felt, right up to where that scarf snapped her neck.

The ride was especially gratifying when we sped by Mrs. Potthoff, out walking her Pekingese, and I yelled, "Hel-*looow* dearie," startling both her and her little dog, too.

All too soon, however, my joy ride came to an end as the motorcycle raced up the steep incline of St. Mary's, coming to an abrupt stop by the church doors, nearly sending me flying. Reckless lad—I might have sprained an ankle!

With some difficulty I dismounted—as out of breath as if I had walked the distance—and thanked the young man, despite the jolt of a stop. He nodded, spun the bike around, and was gone. Just another Good Samaritan whose deed had gone unrecognized. (If I'd thought to ask his name, I could have recognized him here.) (Not a suspect.)

I headed for the administrative building, a small one-story brick structure located next to the main sanctuary. There I found the church secretary, Madeline Pierce, working at her desk in cramped quarters.

"Hello, Mad," I said. Hers was a nickname that suited her put-upon personality. Her features were as severe as her short dark hair and drab brown dress.

I assumed her startled expression was due to my windblown appearance.

"Why, Vivian," the fortyish secretary responded curtly. "How can I help you?"

"Father O'Brien wants to see you right away," I told her, gesturing vaguely. "He's in his quarters."

She frowned. "What about?"

"How should I know, dear? You're his trusted secretary, not I—he just said for you to come."

"I'll get him on his cell." And she reached for the desk phone.

"You can't!"

"What?"

"His cell is dead, dear. That's why he dispatched *me*."

When Madeline hesitated, I said, "If anyone should call while you're gone, I'll be glad to take a message. You'd better hurry—he seemed quite agitated, especially for a holy man."

She got out of her chair. "Well, all right," she huffed. "But I don't know why *he* couldn't walk over here himself. . . ."

I shrugged, and watched her leave, and the moment she disappeared, I took her place at the desk.

She had been working on bills payable—the usual expenses incurred by the church—the only thing noteworthy being a second request from a contractor asking for downpayment on the roof before they would begin.

I riffled through the mail (nothing of interest), checked the computer files (church solvent, but barely), even rummaged in the desk drawers (found several hotel-room-size bottles of vodka hidden in the back of one).

Once, the phone *did* ring, but I picked the receiver up and set it back down. I had no help for them, and anyway I needed to get on with my investigating before Mad returned.

About five minutes had passed before I heard clomping feet in the corridor, the secretary telegraphing her return.

I hopped up from the chair, moved away from the desk, and was studying a framed needlepoint prayer on the wall when she entered.

"He wasn't there," she snapped at my back.

I turned. "Well, isn't *that* odd?"

"*Isn't* it?" she said tersely.

I shrugged. "He probably fixed the problem himself— whatever it was. No harm no foul!"

She glowered at me, and took her rightful place at the desk, eyes sweeping over it, looking for any sign of disturbance among the papers.

Apparently finding none, she asked, "Any calls?"

I smiled sweetly. "No, it was very quiet."

"What are you doing here?"

"Well, I delivered that message, dear."

"Why are you *still* here?"

I frowned at her. "That isn't very Christian."

And with that, I made my exit.

I headed over to the sanctuary, finding the heavy front doors unlocked. I crossed the lobby and entered the dark, gloomy sanctuary. Pausing at the baptismal font, to let my peepers adjust, I heard muffled voices from behind the closed chapel door to my right.

I crept over to listen. There are no secrets in the House of God.

Father O'Brien was speaking, the familiar rise and fall of his cadence punctuated with anger, unusual for this gentle man of the cloth.

Another voice responded, but too muffled for me to determine gender, but I somehow had the impression whoever it was was trying to placate the priest.

Suddenly the chapel door opened, and I jumped back into the shadows of the nearby transept, hiding behind a statue of Mary and the baby Jesus.

A full minute went by before I felt secure to emerge. The chapel door remained open, and I risked a peek.

Father O'Brien was alone, on his knees at the altar, head bowed.

Quietly I backed away, and retreated from the sanctuary. I had gotten as far as the entryway when a voice behind me called out, "Is there something you wanted?"

I turned to face Father O'Brien.

"Uh, yes, yes indeed," I said. "I wondered what time the funeral mass for Madam Petrova is being held tomorrow?"

He had a suspicious expression, for a man of God. "Ten o'clock. It was in the paper. Is there anything else, Mrs. Borne?"

"No," I said cheerily. "See you there!"

I thanked him and left, then hurried down the church driveway to catch the trolley. All the way down I'd felt the priest's eyes on me.

And I could still feel them, all the way home.

Mother's Trash 'n' Treasures Tip

If you bid on the wrong item, tell the auctioneer immediately. And if your bid wins the wrong item, it's at the discretion of the auctioneer whether or not you're stuck with it. So butter him/her up beforehand—just in case!

Chapter Eight

Deviled Eggs

When I got back from my morning visit with Peggy Sue, I began playing with a much-neglected Sushi. She had no idea that a friend of mother's had possibly been murdered just down the block, and the bliss of her ignorance was contagious.

Her favorite game was for me to rearrange the living room furniture, making an obstacle course she would navigate to the grand prize—a doggie cookie. I would say, "Stop," "Left," or "Right," whenever she might bump into something, and she got so good at it, I had to extend the course past the French doors into the music/library room.

By early afternoon, I was returning the furniture to their rightful positions, when Mother came home, looking unhappy—and not a little disheveled—and I surmised that her snooping had not gone at all well.

We'd both blown through the lunch hour, so I made some egg salad sandwiches and served them with potato chips and iced tea on TV trays at the couch, the dining room table being taken up by Mother's cardboard church with its game-token congregation. As I served her a plate, I noticed a faint fragrance of liquor on her breath.

I did my best not to overreact—which is not so easy, off Prozac—and asked her for a blow-by-blow account of her latest downtown excursion, which she did, even copping to having "the tiniest" glass of whiskey, quickly assuring me that her "indiscretion" would not be repeated.

But I wasn't so sure. Extended bouts of depression had been known to make Mother a) stop taking her medication, b) start drinking, or c) all of the above. Mother had by no means ever been an alcoholic, but booze combined with the naturally nutty juices zipping around within her made for a cocktail that gave all around her perpetual hangovers.

To cheer Mother up—and against my better judgment— I said, between delicious bites (Mother's egg salad recipe was to die for), "Maybe we should drop by your friend Henry's hypnosis session this afternoon. Maybe when he's under, his memory could be jogged."

That immediately perked her up. "Together? Mother and daughter? Holmes and Watson? Poirot and Hastings? Archie and Nero? Nick and Nora? Morse and Lewis?"

More like Martin and Lewis, I thought.

She went on like that for a while, while I just ate my sandwich and nodded, as she summoned increasingly obscure detective teams that her Red Hatted League had read about.

Finally she ran out of names and said, "And I need to question Clifford Ashland. He's still on my list."

"I don't know, Mother. Peggy Sue said Ashland's investment firm is doing very well. She and Bob do business with him, and are happy as clams with him."

"Wonderful! Even better!"

"But that means he has no *motive.* . . ."

"You said it earlier! He's the least likely suspect, so he *has* to stay high on our list."

After lunch, I removed the trays and generally cleaned up while Mother went into the dining room. When I joined her, I could see she had written "Least likely suspect!" in the motive column next to Ashland's name. Next to Father O'Brien she had jotted, "Church in need of funds," like a church being in need of funds was a news flash, but also, "Mysterious visitor!"

Keeping my promise, at twenty till three, we set out for the home (and workplace) of Matilda Tompkins, Serenity's resident New Age guru and part-time hypnotherapist. Tilda—as friend and client alike called her—lived across from the cemetery in the kind of white two-story clapboard house that people nowadays call shabby-chic, though I'd say emphasis on the shabby.

I had suggested we call first, but Mother insisted that she and Tilda were good friends and no appointment would be necessary. The woman's surprised expression, however, when she opened her door, made it clear that Mother was not a welcome caller.

The woman's husky, sensual voice mustered, "Why, *Vivian. . . .*"

Which I guess was better than "*Why*, Vivian?" You know, as in "*Why* the hell are *you* here?"

The guru/hypnotist, pushing fifty, could have passed for forty, with her slender figure and long golden-red hair. She wore little makeup, which only enhanced her green eyes, translucent skin and freckles. Her attire, strictly Bohemian, included pastel peasant skirt, funky necklaces, white gypsy blouse, and (yes) Birkenstock sandals.

Mother said, "It's vital that we speak, my dear."

Tilda, opening the screen door just a crack, said, "I'm sorry, Vivian, but I can't see you now—I have a session scheduled with a client, who should be arriving any minute. I *do* wish you had called."

Which is why Mother hadn't.

"Yes, dear, I know," Mother said. "You're expecting Henry—that's why I'm here."

"I don't follow," the woman said.

I smiled. "That's okay—you're a hypnotist, not a psychic. Henry isn't due for another five minutes, right? Can you spare us that? I'll buy something."

"Well," Tilda said, and shrugged, adding, "all right, girls," and allowed us in.

We entered the small living room, a mystic shrine of soothing candles, healing crystals, and swirling mobiles of planets and stars—much of it for sale. Incense hung in the air, and from somewhere drifted the tinkling sound of New Age music. I found it odd that this front room served so many purposes—living space, waiting room, and gift shop.

Tilda shooed a quartet of cats off the floral couch, gestured for us to sit, then took a rocker nearby, displacing yet another cat.

Did I mention she had cats? Did I mention they weren't your ordinary run-of-the-mill felines, but were reincarnates of dead people?

I'd heard all about this some years ago from (who else?) Mother, who had gone to Tilda for hypnotic help to stop grinding her teeth while sleeping (Mother was doing the grinding/sleeping, not Tilda). This had been some time ago, actually, probably ten years at least, since the tooth-grinding problem had long since been solved (not by Tilda—by dentures).

Anyway, it was well-known around Serenity that Tilda believed that spirits from the cemetery—lingerers who, due to unresolved earthly problems, hadn't moved on—regularly floated across the street and took up residence in her cats. Or maybe the cats showed up at her door, bringing the souls with them—I'd heard it both ways.

Anyway, while I didn't find either story particularly disturbing, what *was* disturbing was the woman calling each feline by some actual dead person's full name.

Like she was doing right now.

"*Stop* that, Eugene Lyle Wilkenson!" Tilda said. A yellow tabby was hissing at my feet because I was sitting in his spot.

I sincerely doubted the cat was inhabited by the soul or ghost or what-have-you of the deceased Mr. Wilkenson. I mean, after all—the man had owned a dog kennel!

Mother was saying, "Henry mentioned that he had an appointment with you today."

"Really." Look up "noncommittal" in the dictionary and you'll likely find Tilda's picture wearing the same expression she was now.

"And, as I'm sure you know, my daughter and I have become rather celebrated amateur *sleuths* of late."

I winced. Mother had somehow managed to make me feel embarrassed in front of a woman with a houseful of reincarnated cats.

"So I've heard," Tilda said.

"You may or may not be aware that Henry is what we call in the detective business a 'snitch,' or to be more precise an informant, as snitches tend to be criminals themselves, and of course Henry is a lovely man and hardly a criminal and—"

"Mother," I said. "We only have five minutes. . . ."

"Anyway, Tilda darling, I'm hoping you can help Henry— under hypnosis, of course—remember something lost in the mental mists of boozery that may prove vital to us in solving these terrible murders that have lately occurred."

Tilda frowned, suddenly looking every one of her fifty years. "Well, Vivian, I don't know about the ethicality of what you're requesting. I've never used my powers in such a fashion. I do have a *reputation* to uphold, my *credibility* to think of."

I managed not to say that somebody with a houseful of reincarnated cats might already have reputation and credibility problems. But I was a guest here.

Mother said, "Yes, dear, I do understand—and that's why I've never breathed a word about Henry, and the fact he became a heavy smoker due to a slip-up on your part. Did you later charge him to help him drop *that* habit, as well as his drinking one?"

Remember before, when I advised you not always to believe Mother? This is where I warn you not to rule out anything she says that might seem too outrageous. You never know with Vivian Borne.

Tilda's frown had deepened. "I was . . . addressing an addictive personality. There was no extra charge for—"

"Addicting him to cigarettes?" Behind the big lenses, Mother's eyes were tiny and hard, like bee-bees. "Let's see, what were we discussing just now—ethics? Reputation? Credibility?"

The woman turned her next word, a short one, into a three or four syllables. "Well," she said. Then she went carefully on, "*Only* if Henry agrees—if he is comfortable with the procedure, it would be acceptable with me. I would ask only that we maintain Henry's, and *my*, confidentiality."

Mother said, "Your secrets are safe with me."

I almost fell off the couch onto a cat.

"And Henry *must* agree!" Tilda insisted.

I said, "You could ask him now—he's here." His sharp knock on the front door put a period on the end of my sentence. I wasn't psychic, either—I'd just seen him coming up the walk.

Tilda rose from the rocker, and in another moment

Henry had joined our little group, and after Mother had gone over the same ground with him, he agreed to the mind probing.

"I'd be so glad to help," Henry said. He was in a tidy brown suit with a darker brown tie, looking as professional as the doctor he'd once been. "I was sorry this morning, Vivian, that I couldn't help you. I hate letting you down. Hope this'll make up for it!"

Tilda, however, set a few parameters: Mother and I must remain quiet during the hypnosis, Tilda being the only one to ask Henry the questions (which Mother would present her in advance), and we must leave quietly afterward, so Tilda could continue her regular antiaddiction session with Henry.

We agreed, of course, and Mother set about writing out her questions onto a piece of stationery the hypnotist provided.

In short order, the four of us went through the kitchen to the small hypnosis room, possibly a former sewing room, claustrophobic and dark, the single window shuttered. The only source of light came from a table lamp, its revolving shade with cut-out stars sending its own galaxy swirling on the ceiling. There was a Victorian "fainting couch," where Henry stretched out (wouldn't I have loved to have had *that* piece of furniture for our booth!), and an ornate straight-back chair that Tilda took, pulling it up next to Henry. Swathed in darkness, Mother and I stood silently against the closed door.

Tilda began the session by picking up a long, gold-chained necklace with round disc off the lamp table, and dangled it before Henry's face, then slowly began to swing it like a pendulum do (sorry—I always liked that song).

"Watch the medallion, Henry," she said softly.

His eyes moved back and forth.

"You feel relaxed . . . very relaxed. You're getting sleepy . . . very sleepy." This she repeated, progressively slower, ever more soothing.

Henry's eyelids fluttered.

"Your eyelids are heavy . . . very heavy . . . so heavy . . . so heavy you can't keep your eyes open. . . ."

Henry's eyelids closed.

"I'm going to count backward, from ten to one. When I say 'one,' Henry, you will be asleep, completely, deeply *asleep*. Ten . . . nine . . . eight. . . ."

At "five," Henry's body went limp, but Tilda finished her count.

She consulted Mother's hen-scratching on the stationery on her lap.

"Henry," Tilda said, "you told Vivian Borne that you saw one of the bidders from the auction in town some years ago. Do you remember who it was?"

I could see Henry's eyeballs moving behind the closed lids. An hour seemed to pass before he responded. "Louis Martinette."

I didn't know whether to be excited or disappointed—I'd hoped for a suspect, and instead got one of the murder victims.

"Can you tell me when that was?"

"June. Nineteen ninety-two."

"Where?"

"Hunter's. He came in for a drink."

"Did you ever see him again—before the auction?"

"Yes."

"When?"

Henry's face contorted as he searched the cobwebs of his mind. "December. Nineteen ninety-two."

"You're sure?"

Henry nodded in his sleep. "I remember the Christmas decorations."

"This was at Hunter's again?" Tilda was following Henry's lead now, and not Mother's notes.

Henry said slowly, "In a rear booth. Another man."

"Who?"

"Couldn't see. Hidden. Left before they did."

"Thank you, Henry. Did you ever see this man again, before seeing him at the church?"

"Yes. A month ago."

Hadn't Henry sobered up by then? I thought Mother had said his memory of recent events was flawless.

Tilda was ahead of me. "But you weren't drinking then, were you, Henry?"

"I . . . I fell off the wagon. I never told you. I had a relapse. Just one afternoon. Next morning, I was sick. Very sick. Ashamed."

"Where did you see this man, a month ago?"

"Hunter's again. Alone. He was in the same booth. Maybe waiting for someone. When I left, he was still there."

What would Martinette having been doing in Serenity on those three occasions? Twice in 1992, and again just last month?

"Henry, go deeper . . . deeper. Rest. Rest."

Tilda shot a sharp look our way, and signaled for us to leave; I took Mother's arm in the dark, quietly opened the door, and we slipped out in the cat-strewn front room. I picked out a candle with a nice woodsy scent and left a five-dollar bill.

I was very proud of Mother, and even amazed—she had not interrupted once, or insisted on more questions or tried to follow up or anything.

We maintained silence until seated in the car, when I said, "That couldn't have gone better. Don't you think?"

"Yes."

"Isn't that the kind of information you were hoping for out of Henry?"

"Yes."

Mother was being uncharacteristically succinct, so I twisted to look at her. She had a blank expression, staring straight ahead, a cross between a china doll and an utter idiot.

I'm sure you're ahead of me, but I was astonished and instantly amused—*Mother had been hypnotized right along with Henry!*

The angel on my right shoulder said, "You should wake her up." But the devil on my left responded, "Now wait just one minute! How often does *this* happen? Now's your chance!"

So put me under hypnosis if you like, give me a lie detector test or truth serum, and the answer will be the same: the devil made me do it.

"Who is my real mother?" I asked. I knew, of course, but needed to hear it from her own lips.

"Peggy Sue."

"And my real father?"

"Senator Edward Clark."

So Peggy Sue really *had* leveled with me.

What to ask next?

"You *knew* I didn't like Tiddly Winks, and yet you still made me a Tiddly Wink, didn't you?"

"Yes."

Thought so.

I grinned at her blank face. "How *old* are you, *really?*"

"Don't press your luck, dear."

Mother had snapped out of the trance, jarred back to reality. Self-preservation, I guess—preservation of her true age, that is.

She was blinking. "What . . . what *happened* in there?"

"You got hypnotized along with Henry," I told her.

"Nonsense," she scoffed. "I am far too strong-willed to

be in any way susceptible to such hippy-dippy phony-baloney hocus-pocus."

I started the car. "Then you remember what Henry had said?"

"Of course, dear, weren't you listening? In nineteen ninety-two, Louis Martinette was in town to examine the egg—that much we know. He's obviously the Chicago expert who appraised the item for Madam Petrova. What we *don't* know is the reason why he returned six months later . . . and why he was here a *month* ago!"

"And how do we find that out? Henry didn't see who Martinette had drinks with at Hunter's, back in '92. Would *Junior* remember?"

"No, dear. He and Mary didn't own the store at that time."

"They owned it a *month* ago."

"Yes, dear, and I will follow that up with a phone call, although Junior has the shortest of short-term memories. But I think in any case it's safe to assume Martinette came back to Serenity to see the only person or persons he might have business with."

"Nastasya Petrova," I said. "Or Clifford Ashland."

"Correct, dear. And we can't talk to Madam Petrova, can we?"

"No. But we can talk to your favorite least likely suspect."

She nodded crisply. "So let's drop by Mr. Ashland's brokerage firm and ask *him* what the purpose was for Martinette's trio of visits."

"It's a little late in the day, isn't it?"

It was after four P.M.

Mother's eyes flashed. "We'll take a chance."

"I could call ahead on my cell, and get an appointment. . . ."

"No, dear. He might say no. But with the Borne girls before him in the flesh, he won't *dare!*"

And off we drove.

Ashland Investment Incorporated had recently moved from the top floor of the First National Bank to its own newly constructed glass, steel, and cement building near to the mall. Peggy Sue would appear to be right—business *must* have been good.

We parked, entered the marble lobby, and passed through glass doors to a waiting area, which had all the comforts of home, if you were frickin' rich, that is: thick Persian rug, overstuffed leather couches (money green), cherry-wood armchairs, fresh flowers on the coffee table, a gas fireplace, and even a big flat-screen TV tuned to a cable business news station.

Our tushies had barely touched a two-seater couch when a pretty, young, dark-haired woman in a pin-striped power suit appeared to ask if we had an appointment. She was as friendly as she was businesslike, though, and there was nothing snooty or accusatory about it.

Mother, dragging out her fake Brit accent (*omigod!*), said, "I'm afraid not, my dear—spur of the moment. We wish to offer our condolences to Mr. Ashland on the passing of his beloved aunt." She paused, adding, "We of course *have* done our share of business with Clifford. But we hoped to catch him at the end of the day to deliver our personal well wishes."

By "share of business," I guessed she was referring to the trinkets Clifford bought from our booth, because the only investment Mother made lately (with the exception of antiques, obviously) was in a new mattress where she hid her money.

Taking no chances, the young woman smiled and said

evenly, "Certainly, and we're glad to have you stop by. If you give me your names, I'll let Mr. Ashland know you're here."

"Vivian and Brandy Borne," Mother told her.

I wondered if the names would ring a bell, and not a good one, because we had been in the local media a lot in recent months over Mother's meddling, that is, sleuthing. But the woman must not have lived locally—probably from the nearby Quad Cities.

Before she left us, our hostess asked if we wanted anything to drink while we waited—coffee, espresso, latte, cappuccino, tea, a seemingly endless list that devolved into various soft drinks. I requested a latte, while Mother opted for cappuccino; we might as well get our thirsts quenched before we were thrown out bodily.

Actually, I had little hope that Ashland would see us, and on some level was just humoring Mother, because of her rocky morning. So I was surprised when, after only a few minutes (we hadn't even gotten our drinks yet!), the professional woman returned to escort us to the big man's office.

I think Mother was a little surprised, too, but quickly regained her haughty air, ever anxious to display her theatrical chops. We followed the woman down a plushly carpeted corridor, passing well-appointed executive rooms, where other investment brokers were hard at work.

The last office was double the size of the others, and twice again as lavishly decorated. Clifford Ashland stood by the large window, his back to us as we entered. We were announced by the young woman, who then departed.

Ashland turned slowly. I tried to read his face for some clue as to his temperament, but it was a slate as blank as Mother in her hypnotic state, minus the idiotic part.

He did, however, provide a "tell" as to how our meeting might go—he didn't ask us to sit down.

Afraid that Mother might blow the encounter, or turn a few simple questions into a melodramatic showdown, I stepped forward.

"First, Mr. Ashland," I said, "Mother and I want you to know how very sorry we are about the death of your aunt. She was a lovely, caring person, and we know you will miss her greatly. We deeply regret the inadvertent role we played in arranging the auction that turned out so tragically."

A bittersweet smile etched itself on the otherwise still-blank slate.

"Thank you," he said. "I do appreciate your thoughtful words." Ashland moved toward me. "And please understand, Ms. Borne, that I don't hold you and/or your mother personally responsible in any way. You had an indirect role in all of this, of course, but obviously a well-meaning one. Anyway, what's done is done."

I said. "Thank you for that. We do feel your loss."

He nodded. "Well." The tiniest flicker of a smile. "It was nice of two of you to come by."

When neither of us moved, however, Ashland raised his eyebrows. "Was there something else?"

My look to Mother said silently, *Okay, I softened him up—now* you *take over.*

Mother said, "We do have one, small question to ask you. We were wondering why Louis Martinette would come back to see you here in Serenity, from time to time? Including a visit six months after he was first here to estimate the value of the egg?"

The temperature in the room dropped ten degrees. "And this is your business *how?*"

Nicely done, Mother! She had confirmed with one question that the mystery man who'd met with Martinette at Hunter's was Ashland himself.

I said, "My mother was responsible for the auction, and eventually something will have to be done, assuming the Fabergé egg ever turns up. And, frankly, even if it doesn't. We're trying to gather information about the bidders."

This didn't exactly answer his question, but apparently it was enough. Ashland sighed and said, "If you *must* know, on his second visit, Louis was returning the egg to my aunt."

Mother frowned. "Returning it from where?"

"From Chicago! Where he had it appraised by scholars? Tested for authenticity? Carbon-dated and so on?" These were obvious questions proposed to the simple-minded.

"It took *that* long?" Mother asked. "Six months?"

"Well, you don't think he could do all that here, on the spot, in my aunt's parlor, do you?"

I asked, "And you trusted him with a priceless Fabergé egg?"

Ashland was clearly working not to get agitated, a vein throbbing in a temple. "I had the man thoroughly vetted. He was legitimate. *And* bonded. Besides, frankly, I wasn't convinced at the time that the damned thing *was* authentic. Scholars doubted its existence—why shouldn't I?"

"We weren't suggesting otherwise," I said. "But what was Martinette doing back in Serenity, just a month ago? Meeting you again at Hunter's?"

Clifford's eyes narrowed to where only a tiny glittering indicated eyes were in those slits at all. "As the expert collector who had authenticated the Fabergé egg, Martinette came to see me about the auction."

Nicely done, Brandy! Now he'd admitted to meeting with Martinette a second time, and recently.

"Consult in what way?" Mother asked waspishly. "I

was in charge of the auction. Why wasn't I part of any such meeting?"

"Have you forgotten? We agreed the original appraiser, which was Martinette, needed to provide a current written statement regarding the egg's authenticity."

He was right—neither Mother nor I had remembered that.

But I said, "And he did his appraisal at a *bar?*"

"Martinette asked, as a courtesy, if he might make a preemptive offer on the artifact. Apparently—and I'd quite forgotten this myself—he had asked when he was called in for authentication purposes, back in '92, if he might not be given a chance to buy the egg, should my aunt ever want to sell it."

I asked, "What was his preemptive offer?"

"Martinette said he was willing to offer half a million dollars, if we shut the auction down. I told him I had no authority to accept or for that matter decline his offer. In fact, Mrs. Borne—Vivian—I gave him your name and number. Did he ever call you?"

"No," Mother said. "But I would have turned him down. After all, he ended up paying one million!"

"*Bidding* one million," Ashland corrected. "The fact is, the auction is null and void. Mr. Martinette did not live long enough to sign the paperwork or make out his check. Beyond that, I've been informed that my aunt may well have died *before* the gavel fell, and my attorney tells me that if the egg ever does turn up, it will be returned to the estate."

Mother's eyes and nostrils flared, giving her a dangerous rearing-horse expression. "Then *you* would inherit it?"

His expression grew patronizing. "Should it be found, I suppose so. But whoever killed Martinette presumably stole the egg, and I'm unlikely ever to see it again."

Which made him an even less likely suspect—why steal something you would inherit?

"It's St. Mary's who benefits from my aunt's passing," he was saying, "and I can tell you from personal experience that the church is in considerable financial peril."

I said, "Then you only inherit the house and its contents?"

"Not that it's any of your business, but yes—my aunt's funds and investments and so on will be divided by St. Mary's and her Russian Orthodox church, in Chicago. As a faithful member of the St. Mary's family, I was fully in favor of that bequest."

Mother and I glanced at each other—one least likely suspect was sending us off in the direction of the other least likely suspect: Father O'Brien.

Clifford took a deep breath, let it slowly out. "Ladies, I have been more than patient with you, but I'm not going to answer any more of your questions. I know your reputation, *reputations* I should say, of sticking your nose in, snooping around, and generally being busybodies and nuisances."

Mother said (actually said), "Well, I *never!*"

Me, I was thinking, *That's pretty dead on.*

He raised a gently lecturing finger. "You really should take care. There have been two, perhaps three murders, and why you'd want to put yourself in harm's way is the real mystery here."

Was that a threat?

"Now, if you don't mind, I still have *actual* clients to see yet this afternoon. . . ."

We returned to the waiting area, where our hot drinks—in Ashland logo mugs—had been placed on the coffee table in our absence.

Mother and I picked them up, and made our getaway.

These cups would never be valuable antiques, but who couldn't use an extra coffee mug or two?

A Trash 'n' Treasures Tip

Seating can fill up fast at an auction, so unless you like standing, get there early. Or you could do what Mother does—arrive late, toting a lightweight folding chair, which she puts up in front, making a new row of one, to the consternation of those who have been there for hours . . . and the embarrassment of her daughter, hiding in back.

Chapter Nine

Easter-egg Casket

Back home I found an answering-machine message from Chief Cassato inviting me for dinner at his cabin again— if "this isn't too late notice."

You Know Who was hovering like storm clouds as I listened to the recording, and when it had played, I asked her, "Are you all right with this, Mother? Can you get yourself some supper?"

"Who needs food," Mother said, with a disturbing gleam in her eye (both eyes, actually), "when you have an opportunity to feast upon new information!"

I wasn't sure whether she meant the info we'd gathered from Henry and Ashland, or the even *newer* info that I might gather from Tony. And I didn't ask.

I just called him, apologized for not getting back sooner, and asked if it was too late to accept.

"Not at all. I can come get you in an hour. Okay?"

"Fine."

I went up and took a quick shower and got into skinny dark-washed jeans (to not seem too formal) and a three-quarter-sleeve purple silk blouse (to not seem too informal). I topped it off with black sandals that revealed that I had finally decided to settle on pink-polished toes, and no jewelry at all, other than my Chico's watch.

To perfume or not to perfume? Too strong a signal if I spritzed? Or a bad signal, if I didn't? I compromised by spraying the air with Betsey Johnson and walking through.

I had five minutes to spare before Tony would get here, so I checked up on Mother, who was reigning over her cardboard-and-game-token kingdom. Unbelievably she sensed my presence—must have been the Betsey Johnson.

Mother turned and waggled her black marker pen at me like an extra scolding finger. "I'll be counting on you to pry more out of that brute! He has *some* nerve telling those dispatchers not to talk to me anymore. . . . We'll *see* about that. . . ."

I nodded dutifully. "Yes, Mother."

Her smile was only a little crazed, which was a relief. "Good girl."

I waited on the porch for Tony to arrive, so he wouldn't have to deal with Mother—talk about getting an evening off to a bad start! And as soon as his unmarked car drew into the drive, I hurried down the front steps, then hopped in front—his date this time, not a perp.

"Before we go," I said, "I have something to admit."

His head swiveled. "Which is?"

"My morning sickness seems to have tapered off, so if you're here out of the goodness of your heart, well . . . If you'd like to cancel . . ."

One eyebrow raised, though the steel-gray eyes had no expression. "Do you *want* me to?"

"No! No. Certainly not. I *still* need to gain some weight."

"Okay then."

And he backed the car out of the drive.

On this trip, I tried to pay better attention to where we were going. Last time, I'd been lost the ride *to*; the ride *back* I'd come away with at least a vague sense of where his hideout was. But I wanted a real fix, and there were so many twists and turns onto secondary roads (was he taking a different route?) that finally I gave up, and just enjoyed the springtime scenery.

When we rolled up to the cabin, Rocky—who'd been standing guard at the front door—trotted over to greet us, tail wagging. I got out and the dog immediately began sniffing me for evidence of Sushi, finding none because I'd showered and dressed—if I hadn't changed, after playing with Sushi this afternoon, the chief's pooch might have shoved me to the ground and given a thorough frisk.

Rocky seemed disappointed, so I bent and petted his head by way of compensation.

Inside, Tony got the fireplace going, then allowed me this time to help out in the kitchen, preparing the soup (cream of chicken and wild rice) and Caesar salad, right down to the raw egg. A seven-grain bread was already in the oven, smelling yummy.

Throughout dinner, we instinctively put his work and my Mother on the No Fly List, which limited lines of conversation, but somehow I resisted the urge to chatter about nothing, just to fill the air.

Finally we did find some common ground, starting with the outdoors (me hiking, him biking), antiques (me Deco, him early Arts and Crafts), action movies (me Jason Statham, him classic Eastwood), and raunchy cable comedy (both *Reno 911*). Also, we both shared an interest in and love of animals, and I was impressed to learn that he'd given up hunting after a childhood of growing up sharing that with his father. That he *had* a father was the first substantial new information I'd gleaned, but I took it no further.

After our very pleasant and lingering meal, we did the dishes together (no electric dishwasher in the cabin— pretty much my definition of roughing it), then retired to the couch in front of the fire to share the footstool again.

Rocky joined us, plopping down in his same spot, soon falling asleep and richly snoring.

To get any unpleasantness out of the way, I ventured, "I don't mean to spoil the evening, but I do need to bring up a delicate subject—my mother."

"That's a delicate subject?"

"Actually, yes." I sought his gaze and held it. "I'm worried that a perfect storm is brewing. You know—circumstances that can make her go off her medication. And, well, her rocker. Not as funny as it sounds."

I withheld one piece of incriminating evidence—that she had taken a drink of hard liquor.

Our shoulders were touching. "What kind of circumstances are 'gathering' for this storm?"

I sighed. "A slowdown in our antiques business, her old haunts changing, friends dying—even the community theater where she directs is on hiatus until summer because of the flood. All these things kept her occupied and, if not *completely* out of trouble, busy at least."

Tony said, "And now I've shut off her communications with the police department."

I nodded.

"So . . . if your mother stops taking her pills, it's *my* fault?"

Noting the tension in his voice, I made my response gentle. "No, obviously not—you're completely justified, of course. Mother is a busybody, a fourteen-karat meddler. On the other hand, she *has* been helpful to you in the past with pertinent information."

He grunted. "It comes with a high price tag."

I took one of his hands. "I just don't want any drama with the baby coming."

I hated to keep playing the baby card, but I did have my own mental health to consider.

"Brandy, you can't ask me to tell my people to feed your

mother inside police information. I'm all for her feeding her demons with local theater, and your antiques business should pick up soon, now that the floodwaters have receded, but—"

"You could feed *me* a morsel. You're good at feeding me morsels."

That made him smile. *Point for Brandy.*

"Okay. I can tell you something right now that will be in the media tomorrow."

"What?"

"Maybe you even have a right to know this."

"Know what?"

"Mrs. Mulligan. We got the toxicology report back, and it gibes with evidence at the scene."

"She *was* murdered then?"

He shook his head. "No. Not likely. There'll be an inquest, but she died due to an overdose of her own prescription sleeping meds. They were in her stomach, and they were in the pan of broth in her kitchen."

"Not rat poison."

"No. Very likely suicide, Brandy—she had her wig on, and she certainly didn't wear that to bed. She knew she'd be found, and wanted to look her best."

"Was there a note?"

"No. But suicides don't always leave notes—in fact, the stats are the opposite. We talked to several of her friends who'd spoken to her on the phone the morning of her death, and she was very depressed, and ashamed, or . . . perhaps *embarrassed* is the word."

"She was the one being talked about, and it didn't feel good, huh?"

"It would seem. She didn't answer her phone all afternoon. That was not like her, but calls from her regular contacts—the conduits she used to receive and pass along gossip—she ignored. Coroner puts time of death between eight and nine P.M., by the way. She was gone by the time your mother found her."

"You're sure about this?"

"Yes."

"It wasn't staged?"

"Not likely."

"Then Mother was wrong—she thought a suicide in the midst of murders was too big a coincidence, particularly a second poisoning."

"Different poisons."

"You've made your point, Tony. And it makes sense to me—it must've been just too much for Mrs. Mulligan. She liked getting attention, just not *that* kind of attention. Thank you for telling me."

I leaned to kiss his cheek, but he turned so that my lips met his.

When we finally parted, I whispered, "You know this is a big mistake."

He nodded.

We kissed again.

"You know this will never work," I warned.

He nodded again.

And folded me into his arms. He had me right where I wanted him.

The following morning, a bathrobe-clad Mother, going back on her bargain, roused me from my slumber with her usual "Uppy-uppy-uppy!"

Since it seemed a little early, I muttered, "Unnngh . . . *what* time. . . ?"

"Time to get ready for the *funeral*, dear," Mother chirped, joining in with the noisy good-for-nothing yapping spring birds outside my window.

"But it's not till *ten*," I protested.

Sushi was burrowing beneath the covers, growling, siding with me.

Mother loomed like the Statue of Un-Liberty. "You know I want to arrive *early* to get a good seat."

Only my mother would want seats on the fifty yard line at a funeral.

"So rise and shine and up and at 'em," she said, then lowered her voice an octave to intone, "It's not going to be just *any* day. . . ."

Never the kind of prediction you want to hear my mother make, and hardly an incentive to get up; and yet I took the bait. "*Why*, pray tell?" (When my mother starts intoning things in her octave-lower voice, I find myself using phrases like "Pray tell," and I do apologize.)

Mother perched on the edge of the bed. "Because, dear, someone very important is not going to show today!"

"Who's so important that not being there would be a big deal? Her nephew? Can't be the priest. He's officiating."

"No! Nothing so mundane. *Nastasya Petrova* won't be at her own funeral!"

A Catholic funeral mass without the deceased?

Okay, I was awake. I sat up and frowned at her, disgusted with myself that her tricks still worked on me. "Madam Petrova will be a no-show. At her own funeral. All right. I'll bite. How come?"

Mother shrugged elaborately. "She's in Chicago!"

When I raised my eyebrows, Mother intoned, "On Sunday, the members of her Russian Orthodox church, just a handful you'll recall, held a private wake in the Petrova parlor. Monday, there was a private service held in the mansion's ballroom, again just for the Russian Orthodox members, all fifteen of them, and a bishop came in from Chicago to conduct it. And today, at a Russian Orthodox cemetery in Chicago, there will be a graveside service, though I doubt if any of the local members made the trip—they're all very elderly, you know, and these old people simply can't get around very well. It was all very discreet, dear, in accordance with Madam Petrova's reclusive nature. Even the media was unaware."

I'd only been awake for a few minutes, but I already had a headache. "Then what is *this* funeral for?"

"It's not really a funeral per se, dear, not technically at least—it's a memorial service being held at Clifford Ashland's request. As you know, Madam Petrova had made considerable bequests to both the Russian 'sister' church in Chicago and St. Mary's here in Serenity, where she'd been attending with her nephew, except for the monthly Russian Orthodox service at her own home."

"So she's in Chicago waiting to be buried, and I didn't even *know* about it? Who told *you*?"

"Oh, I knew all the details way ahead of time, dear."

"Who *told* you all of this, Mother?"

"Why, Mrs. Mulligan, of course. She knew everybody's business. Now chop, chop!"

And she sailed out of the room.

I threw back the covers, then sat on the edge of the bed and wondered if I'd dreamed that I had a crazy mother and was going to a funeral for a Russian woman who wasn't there because she was in Chicago. But I was awake enough now to know that, unfortunately, it was no dream—*this, Brandy Borne, is your life.* . . .

Funny thing was, I could remember vividly what I had been dreaming—usually, it would have faded, the mood lingering maybe, but not the particulars. But this dream I remembered. . . .

I couldn't see. I wasn't blind, just couldn't open my eyes, as if they were glued shut, and I couldn't tell where I was going or what was happening.

What did it mean?

Oh, well, rise and shine and up and at 'em and chop, chop. . . .

I showered, dried my hair, slapped on some makeup, then returned to my bedroom to get dressed, where I found that Sushi had hidden one of the shoes I'd set out to wear. I could see it partially showing under the bed—my eyes weren't really glued shut—but I still went, "Now *where* is that shoe?" to give Soosh *some* satisfaction, since she would be left alone yet again.

My cell phone on the nightstand trilled and I was happy to see caller I.D. report my son's number.

"Hey, Jake," I said. "What's up?"

"Hi, Mom. Just checking in. You do remember I'm comin' today?"

As if I could or would forget—my heart was aching to see him.

"You bet. When are you coming in?"

"Late afternoon, I think."

"Land or air?" Roger had his own private plane (he didn't fly himself, just hired on pilots as needed).

"Air."

"Can you call me from the plane, or is that illegal?"

"Naw, it's fine. It's just on the big jets and stuff you can't use cell phones, and Dad says it's cool. You want me to call when we're fifteen minutes out or something?"

"That'd be great. Can't wait to see you." I paused, then added, "I can really use your help to keep Grandma occupied."

"Uh-oh—don't tell me Grandma's involved in another *mystery. . . ?*"

"Afraid so. But please don't tell your father."

"I won't. He's pretty touchy about that stuff, ever since I came home and got kidnapped that time."

"Yeah. That was a little over the line."

We signed off, and I admit to having second thoughts about having Jake drop by at a time when old ladies were dying down the street, even if the police chief assured me it had been suicide.

Though Mother and I arrived at St. Mary's an hour early, the parking lot was practically full, irking La Grande Dame, who demanded that I claim the last handicap parking space, which I obediently did so as not to further annoy her, and to avoid hearing about ingrown toenails again.

Wearing our better clothes—Mother a subdued gray dress and black pumps, me a tailored black pants suit and silver flats—we waited in a short line to enter the church, while above us, a lone, low-pitched tower bell tolled.

Father O'Brien, draped in his ceremonial black cope, stood somberly at the small entryway, greeting the attendees as they passed on through to the lobby, where some lingered, visiting quietly, but not us.

I had to move to keep up with Mother, who made a beeline for the sanctuary. But once inside, she halted by the Holy Water Angel, surveying the pews, scrutinizing the crowd that had beaten her here, painstakingly calculating her next move.

I knew what she was after—a pew from which she could be seen by all and yet *see* all. It was a conundrum, especially with the now-limited seating. Funny how a recluse like Madam Petrova could draw such a crowd. Of course, plenty of people in Serenity had never had a chance to see her in the flesh. I wondered how many of them knew she wasn't even here—surely the biggest subject of whispered conversation had to be the lack of a casket.

Finally, Mother put her two new hip replacements to the test, and I stayed with her as she hurtled down the center aisle, until halting three-quarters of the way down.

Addressing a middle-aged man seated on an end pew,

she intoned in her high-class voice, which was essentially a fake British accent, "Would you mind, *terr*-ibly if you scooted down? My daughter is pregnant and might have to dash out to be sick, and we wouldn't want a *mishap*. . . ."

Before the startled gentleman could respond, Mother said, "Thank you *soooooo* much," and began to squeeze in as he quickly shoved the woman next to him, who in turn shoved over the next person, and so on down the line, like train boxcars bumping each other.

When I squeezed in, it was a pretty snug fit—that last "boxcar" had to get up and find another pew—but at least we were settled. And I had to hand it to Mother—we had a good view of the pulpit as well as all of the suspects on her list, every single game token in her sights.

Two rows ahead, clustered together, were our out-of-town Fabergé egg bidders (the surviving ones, anyway): Don Kaufman, Katherine Estherhaus, John Richards, and Sergei Ivanov, attired much as they'd been at the auction. Across the aisle sat publisher Samuel Woods, nervously fiddling with his suitcoat collar, channeling Rodney Dangerfield.

But our main interest—and that of everyone else in the sanctuary—was the bereaved Clifford Ashland and his wife, Angelica, the couple seated alone in the first-row pew, intermittently dabbing at their eyes with tissues.

At precisely ten o'clock, the funeral mass began, and it wasn't long before I remembered how bored I'd been in services during our Catholic try-out. I began having trouble keeping my eyes open, getting no help from how warm it was in the cavernous sanctuary. This time of year, the furnace wasn't going, but neither was any air-conditioning (if they had it), the purgatory-like temperature due to heat from all of the bodies.

Mother, however, seemed cool, listening intently to every word, as Father O'Brien read from the Scriptures.

" 'You whose rich men are full of violence, whose inhabitants speak falsehood with deceitful tongues in their heads—' "

I nodded off only to be jostled by Mother as she reached into her copious purse to withdraw a pen and small notebook, whereupon she began to scribble.

The priest continued. " 'In a large household there are vessels not only of gold and silver but also of wood and clay, some of lofty and others for humble use—' "

I drifted off again, until my head suddenly dropped and I reflexively snapped it back with a ladylike snort.

" 'But what profit did you get then from the things of which you are now ashamed? For the end of those things is death.' "

Why was Mother paying such close attention to this droning?

" 'Chastised a little they shall be greatly blessed, because God tried them and found them worthy of himself. In the time of their visitation they shall shine—' "

While I didn't fall sleep again, my behind did, anyway the left cheek, and I squirmed, changing positions, and got a reproachful glance from Mother.

" 'No one takes my life from me, but I lay it down on my own. I have power to lay it down, and power to take it up again. This command I have received from my Father.' "

Finally, the priest came to the end of his Scripture reading, and Mother relaxed, returning her pad and pen to her purse.

What happened next was a surprising departure as the priest exchanged the typical nonspecific sermon for a bonafide eulogy that commemorated the life of Madam Petrova. Most Catholic theologians would frown at this, but the audience showed their approval with nods, and murmurs of appreciation, at the priest's kind and personal words.

When the priest revealed that Madam Petrova had already received a Russian Orthodox funeral, and that her earthly remains were not present, as she was being buried today in Chicago, murmurs of surprise rippled through the sanctuary . . . and Mother gave me a very smug sidelong glance.

After the Liturgy of the Eucharist, including communion, we sang a song of farewell—"Jesus Christ Is Risen Today"—and Father O'Brien gave a moving prayer of commendation, followed by an invitation to partake of fellowship, i.e., food.

As the congregation rose, I didn't wait for Mother since a) I was starving as we'd skipped breakfast, and b) Mother would likely dawdle talking to anyone who cared to listen (and many who didn't).

I maneuvered in and out of the slow lane, making for the basement, where I discovered that the lunch was being catered by Mimi's, a popular local bistro. This was yet another departure from the norm, as the women of the church usually provided the funeral meal. Maybe Father O'Brien wasn't taking any chances, after what had happened a few days ago; or perhaps he couldn't bring himself to impose on his ladies so soon after the botched auction.

The food arrayed on a long banquet table seemed fairly rat-poison-proof: crisp lettuce salad bowl, cold meats and cheese platter, crunchy veggie tray, and gooey-frosted white sheet cake. Nothing looked remotely like Mrs. Mulligan's ill-fated final stew. Still, many of the people filing in for "fellowship" seemed to steer clear of the table.

Not Brandy.

I loaded up my plate like a long-haul trucker, making up for the past couple of lean months, then found a table to myself where I proceeded to scarf, keeping one eye on Mimi. I was watching the middle-aged plump caterer (who was obviously fond of her own cooking) for the moment when she'd cut the cake. I wanted to grab a corner piece with its extra frosting.

But her attention had been grabbed by Samuel Woods, *American Mid-West Magazine* publisher, food plate in hand, apparently complimenting her on the spread, judging by the way she had turned all knock-kneed and girlish.

Come on! Funeral's over! Cut the damn cake already.

My attention turned to the Ashlands, who had taken a position near the basement entrance to receive condolences from those coming in. Ashland was letting his wife, an attractive brunette in her forties who was vaguely a Peggy Sue type, do most of the talking.

I'd finished my food, and Mimi *still* hadn't cut the cake, so I went off to use the bathroom—my bladder and my appetite clearly had control of preggers Brandy today. When I returned, I spotted Katherine Estherhaus, Don Kaufman, John Richards, and Sergei Ivanov at a table by themselves. I got myself a cup of punch and hovered near a cluster of people nearby, making no conversation, just keeping an eye on this gathering of Mother's game tokens.

Estherhaus, dressed in a chic black sheath, was eating only veggies. Don Kaufman was working on a sandwich he'd made from the cold cuts and cheese platter. Richards, in a navy suit, had limited himself to salad; but Ivanov, his brute bulk stretching the fabric of his sweater, had two plates going, putting my serving to shame.

Kaufman finished his sandwich and I followed him as he headed back for more grub. He filled a fresh plate, then turned to go back to the table and almost bumped into me.

"Sorry!" he said, and smiled.

Under other circumstances, I might have found the slender blond attractive; he was handsome in a bland kind of way. But I had another agenda.

"Second helping, huh?" I said, friendly. "No wonder you're hungry."

"Why's that?"

"Last time I saw you, your pal Sergei wasn't sharing his ice cream."

"He's a little selfish, at that," Kaufman said good-naturedly. "But he's not my pal. I know the others in our group well enough, but Sergei's an outsider. He's with us sort of by default."

"It was nice of you to pay your respects to Madam Petrova," I said to him.

"Well, it seemed like the right thing to do."

"Shall we sit for a moment?" I nodded toward a nearby table, already abandoned by eat-and-run mourners.

"Sure."

We sat.

I asked, "Besides Ivanov, you and your fellow bidders, you're all friends?"

"Friendly rivals—we work the same circuit."

"How about Martinette?"

"I knew him primarily by reputation. He was a collector and appraiser, not someone who worked for the various auction houses. If you want to know about Martinette, Katherine is the one to talk to."

"Katherine Estherhaus? Why?"

"She knew Martinette well—they were an item once."

I blinked. This was the best surprise since Madam Petrova skipped her funeral. "No kidding? I thought she was from New York."

"She is now. She used to live in Chicago."

We chatted a little, he finished his food, and then he gave me a nice smile and headed back to the bidders' table. Another time, another place, maybe. . . .

Katherine Estherhaus I cornered in the ladies' room at the sink, where we were both washing up. I hadn't been intentionally staking out the rest room, but it worked out that way.

"Ms. Estherhaus," I said, nodding at her in the mirror.

She nodded back, her smile strained. "Ms. Borne, isn't it?"

Like she could forget the Borne girls.

"Yes. I'm surprised you're still here, you and your friends. Haven't the police given you a Get Out of Jail Free Card yet?"

"We're leaving tomorrow, thank God. I can't *wait* to get out of this town. No offense meant, but this has been a most unpleasant trip."

We were drying our hands with a paper towel (one each, actually) when I asked, "So you and Louis Martinette were a couple once, huh?"

"Who told you that?"

"A little bird."

"A little blond bird named Kaufman?"

I didn't confirm or deny, saying, "Interesting coincidence, Martinette being your ex. Does Chief Cassato know?"

"Of course he knows," she said icily. "We've all been thoroughly interviewed."

So Tony was holding out on me. My charms had only worked so many wonders, it seemed.

Outside the ladies' room, I said pleasantly, "When was this, anyway?"

"When was what?"

"You and Martinette. And how serious was it?"

"Why is it any of your business? Anyway, we were . . . close for several years. We even lived together for a time, and then parted ways on very good terms. I had no problems, no negative baggage with Louis. If you're looking for dirt, why don't you talk to Sam Woods?"

"Why Woods?"

"Well, he fired Martinette."

"Fired him?"

"Yes, from his magazine. Louis wrote a column for

Woods, for a number of years—'Collector's Corner.' Woods accused him of giving certain dealers and shops puff-piece treatment, in return for favors and discounts."

"Anything to it?"

"I'm sure there was! But you don't write a column for a magazine like that for the money—it's paltry pay! You do it for your reputation and any other value you can get out of it. If you'll *excuse* me. . . ."

Woods I found at the banquet table, where he was still flirting with Mimi, the cake as yet unsliced. I got a dirty glance from her when I approached him and said, "Got a minute, Mr. Woods?"

He gave me a pale look, like he'd just seen a ghost, but forced a smile and said, "Why, of course, Ms. Borne."

We found a corner and I said, "I heard you and Martinette had a history."

"What? Where did you hear that?"

"Katherine Estherhaus. Why, is she fibbing?"

He scowled. "She's a witch."

"With a 'b'?"

"Yes. *Definitely* with a 'b.' She probably just doesn't want people to fixate on her and Louis, in the wake of his murder. They lived together, you know—and they fought like professional wrestlers."

"You mean they faked it?"

"No! I mean they *fought*. And not just with words. . . ." He made a fist. "They were a pair, all right. I've been in relationships where things got nasty, but never actual, physical violence." He shuddered.

"Did she hate him?"

"I don't know. It was more . . . anyway, really, don't listen to me. They hadn't been together for a long time. It just makes me mad, her trying to make me look bad, just because I let Louis go."

"From his column, you mean?"

"Yeah. You know that term they used to use in the record industry—payola?"

"I've heard it."

"Well, Louis was raking it in, in the antiques game. He did a column for us for several years, and him taking in freebies and favors, it just made us look bad."

John Richards came over and said to Woods, "Sam, we're getting ready to head back to the hotel. Are you ready?"

"Sure." He gave me a nod and a smile, and they were heading off when I trotted up alongside the bespectacled Brit.

"I guess you're pretty happy to be heading home," I said. "Back to the UK, or. . . ?"

"Katherine, Don, and I have another auction to attend this week—in Baltimore, if it's any of your business, which of course it isn't. If you'll *excuse* us. . . ."

But I didn't excuse them. Instead I followed the two men back to the table, where Katherine Estherhaus, Don Kaufman and Sergei Ivanov were preparing to go.

I said to the collective, "I *am* sorry the auction turned out the way it did—my mother and I had hoped to raise some serious funds for flood relief from the sale of the egg."

Ivanov gave me a harsh glare. "You people in this, this provincial gulag make mess of everything. One of *us* should have egg!"

"Who knows," I said with a girlish shrug. "Maybe one of you does."

And I moved away.

Meanwhile, Mother had been flitting from table to table, as if she were the bereaved making sure everyone had been acknowledged and thanked, oblivious to—really, ignoring—cold stares from those who clearly felt she'd played a role in Madam Petrova's death.

I'd had my fill of food, suspects, and funerals in general,

but I knew escape was impossible until *Mother* was ready to go. Which could be a while. I noticed that the cake had finally been cut (what took Mimi so long?) and went over and helped myself to the biggest remaining corner slice.

Looking for a place to alight, I spotted a friendly face—Mrs. Hetzler, my old middle-school math teacher, and I do mean old. Though she was seated, I could tell she had shrunk even more since the last time I'd seen her. But the woman was still as sharp as the tack I'd been tempted to place on her chair after she gave me that "D."

She was one of Mother's cohorts in the Red-Hatted League mystery book club, and a fairly reliable source for information. She also was a member at St. Mary's.

"Mrs. Hetzler," I said, plopping down beside her with my cake, "hello! Nice service, don't you think?"

There was a lag in her response, sort of like on cable news when a guest answers a question over a remote feed.

"Yes," the woman responded, "but I did *not* approve of the selection of Scripture."

"Really?"

"Quite depressing! I would have suggested Isaiah 25, 7–9. And where was the *Gospel*, I ask you?"

Where indeed? And where could you find a retired teacher who didn't think he or she was still in charge of the class?

"Well-attended, though," I said, and forked frosting.

"Yes, yes. Few knew Nastasya personally, but many know of her good heart. *Now* we can get the church roof fixed."

"Pardon?"

She eyed me like the spotty student I'd been. "Natasya is leaving a generous bequest. And heaven knows we can use the money."

"Yes, I *had* heard about that. But I guess you have Clifford Ashland to thank, too."

"Why do you say that, Brandy?"

"Well, he's the St. Mary's member in the family. His aunt came here because her own church could only meet once a month."

"Ah, yes—the Russian Orthodox crowd."

I wasn't sure fifteen members made a crowd.

"He has turned out rather well, our Clifford. He wasn't a wonderful student, you know—no better than you."

That bad, huh?

She was saying, "Nastasya wasn't always overly fond of him, you know. During his college years, she thought he was wild and irresponsible. And later, when he was selling used cars, she thought he was undignified and reckless."

"What changed her mind?"

"He got married and settled down, made a success of himself, and without asking her for any money. Moved from used cars to establishing Serenity's foremost brokerage. That made a big impression on Nastasya. Drew the two of them together, finally."

Like a bad cut in a movie, Mother appeared at my side. "Would you like to *go*, dear?" she cooed. "You look *tired*. . . ."

Since Mother rarely seemed concerned about me, I became immediately suspicious—particularly considering the reception was really just getting started, voices now animated, with some light laugher cutting through the gloom of the occasion, the room taking on a nearly festive air.

But if Mother was ready to leave, I would seize the moment before she changed her mind. I bid Mrs. Hetzler goodbye and soon Mother and I were making our way through the crowd, with minimal stop-and-chatting, then ascended the basement stairs, even as others were descending. In the lobby, church secretary Madeline Pierce was exiting the sanctuary, closing the doors behind her.

Mother picked up speed, approaching her. "Mad, have you seen Father O'Brien? I simply *must* speak with him."

Madeline stood with her back to the doors, as if to bar any entry. "He's meditating," she said coldly, "and does *not* wish to be disturbed."

"I quite understand," Mother replied cordially. "I suppose I can talk to him later. Come, Brandy—let's go home, dear."

If you're thinking Mother gave up a little too easily, you're right, because when the secretary disappeared down the basement steps, Mother did an about-face and marched toward the sanctuary.

I caught up with her, grabbing her arm. "Mother, you heard the church secretary—the father doesn't wish to be disturbed."

She wriggled out of my grasp. "Dear, this is important! They *pay* the man to be disturbed."

"He's *praying*. . . ."

"Let him do that on his own time. Anyway, he's got a direct line to the Almighty, and with privilege comes responsibility."

She yanked open the sanctuary door and charged in, leaving me no option but to follow her.

The sunlight flooding in through the stained-glass windows fell like God's spotlight on Father O'Brien, who knelt in prayer at the communion rail, head bowed.

"Mother," I whispered, "we really should *not* be bothering the father. . . ."

I hung back as Mother pranced down the center aisle, coming up behind the priest. What was I going to *do* with her?

"Father, I'm sorry," she said, her voice seeming to float back to me, "but I simply *must* speak to you."

She touched his shoulder.

He toppled backward, at her feet, staring up at her and me as I approached, too; but he had nothing to say.

Not with a knife sunk in his chest.

A Trash 'n' Treasures Tip

Set a price limit on the item you want to bid on, and stick to it. Remember to allow for extras, like a buyer's fee and sales tax. And three Cherry Cokes, a bag of chips, and a hot dog in a stale bun.

Chapter Ten

Egg on Our Faces

The small chapel off the sanctuary had been turned into an interview room, with a card table and a few chairs set up in back, behind the pews. Mother and I were the first to be questioned by Chief Cassato, who wore his usual white shirt, blue tie, gray slacks, and blank expression.

When he'd first arrived, our eyes met, his asking if I was all right, and mine signaling yes. Then his demeanor changed abruptly from concerned suitor to tough cop.

Now, remaining seated, he was motioning brusquely for us to sit opposite him at the table, a small tape recorder making a clunky centerpiece. The religious setting gave the proceedings an extra somber note, as if they needed one, and it felt natural to be praying, which I was.

I was praying that Mother wouldn't fall into her typical flippant arrogance—I'd seen this from her in the past, when interviewed by police—but she'd been hit hard, finding Father O'Brien, dead by violence in his own sanctuary, sprawled before her like a pagan sacrifice.

She appeared disoriented, her hands shaking, and I could see the mentally ill woman behind the confident, if eccentric, facade showing through.

The chief began, "Interviewing Brandy and Vivian Borne"—he checked his watch—"... at one twenty-two P.M. Who discovered Father O'Brien?"

When Mother uncharacteristically didn't answer, I said, "We did."

"Both of you?"

"Well, *Mother*, really. . . . I was coming up from in the back of the sanctuary. Mother went down ahead, to talk to the father—from where I was, he appeared to be praying—but when Mother touched him, he just . . . fell over. Backward. That's when I saw the knife."

"Mrs. Borne?" the chief asked. "Can you affirm your daughter's account?"

Mother nodded slowly.

"For the record, Mrs. Borne is indicating the affirmative." He went on. "Anything to add, Mrs. Borne?"

She shook her head.

"Did either of you see anyone else in the sanctuary?"

"No," I said. "But Madeline Pierce—the church secretary? She had just come out when we got there."

"And how did she seem?"

"Well, I'd have to say annoyed. But that was probably just because, you know . . . it was *us*. . . . People get annoyed with. . ." I almost said "Mother." ". . . us."

He nodded. I wasn't expecting an argument.

"But, uh, also, Chief?"

"Yes?"

"I, uh, might be reading in, but . . . the secretary did seem nervous. Of course, she always seems a little uptight to me. I mean, I don't want to get the woman in trouble. . . ."

Mother, eyes flashing behind the magnifying lenses, blurted, "She was in *love* with him, you know!"

Tony seemed unimpressed. "Is that right?"

I frowned at her. "Mother, that's outrageous. How can you say that? Who told you that?"

The feistiness was back. "A very reliable source!"

The chief's eyes closed, as if he were taking advantage of the setting to summon the patience of Job. Then he said, "*Who*, Mrs. Borne?"

Her nose and chin went up, the eyes wide now. "I have a right to protect my sources."

"No. You don't. You're not a detective, you're a senior citizen and a person of interest in a murder case."

"I am *not* a senior citizen!"

I said to her, "Mother, the key phrase there was 'person of interest'—that's next door to 'suspect.' Please cooperate."

"Well . . ." She frowned. "I suppose there's no real reason to protect a source that's no longer a source, is there?"

Tony's brow tightened in irritation. "What are you talking about?"

Mother shifted in the folding chair, summoning dignity. "Mrs. Mulligan told me."

"The late Mrs. Mulligan."

"She wasn't late at the time."

He shut his eyes. He opened them. "Mrs. Mulligan told you that Madeline Pierce, the St. Mary's secretary, was 'in love' with Father O'Brien."

"Her exact words were 'That woman has a thing for Father O'Brien, and it's just shameful.' "

"You have no reason to believe that there was any more to this than a rumor passed along by a notorious gossip."

Mother's eyelashes fluttered like twin hummingbirds. "No. I suppose not. But you *could* be more kind to her memory."

His eyebrows went halfway up his forehead. "Mrs. Mulligan's memory? All right, Mrs. Borne, let's *talk* about Mrs. Mulligan."

"Don't ask me to speak ill of the dead."

"Let's talk about *you*—you're alive and well. You're the one who discovered Mrs. Mulligan's body, correct?"

"Of course. Whoever said I wasn't? Anyway, haven't you dismissed that as a suicide?"

"Not entirely. It's possible someone who knew Mrs. Mulligan's habits, her nightly rituals, could have taken advantage of that knowledge to put an overdose of sleeping pills in her chicken broth. Do you know anyone who might have been familiar with Mrs. Mulligan's pattern, Mrs. Borne? Someone, perhaps, who was a close friend and dropped by once or twice a week?"

"You can't fool me, young man. You're *hinting* at something."

"And now you've discovered a *second* body—Father O'Brien, murdered at the altar in his own church."

"Yes. That's why we're talking, isn't it?"

"It is. And it's why you're a person of interest. You were in charge of the auction of a very valuable antique that has gone missing. An auction where over a hundred people suffered from rat poison in their lunch, one of whom died, not coincidentally ingesting a larger dosage of that poison. You were right on the scene when the body of another murder victim, Louis Martinette, was discovered."

"I was not! Not *first* on the scene, anyway."

"Who was, Mrs. Borne?"

"Well, Father O'Brien, of course."

"The same Father O'Brien whose body you discovered not an hour ago."

I said, "If you're really accusing Mother of something, I think we should be allowed to have our attorney present, or you should read her rights or something."

The chief's face smoothed into blankness again. He said, "This concludes the interview with Vivian and Brandy Borne," and shut off the tape.

We stood, but the chief said, "Mrs. Borne, would you please step outside? I need a moment alone with your daughter."

Mother's nose and chin went up again. "Haven't you had quite enough moments alone with her lately?"

"*Mother!*"

She gathered a few more shreds of dignity and went out.

I sighed, shook my head, and said to Tony, "I'm so sorry about her. You don't really suspect her of anything?"

He said nothing, just gestured for me to sit again.

I sat.

And braced for an off-the-record come-to-Jesus meeting.

But instead of a tongue-lashing, he said gently, "I need both you and your mother to write down *who* you saw *where* and *when* at the funeral—and do this *separately*, without discussing it beforehand. In ink, so I can see any changes. Can you go home and do that?"

"Sure. Mother loves homework assignments." I wasn't kidding. And I liked this, too, because it would keep her busy, for a while, at least. Which may have been Tony's intention.

The door to the chapel opened, and a good-looking, sandy-haired, thirtyish plainclothes detective leaned in. Brian Lawson, to be exact.

Remember him? My once and possibly future boyfriend?

"Sorry to interrupt, Chief," Brian said in the doorway, revealing Mother just behind him, wide-eyed and hovering, "but the caterer is out here, and insists on seeing you—something about a missing cake knife."

Mother's ears perked, the way Sushi's did when I opened a bag of Cheetos.

"Bring her in," the chief said. To me he said, businesslike, "We're done for now, Ms. Borne," adding for Brian, "Would you please escort the Borne women off the premises. They've been questioned and are released."

Brian nodded, slipped out briefly, quickly reappearing with Mimi, still wearing her white chef's jacket, her pretty, pudgy face clearly troubled. The detective deposited the woman at the card table, then escorted me out to join my lurking mother.

Except for a path leading from the small chapel to the lobby, the sanctuary had been cordoned off. A two-person forensics team, a man and woman in Kevlar and latex gloves, were working the crime scene. Father O'Brien's body had been removed, but tape outlined where he'd fallen.

When we entered the lobby, Mother scooted ahead, flashing me a glance that said she was giving Brian and me some privacy.

As we walked, side by side but not looking at each other, he asked, "So, Brandy—how are you doing?"

"Fine. How's your daughter?"

"Gaining weight. Not as much as we'd like, but her nutritionist is hopeful."

"Good to hear. How's your wife doing?"

The couple had been separated when Brian and I were dating (I'm not *that* big a creep).

"We're in counseling."

"Good."

I didn't ask for details—part of me, despite the budding relationship with Tony, was not really rooting for the Lawsons to get back together, though I certainly hoped their daughter would get well. Soon.

We stepped outside the church, and I turned to look into those puppy-dog brown eyes. Somehow I could tell he'd heard about Tony and me. The Serenity P.D. was a small world in a small town.

So I said simply, "Hey, the chief and me? I don't know where it's going."

He nodded, understanding. "Same here. I don't expect your life to stop while I try to see where mine is headed.

But as for my marriage . . . we just have to give one last try. Owe that to ourselves, and our daughter."

"I'm glad."

And I was. Kind of. Sort of.

He gave me his boyish smile. "Don't be a stranger."

I smiled back. "No place to hide in Serenity."

"That's the truth. Unless you're a bad guy, of course."

Soon Mother and I were in my Buick, and I turned to her and asked, "Did you get a good look at that knife, Mother?"

"Enamel handle with rosebuds. Was it that caterer's knife, dear? That Mimi woman's?"

"Sounds like it."

Which might explain why the caterer had taken so long to cut the cake, besides flirting with Sam Woods. She'd been looking for her missing knife.

I said, "I saw it on the buffet table when I went through."

And while that flirting was going on, somebody made off with the thing—maybe even Sam Woods.

We were sitting there in the parking lot, engine off.

"Just about anyone could have taken it," Mother said. "Anyone, that is, who partook of the food. Some guests were hesitant, after the *last* meal served at St. Mary's."

I said, more to myself than to Mother, "Let's see—I was about the first, except for—"

"Don't *say* it, dear. Write it down when we get home! Remember what the chief said—we're not to influence each other."

I glowered at her. "You weren't even *there*—how did you hear that?"

"I have exceptionally good hearing, dear."

"No, you don't. Who was guarding that door?"

"Your nice friend—Brian. I'm not sure trading him in on an older model like the chief is a good—"

"Don't tell me—you sent Brian off on some errand, glass of water or who-knows-what, then you cracked the door and eavesdropped."

Her smile betrayed a not-so-secret satisfaction. "A good detective doesn't reveal her secrets, dear. You must develop your own techniques if you want to make it in this game."

"Game. You can call it a 'game' after what we found in the sanctuary? That's no cardboard church, Mother, and the man bleeding there was no game token."

She swallowed and turned and looked out the window.

It's just possible I'd made her tear up. Whether that was a good thing—getting her to take this situation with the seriousness it warranted—or just further edged her to the abyss of a full-blown breakdown, well, I didn't have the detective techniques developed yet to make that call.

I fired up the car, and we drove home in silence, each lost in our own thoughts.

Every suspect on our list had an opportunity to take the knife, even Clifford Ashland. While I hadn't seen him go through the food line, I had noticed him walking by the banquet table on his way to the kitchen, shortly after he and his wife had arrived. Later I noticed Mrs. Ashland greeting mourners as she held a glass of water, which must have been what he'd fetched.

The bidders I'd spoken to had not been glued to that table of theirs, getting up and around to hit the food table or go to the bathroom or out for a smoke, as far as I knew. Anyone who knew Father O'Brien might be praying in the sanctuary could have copped the knife, slipped out and upstairs and done the deed, and come back down to join the food fellowship. At this kind of event, anybody could excuse him or herself long enough to dispatch Father O'Brien, attracting no attention at all.

Whoever that was, he or she was a cool customer. Make that *cold* customer. . . .

At home, I tended to Sushi, while Mother scurried to find two legal pads and several pens, and then we went to separate rooms—me, my bedroom, Mother, the dining room—to do our assigned homework.

We were still at it when, at about four that afternoon, Jake called saying his dad's plane had just crossed the Mississippi River, and I should head out to the airport pronto.

As soon as Sushi heard my car keys jingling, she started dancing at my feet, hoping to go with, so I got her Fi-doRido car seat from the front closet, and she *really* went ballistic. It took several minutes to calm her down enough that I could pick her up. And then when I did, she pee-peed in excitement, a little, on my top.

That's what I got for not taking her along more. You get pee-peed on and so it makes you gun-shy to take her, so you take her along less, and then when you finally do, she's so excited that she. . . . You get the picture. This is that vicious circle you hear so much about.

Anyway, I hauled her upstairs and she danced on the bed while I put on another top, and this time, when I picked her up, all I got was kisses for my trouble.

It used to be a quick ride south to the airport on the treacherous bypass, but now—in the wake of so many accidents—nearly every intersection had a light, and I managed to hit them all. I was bemoaning the lost time to myself when a little rational voice reminded me how much time had been lost by the fatalities who'd inspired these stoplights.

I glanced in the rearview mirror at Sushi in her car seat; she had been to the municipal airport only one other time, so I wasn't sure she knew where we were going. But since Shoosh wasn't shaking in terror, she at least understood that we weren't headed to the veterinary, a.k.a. the House of Pain.

My thoughts drifted to Jake. Would I notice any changes

in my son since I'd seen him at Christmas? Would he be taller? More young man than child?

We were in the sandy-soil area south of Serenity, famous for growing melons (watermelons and cantaloupes, especially). Farmers, idle in the fields since fall, were out on tractors turning the fertile soil. But planting wouldn't happen for another month, due to the chance of late frost.

As I approached the airport—used only by private and corporate planes—Sushi began to whimper with excitement, which increased into little yaps when I pulled off the highway and drove up to the small, one-story brick administration building. To the right of the building loomed two large hangars; to the left, one landing strip, where a wind sock flapped in the breeze.

Surprisingly, I had beaten Roger's plane here. After gathering a wiggling Sushi from the backseat, I headed to the gated area by the landing strip, where I waited by the fence.

Soosh heard the distant drone of the engine before I did, and began to get squirmier.

"Stop that," I said firmly.

She didn't.

"No more *car* rides!"

She did.

The plane came into view, a silver speck in the sky that grew into a twin-prop aircraft, dropping lower, and lower, as the pilot lined up to land. I held my breath until the wheels hit the ground, then sighed with relief. Can any parent watch their child (of any age) come in for a landing without dying a little?

The pilot taxied toward us, the propeller blowing my hair around like Ingrid Bergman's in *Casablanca*, and then the engine stilled, and Roger was getting out, and turning to help Jake down, my son hauling a small duffel bag.

And I was running through the gate toward Jake, with

Sushi bumping against my chest, the pooch making no noise, just going along for an out-of-the-ordinary ride.

I gave my son a one-armed hug, while Soosh frantically licked his face, then Jake, laughing, took the dog so I could talk to Roger.

His hair was a little grayer at the temples, but otherwise he hadn't changed, wearing a tan leather jacket, designer jeans, and expensive Italian shoes—his idea of casual. (To any females in the audience who are thinking, "Brandy, you blew it," I can only say, "Girlfriends, you are right.")

We exchanged polite how-are-you's, and I'm fine's, then got down to the parameters of our son's stay, which was four days.

After that, I said, "Say, Roger—can I ask you something a little out of left field?"

"Sure. Don't you usually?"

"You ever hear of Clifford Ashland? A broker here in Serenity?"

"Yeah. Pretty successful one—we've dealt with him ourselves."

"Really! Would you say he's got millions?"

"Well, he and his partners own a company worth millions, certainly. So is *mine*, but don't get any new alimony ideas. I don't have millions lyin' around, you know."

"I know. But he's not one of these successful guys who's gone under because of the stock market."

"No. We've dealt with them several times since the you-know-what hit the fan. He's solid. Nobody's liquid right now, but Brandy, if you're thinking of investing, why not come to your own kid's dad?"

"Maybe I'm afraid you'd pay me off in pennies."

He winced but smiled. "Ouch! You ever going to forgive me for that?"

I'd once received an alimony payment from him in that form. But we were getting along better these days.

"Never," I said, and gave him a quick kiss on the cheek.

He was brushing hair from my face, giving me a fond look when Jake, anxious to get going, said, "Get a room, or hurry up! I wanna see Grandma!"

And so ended my most recent reconciliation with my ex.

Which was maybe a good thing. I wouldn't have wanted to answer too many "What's new?"-type questions.

In particular, I had not yet told Roger about the baby. Jake knew, because I'd wanted his approval before going ahead with the surrogacy—I'd be having a baby brother or sister for him that would immediately leave both our lives, and I'd figured he had the right to know.

But since Roger hadn't alluded to it, I could safely assume Jake hadn't spilled the beans. I just had to pick the right time to tell my ex. And now was not it.

On the ride home, while Jake held Sushi, I questioned him about school, what new video games he was playing, if there was a girl he liked, and other mother-intrusive things, since he was a captive in the front seat, and I was hungry for any insight into his life.

A few blocks from home Jack said, "Okay, back off! That's all you get. I wanna hear about this latest murder."

"How'd you know about *that?*"

"Grandma texted me this morning."

"Oh, she did, did she?"

"Uh-huh. Pretty tech-savvy old girl."

"Look, Jake," I said, "you're supposed to be helping me keep her *out* of trouble, not encourage her to get into more. I don't want us involved in this 'mystery' anymore."

"But you're *already* involved. It's like . . . you can't be a *little* pregnant."

"Don't get smart. Anyway, we're gonna get *un*involved. Understand?"

"Okay, okay." Sushi was whimpering for attention.

"Quiet, girl! I'll play with you when we get home! Mom, it's okay, isn't it, if Grandma tells me all about it, kind of fills me in? *That* wouldn't hurt, would it?"

"I . . . I guess not."

Later, after dinner, against my better judgment (as if I had any), Mother did indeed entertain Jake in the dining room, regaling him with her version of the events, from the poisoned audience, the murdered Madam Petrova, the murdered bidder Martinette, the suspiciously deceased gossip down the block, the priest stabbed in his own sanctuary, and of course the fabled, incredibly valuable, missing Fabergé egg.

I chose not to be present for much of it. I had to field phone calls once again from a concerned Peggy Sue and an at least as concerned Tina, who'd heard about the latest murder at St. Mary's. But several times I watched through the closed French doors, where Jake, riveted to his chair, was hanging on his grandmother's every word.

That was when I realized I couldn't count on Jake. Apparently the same Curiosity DNA that ran through Vivian Borne had gone on to infect me and now my only son.

Exhausted from the long day, I went off to bed, taking Sushi with me, and fell asleep almost immediately. . . .

I was at St. Mary's, climbing the spiral staircase, which broke away from the wall, taking me with it, in a crash of metal gnashing on metal and on an endless slow-motion fall. . . .

Willing myself to wake up, I became aware of another presence in the room.

A dark figure was reaching for me with clawed fingers.

Which was when I did what you would done.

I screamed.

A Trash 'n' Treasures Tip

When going to an auction, come prepared—this means comfortable clothes, water, snacks, a book and, most important, a soft cushion. You picture yourself on your feet, waving your auction card or going off to collect your prize; but mostly you'll be on your backside, for a long, long while.

Chapter Eleven

Egg Hunt

The figure gripped my shoulder and shook.

"*Wake up*, dear! It's me—*Mother!*"

All right, I realize some of you (perhaps all of you) are thinking, *What a cheat!* You end a chapter with a spooky scare, and then it's just your mother. Like one of those cheesy fake "boo" moments in a movie, where it turns out to be some good guy coming up behind another good guy, in a sudden and unjustified manner; or the frightening sound, the metal clunk that echoes maybe, or the ominous rustle of drapes, and then it's just a cat.

Fine. But remember two things: people were dying mysteriously, including Mrs. Mulligan down the street; and, anyway, with apologies to Count Floyd of *SCTV*, if you don't think my mother coming up on you in the dark is scary, kids, then you haven't been paying attention.

I sat up in bed and said, "I'm *awake,* already! I'm awake! You wanna give me a damn heart attack?"

Despite the darkness, I could tell Mother was shaking her head at me. "*Language*, dear—and in front of the boy. . . !"

Jake materialized, shining a flashlight my way.

I squinted. "Okay, it's not *X-Files,* you two—get that

out of my face, please! And someone feel free to turn a light on."

"Better to light one small candle," Mother said, "than to curse the darkness!"

It wasn't the darkness I felt like cursing.

Jake retreated to the wall switch, turning on the overhead light. Immediately I wished I could switch it off—he and Mother were dressed all in black, Jake in a black sweatshirt and jeans, Mother in a black turtleneck with sweatpants, both with black commando smudges under their eyes.

"All right," I demanded, "what are you trick-or-treaters up to? Haven't you even been to bed? What time is it, anyway?"

Mother said, "Taking your questions in order. First, no, we haven't been to bed, we've been in a planning session, and second, as for the time, it's a little after one A.M., dear—there's a clock on the nightstand, if you'd care for something more precise."

I pointed at Jake. "Wash your face and go to bed." I pointed at Mother. "Wash your face and go to bed."

Jake was frowning in disappointment, Mother frowning in irritation. She said, "We need you to drive us to St. Mary's."

"No!" I got the covers up over my head. My voice, muffled but my crisp delivery cutting through, said, "Turn the light off on your way out, one of you."

"Perhaps you didn't hear me, Brandy. We need you to drive us to St. Mary's."

Under the covers, I said, "Like *that's* going to happen."

"If you'd rather *I* drive, dear, because I consider this an emergency, and could do so, unless . . . Jake, darling, do you have your learner's permit?"

"I'm only twelve," Jake said, "but I've played lots of driving games."

I was out from under the blankets. Realizing I was dealing with *two* twelve-year-olds, I decided a calmer, more rational approach was needed.

I asked, "Why St. Mary's in the middle of the night?"

The Mutt and Jeff commandos exchanged looks, then G.I. Joe Mutt said, "We have to, 'cause Grandma figured out where the egg is hidden. You know, the valuable fabric egg?"

Patiently, Mother said, "Fabergé, Jake. Fabergé."

"Mother," I said, "why would you fill Jake with such nonsense?"

"Because I *do* know where the egg is, dear."

"After all these days, it just *came* to you?"

Mother sat on the edge of the bed; in her commando outfit, she looked crazier than usual, which of course was saying something, but the tone of her voice lacked hysteria. She seemed alarmingly self-composed.

"Because of the *Scriptures*, dear—haven't you been paying attention? That's why I wanted to talk to Father O'Brien, until some thoughtless person killed him."

"You mean, the Scripture lesson Father O'Brien read at the memorial service?"

I did remember she'd gone on about it, though the topic had fallen by the wayside when police interrogation at the murder scene kicked in.

"It's not what he *read*, dear."

"Then what is it?"

"It's what he *didn't* read."

"You lost me."

"At what point, dear?"

"Somewhere around when Jake switched on the light."

Mother frowned. "Be serious, you imp."

Imp? Now I was an imp?

Jake was frowning, too. "*Show* her, Grandma."

Mother withdrew a folded sheet of paper from her black sweatpants' pocket, and said, "I was troubled by Father

O'Brien's choice of Scriptures. If you'll recall from your Catholic upbringing—"

"*Brief* Catholic upbringing," I corrected, yet I was paying close attention, remembering that Mrs. Hetzler had complained about the Scripture reading, as well.

"Yes, dear, brief upbringing, but not so brief that *I* didn't remember that the correct procedure at funeral mass is to read Scripture from the Old Testament, New Testament, and the Gospel."

Same complaint Mrs. Hetzler had made!

"All right," I said. "I'm listening."

"Well, besides leaving out the Gospel *entirely*, the late father was combining verses while leaving others out."

My eyes tightened. "Why would he do *that?*"

"I don't believe out of carelessness. I think this was a well-considered revision."

"Why?"

"I can't be sure, dear. But my guess . . . my *educated* guess . . . is that he wanted to put the murderer on a kind of notice."

"You're saying Father O'Brien knew who killed Martinette?"

Mother's eyes narrowed and, with the commando black beneath, they seemed to disappear, despite the magnifying eyeglasses. "He may have. I think it's more likely he suspected someone, suspected them strongly."

"If he knew for sure, wouldn't he have told the police?"

"That's my view. But then again, the other day I heard him in a heated discussion with someone—wouldn't go so far as to characterize it as an argument. Still, he may have been confronting the killer with his suspicions."

"And the killer was threatening him?"

"No. I would say the killer was reacting with indignation. Trying to intimidate the good father into forgetting about these suspicions."

"But Father O'Brien *didn't* forget."

"That's right, dear, and he restated them in public—granted, in a disguised fashion, but enough so to inform the killer that he must come forward and tell the truth, else the father would go to the authorities with his suspicions."

Jake jabbed at the paper Mother held. "The *line*, Grandma—read Mom the line!"

Mother unfolded the note. "I wrote down Scripture from the Old Testament that he read—from the *Book of Wisdom*, Chapter Three, verses one through nine." Mother raised a finger. "But Father O'Brien made a significant omission—he left out verse *six*."

When Mother paused, I said, "Please don't make me ask."

Which was sort of asking.

"The missing verse," she said with just a hint of triumph over me, "reads: *'As gold in the furnace, he proved them, and as sacrificial offerings he took them to himself.'* "

When I remained mute, Jake said, "*Well?*"

I said, "Let me read."

Mother handed me the sheet of paper.

"Mom?"

"I'm thinking. . . ."

Prozac Brandy would have nixed this middle-of-the-night Easter egg hunt; but the unmedicated Brandy felt Mother might be on to something.

I said, "Would be pretty cool to find it."

"Think of the money it would mean for flood relief," Mother said. "And think of what a *clue* it will be to the murderer's identity."

"Yes!" Jake pumped a fist.

"But how are we going to get into the church at this time of night?"

"God works in mysterious ways, dear."

I raised a stop palm. "I'm okay with entering, it's *breaking* and entering I'm not on board with."

"Dear, how often have I instructed you in the need to think and plan ahead?"

"Never?"

"How often have I made the point that life is a game of chess, and you must always plan ahead?"

"You don't play chess. You get a migraine over checkers."

"Shush, dear." Her smile turned devilish. "When I was in the church secretary's office the other day, I thought ahead and borrowed an extra *key* to the back door . . . just in case we might need it."

Mother always "borrowed," by the way, and had never been known to filch, pilfer, swipe, or steal. Semantics were everything to Vivian Borne.

"All right!" Jake said, with a grin and a swing of a fist. "We're in like Flynn."

I squinted at him. "Where did you hear *that* saying? Your grandmother?"

"No," he said, and pointed at me. Gently, but pointed.

"Oh. Well. It is colorful. Do you know who 'Flynn' was, Jake?"

"No."

"Or what exactly what it was he was 'in'?"

"No."

"Good. Keep it that way." I threw back the covers. "Just one condition, before I join *Farce Ten from Navarone*—I do *not* wear commando grease under these eyes. Capeesh, gang?"

"Capeesh, Mom."

Mother said, "Ditto, dear."

"Okay, then. Go downstairs and wait for me. I have to find something black to wear."

At this early-morning hour, the streets of Serenity were deserted, stoplights flashing, houses dark, sane people in their beds. A spring shower perhaps an hour ago had dampened the streets and made them black and glisteny under the streetlights. There was an unreality to it, a quiet surrealism heightened by our black commando garb, and I felt in a sort of dream state. But reality kicked in when we came to the hillside drive up St. Mary's.

A floodlight gave modest illumination in the parking lot, and I didn't want to leave the car there, not caring to be spotted—by whom, I couldn't say. Might be the church was on a security firm's rounds or a police patrol car's or even a night watchman wasn't out of the realm of possibility.

So I drove around to the rear of the church, taking a gravel service road, then parked the Buick along a row of bushes.

Mother, "borrowed" key in hand, led the way, unlocking the back metal door, where, in less time than it takes to say, "In like Flynn," we were in like Flynn. (*Really* had to learn to watch my mouth around Jake. . . .)

Our flashlights did their light-saber number, even crossing sometimes, on the stone walls, racks of hand tools, stacked boxes, our beams landing simultaneously on the ancient furnace hunkered near the spiral staircase. It felt as if the furnace had been sneaking around and froze in our lights, like an escaping prisoner about to go over the wall.

With hushed excitement and not a little trepidation, our little group approached the slumbering beast, with its large round heat ducts bound in tattered insulation tape reaching like agonized arms severely injured in battle.

We circled the furnace, our flashlights probing, looking for any possible hiding place that might conceal the precious little item that was the Fabergé egg.

Finally, Mother whispered, "I wonder if it's in with the pilot light?"

Her beam found a rectangular panel, about six inches

by eight. Unlike our furnace at home—which required a screwdriver to remove the pilot-light panel—this one had no such safety feature, and popped open on hinges.

Mother reached a hand in.

"I hope it's there," Jake whispered.

She fished around.

And pulled out nothing but a dirt-smudged paw.

"Try again, Grandma!" Jake said. "Stick your hand *way* in, way back, this time. . . ."

She obliged, and we watched in wide-eyed silence as she reached and probed and frowned and fished and I was just wondering if she was milking it when she said, "Bingo."

Jake and I crowded around her as she withdrew her hand, revealing the missing if unimpressive-looking Fabergé egg. The light-wooden treasure was dirty from its nesting place, but seemed to be in one piece. Not a crack.

Jake asked, disappointedly, "That's *it*? That piece of junk is worth a million bucks? I thought the Bible said there was *gold* in the furnace—"

"There *is* gold inside, young man," a male voice said, and we three jumped, with Mother almost dropping the egg, even bobbling it in a one-handed juggling act that caught everyone's breath.

John Richards—the slender, boyish bespectacled Brit, attired in a black long-sleeved t-shirt and black trousers (but not commando eyeliner)—stepped from the darkness and into the outer rim of our lights.

He held out a palm. "*We'll* take that. . . ."

We?

He was quickly joined by Katherine Estherhaus, looking curvy in a black pants suit, and Sergei Ivanov, who wasn't quite with the program, his shirt navy and his slacks a dark shade of charcoal. Every commando unit has one screw-up.

Mother, rarely one to stammer, was so flabbergasted by

these interlopers that she said, "You . . . you . . . you're *all* in this *together*?"

"That's right," Estherhaus said. "Now hand us the egg."

"*Da*," the stocky Russian said, scowling, looking pretty formidable. "We want egg!"

Mother thrust her hand-with-egg behind her back and her chin went up and her bosom went out. "*Never!* You'll have to kill all *three* of us first!"

"No, you won't," I said, and took the egg out of Mother's hidden hand.

She gave me a pop-eyed look that called me a betrayer, but I simply said, "But before I hand it over, what right have you to it? What are you, a bunch of thieves?"

The trio of bidders traded alarmed looks.

I went on. "Because, hey—my kid and I are willing to cut a deal and keep our mouths shut, to save our skins. The two of us can sit on Mother, and you three can skate."

"Brandy!" Mother said, as ashamed as she was angry.

"Yeah," Jake said, going right along with his mom, "I'm no snitch."

He made a zip sign at his lips.

Estherhaus had her hands on hips. "What are you *idiots* taking about? We want to turn that precious artifact over to the authorities. We certainly don't want to leave it in the protective custody of your Looney-Tunes mother, whom you may have noticed almost dropped it, a minute ago."

Mother frowned. "Then you're not the killers? Any one of you . . . the killer?"

I said to Estherhaus and company, "I get your point. But why are you guys here playing ninja?" I jerked a thumb at Mother. "*I* have an excuse."

The brunette gestured to the Brit. "We're both Catholics, and when we heard the priest's Scripture reading, we knew something was amiss. We looked the passage up, courtesy of the Gideons providing a hotel-room Bible, and determined that Father O'Brien was sending a message about where to find the egg. We had no idea why he did it that way, but we decided to take a look—only after dark, and carefully. We're hardly killers, but somebody seems to be. Discretion is the better part of valor, after all."

"And *Nikita?*" Mother asked, gesturing contemptuously toward Ivanov. "What is *he* doing here? He claims he only wants the egg to *destroy* it!"

The Russian thumped his chest. "I break down door, if need. We all come great distance for auction—egg must be found before second auction can take place."

Richards stepped forward. "We were just about to have Sergei perform that service for us, when your car came driving up, and we took shelter in the bushes. You had a key, and saved us the trouble."

I said, "If you're just planning to do the law-biding thing, and turn this egg over, then how did you intend to justify breaking into the church? How do we know you weren't going to disappear with it—sell it to some private collector, and get very, very rich?"

"I would say," Richards said rather jauntily, "the point is moot. We're all here and in agreement that the artifact must be turned over to the police." He reached for his pocket and said, "Don't get worked up—I'm just after my cell phone."

Estherhaus said, "May I see the egg? I just want to make sure it's not damaged. Whoever took it off Martinette's body would have only had moments to conceal it, and it might have been harmed in the rush. . . ."

Mother was shaking her head, Jake was frowning, but I went to the woman and held the thing in my palm like, well, like an egg.

"Go ahead," I said.

The brunette asked, "Anyone mind if we get some lights

on in here? If it attracts any attention, we should be all right, since we intend to call the police, anyway."

No one had any problem with getting some light on the subject, and I sent Jake running over to a wall switch, which he clicked, then came running back.

Everyone blinked momentarily, getting accustomed to the illumination, then gathered around Estherhaus, who held the egg, turning it over, examining it closely. She was frowning. She handed it to Richards, and Mother protested but I let it happen.

The Brit gingerly examined the egg, opening it to have a look at the delicate crystal bird with the gold wreath in its beak. Then he looked at Estherhaus, and from her returned gaze I could tell at once that something was wrong.

"It's a copy," she said, with a glum nod. "A good one, a first-rate job of it—still, even in this limited light, without any tools, easily discernible as a fake."

"*What?*" Mother shrieked. "Are you sure?"

Richards and Estherhaus nodded in tandem. Then Richards said, "This is *not* the Fabergé egg we examined at Madam Petrova's home that morning, before the auction."

The Russian was frowning. "How is *possible. . . ?*"

I said, "Well, obviously, the real egg was switched with this copy, some time after the bidder viewing. Maybe here at the church."

"All right then," Richards said evenly, calmly, "where is the original?"

Jake, who had been listening intently, said, "Maybe *it's* here, too."

All eyes went to the boy.

Mother said, "My grandson may well be right. If the switch was made here at the church, and if we can take the leap that the killer is the same person who *made* that switch, then after getting rid of Mr. Martinette, he or she hid *both* eggs."

Richards seemed bewildered. "Why on earth. . . ?"

"Because with the police around, questioning everyone, possibly conducting a search, the safest procedure would be to hide *both* eggs and retrieve them later." Mother raised a finger. "And since the copy was still here, we can assume the original is, too. But one thing we *do* know—it's not in that furnace."

"You're sure?" Estherhaus asked.

Mother shrugged. "Check if you like, dear, but I found only just this one."

"Cool!" Jake said. "That means another Easter egg hunt!"

I wasn't as convinced about Mother's theory, but it held enough water that I suggested, "We should search only where the real egg *could* be—the inner sanctuary, the choir room, this room, and there."

I pointed to the spiral staircase leading to the walkway and bell tower.

"We should turn on more lights," Katherine said.

Mother nodded, but then qualified it. "Only the choir room and here—the sanctuary and walkway have windows, and the lights would be noticed. No need to go out of our way, attracting attention."

"Dibs on the walkway," Jake exclaimed.

"Oh, no," I said, latching on to his arm, "*you're* staying with *me*."

But he wiggled out of my grasp and ran for the staircase.

"I'll be careful, Mom," he called back.

Richards said, "Katherine and I will take the sanctuary—two people can cover it better with flashlights."

"I take choir room," Ivanov said.

"That leaves Mother and me here," I said.

After the others departed, and I'd seen that Jake was safely on the walkway above, Mother and I surveyed the room.

We had already examined the furnace, but there were other areas of interest, including several storage cabinets of hand tools, paint cans, and such, plus a wall of stacked, labeled boxes containing old music, costumes, decorations, and overflow from the choir room.

"Where should we look first?" I asked.

Mother nodded to the boxes. "These don't seem to have been disturbed for years—a perfect place to stash the egg without fear of discovery until it could be safely retrieved."

We dug in, and were into the third box, sitting on the hard, cold floor, when I told her, "You know, the egg may not be here."

"Well, certainly it's *somewhere* here in the church."

"Is it? Why did it have to ever be in the church at all? Consider—Martinette obviously had the counterfeit Fabergé fabricated during the six months he held on to it for 'authentication.' He returned it to Madam Petrova, who was no expert, and who assumed she'd received the original."

Mother had frozen in her efforts and was paying me uncharacteristic close attention. "Go on, dear."

"Martinette needed to win the bid and retrieve the bogus egg, to cover his long-ago crime. Then, after the auction, during the commotion of rampant food poisoning, someone killed Martinette—someone who did not know the egg was fraudulent, and hid it in the furnace, for later retrieval. As for the real egg, Martinette could have sold it years ago to some collector. . . ."

Mother's eyes were flashing. "The Maltese Falcon was a fake, too, dear, remember! The stuff that dreams are made of, Bogie said!"

"Right. On the other hand, the Fabergé could still turn up in Martinette's estate, in a safe or in a lockbox."

"And the murders were committed by someone who didn't realize the egg was a fake!"

"Maybe."

"But who could it have been, dear?"

"I think I know. But there is one other possibility about the real egg's whereabouts—there was another time it could have been switched, and another place where it may be right now."

I told her.

Her eyes danced behind the thick lenses. "My dear, you are a *genius* off your medication! Forget I *ever* complained about your behavior! You are a detective worthy of . . . well, your mother."

"Gee, thanks for—"

"*Nothing!*" Jake yelled down from the top of the staircase. "Not a darn thing up here!"

Soon the others had returned from their equally unsuccessful egg hunts. I wasn't surprised—the police had given the church a fairly thorough search. I qualify that with "fairly" because the long arm of the law hadn't been as long as Vivian Borne's, reaching into that pilot-light nook.

Estherhaus asked, "What now?"

Richards answered her. "Now we call the police."

"Yes," Mother said. "But there's something you should know—my daughter came up with a very interesting alternate theory."

And she shared with them my scenario in which Martinette had switched the egg years ago, after he'd had the fake fabricated, and that the real egg had never been in Serenity at all, much less the sanctuary at St. Mary's. That the killings were the work of a thief unaware that the egg was a fake.

Estherhaus began to object on some point or other, but Mother cut her off. "Here's how we're going to do this. I am calling the police, or at least my daughter will. You,

Ms. Estherhaus, will return the fake egg to Brandy, and the lot of you will depart, otherwise we will inform the police of your intention to break and enter . . . no! No discussion for now. Go back to your hotel, and wait to hear from me. We will meet tomorrow and discuss the details of this case, and perhaps unveil a murderer. *Where* and *when* to be disclosed at a later date."

There was grumbling, but the trio departed.

"What do you have in mind, Mother?"

"A Rex Stout–style charade, my dear! Full-blown and with Chief Cassato in attendance . . . *and* a murderer."

"I thought we were doing Agatha Christie."

"What we are doing," she said, and she put her arm around me and gave me a hug, "is a *Borne Girls* mystery, in our own inimitable style."

Jake popped in with "What style is that, Grandma?"

"No one knows, dear. No one knows."

A Trash 'n' Treasures Tip

Don't bid immediately on the item you want, because the auctioneer often starts too high—wait for the bidding to come down. I know a woman who jumped the gun and bought a pair of ugly old drapes for fifty dollars. They're in Mother's bedroom.

Chapter Twelve

Ham and Eggs

Before we continue, I should mention that Mother wrote an additional chapter, also labeled "Chapter Twelve," which does not appear in this book. She is not happy with me, and I believe she feels that if enough complaints are registered with the publisher, her twelfth chapter ("Eggs-xamination") might appear in some future edition. She is wrong.

Instead of just calling the police, after finding the (fake) egg at St. Mary's, I called and woke up Chief Cassato, and he arrived at the church shortly after the patrol car he'd dispatched. We went to the "cop shop," as Mother insisted on calling it, which is to say the police station, and had a conversation with Tony in his office that lasted better than two hours. It covered everything we had learned and seen and done at St. Mary's, and it encompassed as well Mother's plan to hold what she insisted upon calling a "charade," in which she would unveil the murderer.

It took much wheedling on Mother's part, and cajoling on mine, to get Tony to go along with the charade, and even more to get him to help organize it, the chief himself asking the participants to come at two P.M. to the home of the late Nastasya Petrova.

Why he went along with us on this stunt, I'm not quite sure. I believe on the one hand, Tony was fond enough of me to put up with us and our scheme; and, on the other, he saw that Mother's plan was just crazy enough (as the saying goes) to work. Also, should this not pan out as planned, Mother had promised the chief to "hang up" her "sleuthing togs" (whatever those were) and never intrude on his investigations again . . . which may simply have been too tempting for Tony to resist.

Anyway, I'm skipping that scene. As indicated, I let Mother try to write it, but have made the executive decision to exclude her chapter because (a) it was seventy manuscript pages long, single-spaced, (b) perhaps sixty percent invention with Mother padding and rewriting her part, and (c) gave away all of the information you are about to learn in *my* chapter.

When we returned home from the police station, not long after dawn, Mother insisted upon ensconcing herself in the music/library room to write (in longhand on a yellow pad) what she was now calling a play (entitled "Rotten Egg: How Louis Martinette Made a Switch and Got Himself and Several Others Murdered," her longest title to date).

This took perhaps three hours, during which time I napped on the living room couch nearby with Sushi curled to me, and after which I convinced Mother to get some sleep while I helped prepare for the show.

Mother insisted on having refreshments served precurtain time—there would be no growling stomachs in *her* audience!—and I enlisted Jake's help in creating little bags of popcorn and making a big jug of lemonade. In part I was trying to keep my son busy, and a part of things, because I knew he was about to be very disappointed.

We went through four bags of microwave popcorn, the

smell of which drove Sushi mad, capering at our feet as if inflicted with St. Vitus' Dance. At one point she scavenged an empty microwave popcorn bag, burrowed in for a stray kernel, and got the small bag stuck on her head. This was fairly amusing, and Jake laughed and laughed while I dreaded what I would soon have to do.

As I sampled his lemonade with a wooden spoon, he watched in wide-eyed anticipation for my reaction. I gave him the thumbs up, though it was a little sweet for my taste, and asked him to load up the car with a cardboard box of the popcorn bags as well as his jug of lemonade.

When he returned to the kitchen, all smiles, I broke it to him. "Sweetie, you have to stay and sit with Sushi."

"What! No *way!* I am *in* on this! I was at the church, and I helped find the egg, and—"

"There will be a murderer present this afternoon. A killer who has caused, directly or indirectly, three deaths. I can't in good conscience let you come along. I just can't. Somebody would kill *me*, and it wouldn't take much of a detective to figure out it was your father."

Five minutes of back and forth followed, but I won, after he pleaded his case to his grandmother only to have her (astoundingly) agree with me.

"I do wish you could see my performance," she said, "and I promise you a reenactment later. But your mother is right, Jake—this may be *very* dangerous."

"But the police will be there!"

"So will the murderer. No. Anyway, we need someone to watch Sushi—she's been very naughty lately when we've been away."

Around one o'clock, we arrived at the big old mansion, pulling up at the portico, where Clifford Ashland met us, opening the car door for Mother. As on our first visit here, he wore resort-style clothes, looking dapper in a brown jacket with darker brown elbow patches, off-white open-collar shirt, light tan slacks, and white deck shoes, sockless. Again, I recalled the old swashbuckling British actor, Stewart Granger—handsome, mildly amused, vaguely aloof.

"You're the first to arrive," he told Mother.

Credit the guy for not commenting on Mother's appearance—hair in curlers, she was wearing her pink fuzzy bathrobe and matching slippers, same as the night she'd gone to visit Mrs. Mulligan and had found a corpse. Her wardrobe for the play was in the backseat in a garment bag.

"You're very generous to provide this venue," Mother said.

He shrugged, smiled a little. "Chief Cassato told me it would help clear things up. And, at the very least, help the bidders who came to participate in the auction finally leave Serenity."

I was coming around to open the trunk. "You're very kind to put up with this . . . and us."

"Can I give you a hand?"

"That'd be nice."

I was already getting Mother's cardboard replica of the church out of the trunk; there was a little box with her game pieces in it, as well.

"Good Lord, what's this?" Ashland asked, half smiling but obviously somewhat aghast as he regarded Mother's masterwork.

"A little show-and-tell for Mother," I whispered. "Please don't mind her."

Between Mother's props and the refreshments, it took several trips, even with our host's help.

"I'm sorry the house is so musty," he said in the kitchen, helping me with the cardboard box of popcorn bags and Jake's big jug of lemonade, which went into the refrigerator. "It's been closed up all week."

"What are your plans for the place?"

"I hope to restore it, maybe to live here at least for a while, perhaps eventually to make a museum out of it. Beyond that stupid egg, my aunt had a lot of interesting artifacts from Russia and the early days in Serenity."

"Chief Cassato filled you in. . . ?"

Ashland nodded, leaned against the counter, a hand casually on a hip. "Hell of a shock to find out that that egg is a fake. I wonder who the phony belongs to, anyway?"

"That's a legal issue, I guess. Maybe to you."

"Be a nice exhibit for the museum, if I could make that happen." He nodded toward the popcorn bags. "You know, if I'd known you wanted refreshments, I could have—"

"No! You've done enough. That's just Mother's eccentricity. I learn to pick my battles with her, and little stuff like this. . . ? I just give her."

Speaking of which, my next job was to arrange the seating, complete with cards attached to the back indicating where each suspect, that is, *guest* was to sit. The play or charade or show or whatever Mother was calling it at any given moment would take place in the parlor, where everything had begun. Wooden folding chairs that Ashland had led me to, in a closet off the kitchen, were arranged in a single fanned-out row, putting the unlighted fireplace at Mother's back.

A card table we'd brought with us was home to her cardboard masterpiece of the church. The replica had needed minor repairs just before we left, because Sushi had eaten the little boxes representing the pulpit and lectern, as Mother hadn't taken the cereal out of them.

Mother's audience would be seated, left to right facing la Diva: Don Kaufman (Forbes family rep), Katherine Estherhaus (Christie's), John Richards (Sotheby's), Sergei Ivanov (collector), Samuel Woods (*American Mid-West Magazine* publisher), and Madeline Pierce (church secretary). Chief Cassato, when he got here, would take one of the chairs or sofas in the Victorian chamber, with its religious icons and framed photo of Tsar Alexander and his ill-fated clan.

I set up a second table for the bags of popcorn and disposable cups of lemonade, very low-end hors d'oeuvres for so grand if gloomy a parlor.

Tony arrived at a quarter till two, and two uniformed officers were with him, positioned outside. He wasn't wearing a sport coat, his short-sleeve white shirt cut by the leather of his shoulder holster, .38 pistol butt jutting threateningly from under his left arm. I wondered if that was to give him easier access, should he need it, or just tell any murderers present that he meant business.

Whichever, I didn't ask.

I went up to him and said, rather timidly, "Thank you for this."

"I can't believe I'm doing it," he said, and rolled his eyes. "She just wore me down, finally."

He meant Mother, of course.

"I've been there," I said.

The house was indeed musty and I opened a few windows, then went outside to get some fresh air. I saw the various bidders arrive, with Estherhaus, Richards, Kaufman, and Ivanov showing up in a shared rental Lexus, and Woods in a BMW that was presumably his own, judging by the Illinois license plate, anyway. Dowdy Madeline Pierce arrived in an old Chevy and a bad mood.

The bidders were rather informally dressed, much as they'd been at Ivanov's birthday party out at the mall, and looked bone-weary, to a man and woman. Their collective visit to Serenity had not gone as advertised. Soon they were in their seats, with everyone partaking of Jake's lemonade but only the Russian chowing down on the popcorn. I had a chair near where Mother would be standing, my back to the fireplace as I faced the single-row audience. Over at the left, the chief and Ashland were seated on a horsehair sofa.

At precisely two P.M., the parlor doors swung open, and Mother, wearing her favorite emerald-green pants suit, her hair beautifully coiffed, swept in. She had even worn a pair of pink-framed eyeglasses with occasional rhinestone touches that were just a little too garish for Dame Edna Everage.

She had wanted me to clap, and prime the pump, because after all, applauding is what one does when the star first comes on stage. But I'd told her no way, and she hadn't pushed the issue.

"I would like to thank all of you for attending," she said regally.

She was not working from her script; she'd spent an hour memorizing it. I had her yellow pad to refer to, however.

"I know it's an imposition," she continued, "but I promise you it will be a worthwhile expenditure of your valuable time. Chief Cassato, thank you—Mr. Ashland, our gracious and generous host, my sincere thanks."

Ashland nodded. Tony sat stone-faced.

"You're very welcome, gentlemen," Mother said. Actually, the two hadn't thanked her, but they weren't aware there was a script to stick to, and that they'd missed their lines.

From where I sat, I had a good view of the audience, and their expressions ranged from dumbfounded to horrified—why in the hell had the local chief of police asked them to come and be subjected to this nonsense? As for me, whenever Mother goes into full-throttle performance-art mode, I am no longer embarrassed, rather viewing her antics as free entertainment, and taking a perverse pleasure watching her victims squirm.

Mother began: "Act One, Scene One. The time is nineteen ninety-two. The place, Nastasya Petrova's parlor—this very room."

Maybe I should have handed out programs. . . .

"Our host, Clifford Ashland, was not yet the successful broker we've come to know—he was, in fact, a used car salesman, considered by his aunt . . . with my apologies, sir . . . as something of an underachiever in business, and rather a loose cannon in his personal life. Do I overstate?"

With a trace of a smile, his voice filling the parlor, Ashland said, "No. You're quite correct, Mrs. Borne. I was fairly wild as a young man."

"At any rate, Clifford suggested to his weathy aunt that she have her one-of-a-kind Fabergé egg appraised for insurance purposes. He made contact with Louis Martinette of Chicago, Illinois, a specialist in the works of the House of Fabergé, to come and view the egg. I have a feeling that Mr. Martinette may have been a member of the Russian Orthodox Church—is that correct, Mr. Ashland?"

"It is," he said. "Very perceptive, Mrs. Borne. My aunt wouldn't have given her trust over to just anyone."

"Unfortunately for you both, Martinette should *not* have been trusted. Martinette told both Madam Petrova and her nephew that he needed considerable time to authenticate the egg, and was allowed to take it back with him to Chicago for that purpose. His real purpose, however, was to have a copy made, to create a counterfeit egg that would fool the untrained eye. So—years ago—Madam Petrova placed that false egg in the wall safe in this very room, where it stayed, until my daughter and I . . . in Act One, Scene Two . . . convinced the generous mistress of this house to put it up for auction, for charity."

She smiled at everyone. And everyone just looked at her.

"Act One, Scene Three!" she blurted, and her audience jumped a little. "When Martinette heard of the intention to auction off what he knew to be a fake, he was under-standably alarmed. He still possessed the valuable egg—he was a *collector*, after all—but he knew that when the ob-ject was put up for bid, experts like those in this room would quickly discern that the egg Madam Petrova had so generously donated was a forgery. He needed to insert himself into the proceedings, because the only way he could protect himself from scandal and perhaps criminal charges was to make the winning bid on that egg."

From the back of the room, Ashland said, "As I told you, Mrs. Borne, he came to see me, a few weeks before the auction, to reauthenticate the egg, and make a pre-emptive offer of half a million. I turned him down, of course. Finally he had to offer much more."

"Yes. A million. Chief Cassato confirms that Mr. Mar-tinette indeed was very wealthy, and had a vast collection of antiques and objets d'art, which are the kind of much-in-demand items that are easily liquidated. So for Mar-tinette—with everyone's permission, I will dispense with the 'mister' for this miscreant—raising a million dollars would not have been a hardship."

Was it my imagination, or was Mother *sounding* like Nero Wolfe?

From over at left came Katherine Estherhaus' slightly patrician tones: "But, Mrs. Borne, all of us seated here *saw* the egg, right in this parlor, just as you say . . . and it was real. Very real."

All along the row of expert bidders, heads bobbed. Only the nonexpert publisher, Woods, and the church sec-retary, Mad Pierce, did not join in.

Mother raised a finger and waggled it. "Precisely right! And that is why we know there were . . . there *are* . . . two eggs! Ms. Estherhaus, could you describe the particulars of the showing of the egg, on the day of the auction? Which would be Act Two, Scene One. . . ."

"It began early," the brunette said thoughtfully, "eight A.M. Local police escorted the egg from the bank, where it had been in a safe-deposit box, into the parlor . . . *this* parlor. Then, we went in one at a time, and . . ." She frowned. ". . . why, of course—*Martinette* was *first!*"

"Was there any special reason he went first?"

"Well, he was here first. Mr. Ashland just took him in for his private viewing, right away—I remember vaguely thinking, or perhaps someone saying, that it was probably out of courtesy to him, because Martinette had originally authenticated the object. I really didn't give it any thought."

Mother asked, "Mr. Ashland, you were present?"

"Yes. For all of the viewings."

"And your aunt?"

"No. She was upstairs, in her bedroom, preparing for the auction."

"*Could* Martinette have switched the eggs?"

"Frankly . . . yes. I was watching but not that closely. He could have turned away from me while he was making his examination and . . . yes, switched the false egg for the real one."

From over at the left, Kaufman cut in. "Then, Mrs. Borne—you're saying Martinette switched the false egg with the *real* one, and then *after* we'd seen it, knowing that we wouldn't get another close look, he . . . somehow switched it *back*?"

Mother nodded, her eyes narrow and knowing. "Yes. The imitation Fabergé egg was indeed the one ushered grandly down the center aisle at St. Mary's, on its tiny velvet pillow. My daughter and I do not believe the real egg ever was *in* the church."

Kaufman was on the edge of his chair. "Are you implying that these are separate matters? Separate crimes? That Martinette stole the egg years ago, and was covering up for it way after the fact? And that he was killed for that egg by someone who didn't know it was a fake?"

"Very possible," Mother granted. "And I would think that would be good news to you all. Any assumption that our out-of-town bidders are the prime suspects here is a faulty one."

With the exception of local girl Mad Pierce, smiles gradually blossomed along the row of chairs, except for Ivanov, who was too busy chewing popcorn.

Mother continued. "Everyone in Serenity knew that egg was valuable. And it would have been much easier for a Serenity resident to know his or her way around St. Mary's Church, and be the one to engineer the mass poisoning of those attending. In fact, I am recommending to Chief Cassato that he allow you good out-of-towners to go on with your lives—to leave Serenity today, and attend other auctions with our blessing."

Madeline Pierce said tightly, "What are you implying about me, Vivian?"

"Why, nothing, dear."

Woods, way over right, said, "Do you know who the murderer is?"

"I believe so."

"But do you know why he *killed* these people? I mean, someone killing Martinette is understandable. Some of us, Mrs. Borne, have a motive for that, quite apart from any egg."

"Yes, I am well aware. First, let's get Mrs. Mulligan out of the way. The chief has confirmed that she committed suicide—she was embarrassed by the negative attention her 'famous' stew had engendered, specifically thinking she had accidentally killed Madam Petrova. The poison that took Mrs. Mulligan away was her prescribed sleeping medication, an overdose she cooked up on her own stove."

Madeline Pierce asked, "Why Father O'Brien? Why *him?*"

"I believe the priest came upon the murderer near Martinette's body, and very likely saw the murderer hiding the egg in the furnace. Why did he not report it to the police? I'm not sure. But my guess is that the murderer was a trusted member of the St. Mary's congregation, and one who had been generous with donations—perhaps even had promised a donation sizeable enough to fix the church roof."

The church secretary said, somewhat derisively, "You're saying, Vivian, that Father O'Brien would have covered up for a *killer?*"

"I am saying, Mad, that the killer told the priest that Martinette had fallen to his death tragically, accidentally. That he or she asked Father O'Brien not to say anything about what he'd seen, and that she or he would explain in detail later. As it happens, I overheard part of that later conversation, though it was badly muffled and I was unable to discern the second speaker."

"So," Ivanov said, wadding up his popcorn bag, "we are clear of wrongdoing? We may go?"

"That's not for me to say, but Chief Cassato has indicated that your Get Out of Jail Free cards are in the offing. But I thought perhaps you might like to see the *real* Fabergé egg, before you go. You came a long way, after all, and it will be your last chance until there is a second auction, once the legalities are sorted through."

Silence.

Had to hand it to Mother—she had showmanship.

Finally Richards said, "The egg—you *have* it?"

"No. But I believe I know where it is. I can't be sure until we look."

"Look where?"

Mother walked to the framed picture of the tsar and removed it, revealing the wall safe. "We need to look in there. . . . Mr. Ashland, do you mind? And perhaps you would like to open it?"

Sitting forward on the horsehair sofa, Ashland was ashen. "No. I'm afraid you've gone too far with your charade, Mrs. Borne." (You have no idea how delighted Mother was to hear Ashland use the word "charade"—later, she went on and on about it.) "This is my home, and you're here at my sufferance."

"Actually," Chief Cassato said, seated next to him, "no. I have a search warrant."

Which he produced from his back pocket.

Obviously shaken, Ashland said, "Well, I'm still not opening it. I am calling my attorney, and you can get a locksmith and—"

"*Not* necessary!" Mother said, gloating. "I saw your aunt open the safe, Mr. Ashland, and I miss very little."

Mother placed the framed picture on the floor and then slowly but confidently turned the dial right and left and right again and finally a *click* announced her success.

Everyone was on their feet, with the exception of Ashland, who remained seated next to the chief, our host now hunched and hang-dog.

Within the small safe, the egg nested on the piece of green velvet that Mother and I had seen when Madam Petrova first attended us in this parlor. The unpretentious light-colored wooden object drew gasps as if it were a more representative Fabergé egg, adorned with diamonds, emeralds and rubies and intricate work in gold.

Tony was reading Ashland his rights while Mother and I, supervising carefully, allowed the expert bidders to examine and confirm this egg as the real thing.

Everyone took their seats. Ashland was seated, too, but uncomfortably on that horsehair couch now, as his hands were cuffed behind him.

"Back in nineteen ninety-two, Clifford Ashland," Mother said, "arranged to sell the egg to Martinette for a large sum, which Ashland used to start his investment company. Part of the arrangement was that Martinette would provide a convincing copy to 'return' to Madam Petrova, after authentication. Since the counterfeit egg had only to fool the eyes of an elderly woman, the switch went undetected, with no one the wiser. In Ashland's mind, the deception was justified, because he was able to strike out on his own in his new business, to win him back the respect and even love of his aunt. He figured the egg *would* have been his one day, anyway—he was just skipping a step, so in his mind, it was not a theft at all. And for decades, all was quiet . . . until *Vivian Borne* came along to overturn the egg basket."

Mother was relishing the moment, so I stood and said, "The thing is, Martinette might well have stonewalled Ashland—could have told Ashland the problem was his alone, and stayed out of it. With so many years having passed, how could it have been proved that Martinette had once upon a time substituted a false egg? Martinette apparently agreed to help Ashland out *only* if Ashland would front the million."

Kaufman said, "All right, but isn't Ashland wealthy and successful?"

"Sure," I said. "But in this economy, with the stock market down, how could he have put together a million dollars? My ex-husband is in the same business, and he made the point casually to me that even a multimillionaire can be very cash poor. Ashland assigned Martinette to *bid* a million, knowing that the auction would be scuttled by poisoning and death, and the million would never have to be paid out."

Estherhaus had lost her patrician poise. "Then Ashland killed his own aunt?"

"Yes—he sat with her at the luncheon and had plenty of

opportunity to add even more rat poison to her stew—with the reasonable expectation that his aunt's death would be written off as just an unfortunate elderly fatality of the food poisoning breakout."

"And Father O'Brien, too?"

"Father O'Brien, too, when the priest seemed about to expose him. I think the police will be able to confirm that Ashland has been a major donor to St. Mary's, and Father O'Brien would have been anything but eager to kill the goose that laid the golden . . . you know the rest."

At this point, Mother invited her guests to gather around her cardboard church. She began to place game tokens here and there, moving them about as necessary, to provide details.

"Act Two, Scene Two," she said. "The time, last Saturday. The place, St. Mary's Church. After the early-morning egg-zibit here in the parlor, Clifford Ashland goes to St. Mary's and helps set up for the auction, arranging the seating, talking to the media, discussing the procedure with Father O'Brien, but mostly just staying visible. At some point—probably around ten-thirty—he slips down to the kitchen via the connecting passageway here . . ."

Mother pointed to the cardboard wall behind the Popsicle-stick choir benches on the left side of the replica, and everyone (except me—I'd seen it) leaned forward.

". . . and, using the chaos in the kitchen as cover, sprinkled rat poison into Mrs. Mulligan's stew."

Mother moved around the card table, so she could illustrate better, shifting her game pieces.

"Ashland—*here*—watched from the rear of the sanctuary as the drama unfolded, seeing Martinette rise from his seat, claim the egg, and head toward the choir room—*here*—to escape the pandemonium. Then Ashland, knowing that the furnace room door was locked, seized the opportunity to get rid of Martinette."

I pitched in. "Ashland dashed to the lobby and took the stairs up to the walkway and across, past the bell tower, to catch up with Martinette, whom he'd seen apparently heading for the backroom exit. From the walkway, he called down to Martinette, who was dead-ended at the locked rear door, to come up and join him, indicating another way out."

Mother picked up. "Martinette climbed the spiral staircase only to have Ashland push him over the railing to his death."

Kaufman said, "The fake egg must have gone over with him, meaning Ashland risked breaking it."

"So *what* if it had broken? Ultimately, Ashland intended to get rid of the fake. Someday the real egg might have been 'found,' and our host, set to inherit the contents of this house after all, could claim the valuable object for himself . . . being not necessarily bound to any auction his aunt put in motion. Or he might *never* 'find' the egg, and instead secretly sell it to a private collector."

Kaufman seemed to be following this, but asked, "Then why hide the fake?"

"Because it *couldn't* be found with the body—it would be identified as a fake, and the entire box of worms would be emptied and its contents wriggling. So Ashland hurried down the spiral stairs, made sure Martinette was dead, hid the fake egg in the furnace, then raced back up and across the walkway, and down to the lobby, where he busied himself helping the poor souls he'd poisoned."

A now badly dehydrated Mother held her hand out and I filled it with a cup of lemonade; she swigged it down, an athlete pausing in a race.

"Act Three, Scene One—*yesterday*—Natasya Petrova's funeral. Father O'Brien hints in his reading of the Scriptures as to the whereabouts of the egg. Ashland felt threatened enough to employ his earlier tactic—appearing to be somewhere else to all and sundry—at the time the murder of Father O'Brien took place. Witnesses would remember Ashland spending the entire reception downstairs, when actually he had gone into the kitchen to get his wife a glass of water, and was absent just long enough to slip up to the sanctuary through the passageway, plunge the caterer's cake knife into Father O'Brien's chest, then position his victim as if praying, to allow more time before the priest would be discovered."

Madeline Pierce said, "I must've spoken to him just moments before he was killed," and broke into tears and ran out. I followed her but she got to her car and was gone.

Back inside, there were other questions, which Mother answered, moving game tokens as necessary, but the show was over, or anyway winding down.

I went over to see how Tony was doing. Ashland had already been escorted out by the pair of uniformed officers.

"Thanks for this," I said.

"Don't tell your mother," Tony said, "but she really did fill in some gaps."

"Don't you mean, handed you the killer on a silver platter?"

He actually smiled. "You were the one who figured out the real egg would be in the safe. Anyway, just don't you two make a habit of it."

Mother had completed her charade and was chatting amiably with the bidders and publisher.

"I hope," she said, "that this experience hasn't given you sophisticates the wrong idea about the Heartland. We are not simple, inbred souls to whom murder and larceny are everyday matters—Serenity is really quite peaceful."

Except for half a dozen murders or so, since I'd come home.

Richards admitted, "I've been to *duller* auctions."

Estherhaus raised an eyebrow. "I hope never to attend one *this* 'dull' again!"

Mother asked, "What kind of money do you think the real egg will fetch, next time around?"

Richards and Estherhaus exchanged glances, then the latter answered, "Hard to say. If you can organize enough *interest*, and *publicity*—"

I cut in. "*Please* don't go there. . . ."

Richards smiled. "You're right, Ms. Borne—maybe your next auction should take place in New York, or London."

"But first," Katherine said, "there's the legality of who actually owns the egg. I understand the police have it now."

Mother said, "It certainly doesn't belong to the 'loyal, loving' nephew—you can't inherit something you killed to get. I feel confident the courts will award the egg to the auction committee so that it may provide the flood relief its real owner intended."

(She was right. Three months later, an auction was held in New York that brought in $650,000 for the egg, and another $25,000 for the now-celebrated fake. Kaufman landed both for the Forbes group, which was fine with me. After all, that blond was the cutest of the male bidders.)

By midevening, we were back home. There had been formal statements at the "cop shop," and local media and Quad Cities TV for me to contend with and Mother to woo. Also, Mother and I posed for a photo session for Sam Woods, who contracted with me to write up the Fabergé egg story (in much shorter form than you've just read) for *American Mid-West Magazine*.

As promised, Mother performed an enthusiastic reenactment of her charade for Jake, while I had a nice, long

supportive call from Tina, who made me promise to tem-
porarily retire from detection and devote myself to eating
and loafing and watching cable TV for the duration of
"our" pregnancy.

Around nine P.M., I was alone downstairs—Jake out
walking Sushi, an exhausted Mother already in bed—
cleaning up in the kitchen. That was when I noticed that
Mother's weekly pills case, containing her bipolar medication, was full. That meant she had missed three days of
medication—which was understandable, considering the
events of the past week.

Knowing how quickly her illness could kick in, I went
upstairs to get her back on track.

She was snuggled under the covers, but not yet asleep.

"I brought your pill and some water," I said from the
doorway. "You missed a couple days."

"No, dear," she said, her voice emphatic. "I did not
'miss' any pills. I've decided not to take them anymore."

Then she told me "good night," and rolled over with
her back to me.

I rushed downstairs and got Peggy Sue on the phone.

"Sis," I said, "we have *got* to talk about Mother."

"That's funny—I was just going to call you about your
father."

"Why, did you and Bob get out the Ouija board again?"

"No, not Jonathan Borne—I mean, your *biological* father, Edward Clark."

"Oh." The esteemed United States senator. "What about
him?"

"I just heard from him, and it seems he, too, recently received one of those nasty anonymous letters."

"You mean—telling him about you . . . having *me*?"

"Yes. Can you come over tomorrow morning so we can
hash this out? And what was it you wanted to tell me
about Mother?"

"It'll wait till tomorrow morning, Sis."

After I hung up, I could only wonder what the senator's reaction would be to his "new" daughter—thirty-one-year-old, divorced, pregnant, unemployed Brandy. And where would we go from there?

But more important, how many more lives would be disrupted or even ruined by that anonymous letter writer? Couldn't *somebody* do something about it?

Tune in tomorrow—same batty time, same batty channel.

A Trash 'n' Treasures Tip

Auctioneers have the power to reject any bid that slows down or disrupts the bidding process. More than once, Mother has been thrown out of auctions when she insisted on topping the last bid by one dollar.

BARBARA ALLAN

is the joint pseudonym for husband-and-wife mystery writers Barbara and Max Allan Collins.

BARBARA COLLINS is one of the most respected short story writers in the mystery field, with appearances in over a dozen top anthologies, including *Murder Most Delicious, Women on the Edge, Deadly Housewives* and the bestselling *Cat Crimes* series. She was the coeditor of (and a contributor to) the bestselling anthology *Lethal Ladies*, and her stories were selected for inclusion in the first three volumes of *The Year's 25 Finest Crime and Mystery Stories*.

Two acclaimed hardcover collections of her work have been published—*Too Many Tomcats* and (with her husband) *Murder—His and Hers*. The Collins's first novel together, the Baby Boomer thriller *Regeneration*, was a paperback bestseller; their second collaborative novel, *Bombshell*—in which Marilyn Monroe saves the world from World War III—was published in hardcover to excellent reviews.

Barbara has been the production manager and/or line producer on various independent film projects emanating from the production company she and her husband jointly run.

MAX ALLAN COLLINS, a five-time Mystery Writers of America "Edgar" nominee in both fiction and nonfiction categories, has been hailed as "the Renaissance man of mystery fiction." He has earned an unprecedented fifteen Private Eye Writers of America "Shamus" nominations for his historical thrillers, winning twice for his Nathan Heller novels, *True Detective* (1983) and *Stolen Away* (1991), and was presented the Private Eye Writers of America's Lifetime Achievement Award, the Eye.

His other credits include film criticism, short fiction, songwriting, trading-card sets, and movie/TV tie-in novels, including *Air Force One, In the Line of Fire*, and the *New York Times* bestsellers *Saving Private Ryan* and *American Gangster*, which won the Best Novel "Scribe" award from the International Association of Tie-in Writers.

His graphic novel *Road to Perdition* is the basis of the Academy Award-winning DreamWorks feature film starring Tom Hanks, Paul Newman, and Jude Law, directed by Sam Mendes. A nominee for both the Eisner and Harvey awards (the "Oscars" of the comics world), Max has many comics credits, including the "Dick Tracy" syndicated strip (1977–1993); his own "Ms. Tree"; "Batman"; and "CSI: Crime Scene Investigation," based on the hit TV series, for which he has also written six video games and an internationally bestselling series of novels.

An acclaimed and award-winning independent filmmaker in the Midwest, he wrote and directed the Lifetime movie *Mommy* (1996) and three other features, including *Eliot Ness: An Untouchable Life* (2005). His produced screenplays include the 1995 HBO World Premiere *The Expert* and *The Last Lullaby* (2008) from his novel *The Last Quarry*.

"BARBARA ALLAN" live(s) in Muscatine, Iowa, their Serenity-esque hometown. Son Nathan graduated with honors in Japanese and computer science at the University of Iowa and works as a translator of Japanese to English in the video-game industry.